The Nightcrawler

The Nightcrawler

Mick Ridgewell

*For Dave,
Enjoy the ride but don't look in the back seat.
With thanks,
Mick Ridgewell
11/29/12*

SAMHAIN
PUBLISHING

Samhain Publishing, Ltd.
11821 Mason Montgomery Rd., 4B
Cincinnati, OH 45249
www.samhainpublishing.com

The Nightcrawler
Copyright © 2012 by Mick Ridgewell
Print ISBN: 978-1-60928-920-1
Digital ISBN: 978-1-60928-912-6

Editing by Don D'Auria
Cover by Kanaxa

This book is a work of fiction. The names, characters, places, and incidents are products of the writer's imagination or have been used fictitiously and are not to be construed as real. Any resemblance to persons, living or dead, actual events, locale or organizations is entirely coincidental.

All Rights Are Reserved. No part of this book may be used or reproduced in any manner whatsoever without written permission, except in the case of brief quotations embodied in critical articles and reviews.

First Samhain Publishing, Ltd. electronic publication: May 2012
First Samhain Publishing, Ltd. print publication: September 2012

Dedication

For Lynn, Cory, and Lauren.
I love you all.

Special thank you to Laurie Smith for the great advice, and Don D'Auria for giving *The Nightcrawler* a chance.

Chapter One

When the elevator doors opened, Scott Randall stood just fifty feet from sunshine and freedom. His mood lightened as he padded toward the glass doors leading to the street. The late morning traffic in Detroit ran steady in both directions and pedestrians crowded the sidewalk. When he reached for the handle to open the door, his cell began to ring. The display identified the caller to be Thomas Andrews.

Scott's shoulders slumped and his gaze shifted from the phone, back to the door and the sunny day beyond. However, it was not the bustle of Woodward Avenue he saw. He saw a man, a man whose appearance was so eerie and sudden it gave Scott a start and he dropped the phone. At the same time, he muttered an involuntary "eeah." To describe this man as an unpleasant sight was like calling a hurricane 'breezy weather.'

A sudden sense of unease came over him. He retrieved the phone and flipped it open. "Scott Randall."

"Scott, this is Sarah. Thomas asked me to let you know that we added your copy of the amended contract to Bill Wheaton's folder in error. Would you like us to deliver it to your hotel?"

"That won't be necessary, I haven't left the building yet. I'll be right up." He ended the call not waiting for a response then looked through the door. The ugly man had disappeared. He didn't come in. Scott was sure the doors hadn't opened while he spoke to Sarah. He leaned toward the glass and looked north, then south. The entire front of the building was glass. He saw no sign of the guy. *He should be there. How could there be no sign of him? He must have blended with the rest of the foot traffic.*

When the elevator opened on the top floor, Scott walked into the lobby of Campbell, Sawyer, and Thomson, an industry leader in computer graphics and web design. The walls were covered with awards: plaques of bronze and pewter, on polished wood backings. Hung on the walls flanking the elevators, framed poster size prints of successful campaigns were each illuminated by a mounted halogen lamp. Directly opposite a polished oak reception desk and behind it, glass shelves displayed more awards of etched crystal and polished silver, mostly for computer graphics design.

Scott set his briefcase on the crescent shaped reception desk in front of Sarah, an attractive young woman with dark hair, green eyes and an inviting smile.

"You called?"

She handed him a folder, which he secured in his briefcase, then placed it on the floor and immediately returned his gaze to her.

"I have an afternoon to myself, can I buy you lunch? That place we ate at yesterday was nice."

The raised panel doors of the boardroom closed with a thud. Sarah's face flushed and they both turned in the direction of the noise. Scott nodded to the four men and two women from the meeting he had been in ten minutes ago. They were all dressed in dark designer suits. Bill Wheaton, a pudgy balding man, nodded back then returned his attention to the five gathered around him. They all spoke in hushed tones, all the while referring to the maroon folders in their hands. Embossed on the cover of each folder was a silver cobra, its hood flared and ready to strike.

Scott watched Bill's every movement while he doled out tasks and poked the folder with his index finger. Bill's eyes locked on each member of the assembly when he addressed them. The gleaming marble floor reflected their every move. When the gathering finished, all but one dispersed in smaller groups. Office doors opened and closed in the distance, the buzz that flooded the lobby with their appearance now gone. The mundane click clicking of keyboards and chatter of faint voices somewhere beyond the reception desk was the only sound left.

With the others in Bill's huddle gone, Thomas Andrews crossed the lobby to join Scott. He smiled but the smile hadn't reached his eyes. His eyes held a look of relief.

"Wow, some meeting."

"An excellent result for both sides, though," Scott answered.

"No doubt about that." Thomas led Scott away from the desk. "I'm glad I caught you before you took off. You can't leave Detroit without seeing her."

"I'm sure she's a great ride," Scott replied, his impatience unnoticed by Thomas.

It wasn't that he didn't want to hear what Thomas had to say, he just wanted to get some sun. After spending months preparing this deal and the last two days locked in negotiations, Scott was ready for some relaxation.

"I'm serious, Scott," Thomas continued. "The 69 Charger is in my opinion the best muscle car that Chrysler, or anyone else for that matter, has ever made."

"The Charger is a great car, but most of our clients aren't looking for old muscle cars. They all want flash. They see James Bond driving the newest Aston Martin, and they have to have it yesterday. At Cobra, we find a way to get it for them without waiting in line for a year or two."

"All I'm asking is you see the car. Make a few calls. If you think you have a client interested, drive her to LA. See the country from the ground instead of thirty thousand feet. You said you were due some time off."

Thomas, a tall man with dark blond hair and blue eyes, hadn't made Junior VP of Graphic Design by taking no for an answer and he wasn't going to start. Scott looked short standing next to him, but he could have been one of those guys; the men you see plastered all over the walls of hair salons, deep set dark eyes, chiseled features, flawless complexion, shiny dark hair. They were both handsome, athletic and looked like poster boys for Hugo Boss.

Scott stood listening to Thomas with something less than rapt enthusiasm. His focus repeatedly wandered to Sarah.

Sarah stopped typing and looked up. Scott sent a wink her way and she returned a flirtatious smile.

"What time does your flight leave?" Thomas asked.

"Just before 7:00 am."

"Well, enjoy your afternoon. Tonight if you don't have plans, we can meet for dinner, say sixish. It's on me. I can pick you up in the Charger. We can cruise for a while after dinner. Show you what a cherry ride she is. You have to eat. Right?"

"Sounds good, Thomas. See you at six."

"Awesome."

After Thomas left, Scott returned his attention to Sarah.

"So, about lunch?"

"I can't today. We have a staff meeting. Attendance is mandatory," she said, rolling her eyes. "But I can meet for a drink after work if you want."

"Can't. I just told Thomas I'd meet him for dinner. Can you meet me for drinks after dinner?"

She slid a Post-it across the desk and whispered, "My cell number."

Chapter Two

Growing next to the pasture fence on the westbound side of I-80, a large bush was the only green visible in any direction. It stood about seven feet tall and just as big around.

Seated crossed legged in the small patch of shade the bush provided, a young man sipped water from a flask. The small pointed leaves on the bush providing Roger Morris some shelter from the sun hung slightly limp, distressed and thirsting for rain. Roger wore khaki knee-length shorts and a white Aerosmith T-shirt. His short light red hair lay flat on his head. Roger left his home in Vermont three weeks ago, sometimes hiking and other times hitching across the country for the summer. On the ground in front of him lay a large blue backpack. The type of pack the sporting good stores sold to serious hikers, campers and rock climbers.

In July, the late afternoon sun blazed high above the horizon in the heartland. A small sign beside the highway read "York County". The highway cutting through the Nebraska landscape looked like two lines painted on a sheet of plywood, angling slightly inward. In the distance the lines became one and terminated where the ground met the sky. As straight as the edge of a ruler the horizon stretched on in endless monotony. Above the line the sky was completely blue, any clouds that lingered after sunrise long burned off by the scorching rays. Below the line, an endless sea of yellow, sun dried pasture.

There was little to break the boredom of this near barren landscape. The fence poles that stood like sentinels on each side of the highway only accentuated the monotony. There were cattle in the distance. Most were lying down, lethargic from the heat. Cars sped along the interstate at seventy or eighty. It was easy to see how the dotted white line and relentless dull grey strip could be mesmerizing. Weary motorists would not even notice the speedometer climbing until the unwelcome flashing lights of a state trooper brought them out of their mind-numbing trance.

Roger took a sip of water from a flask, replaced the lid and put it in a side pocket of his pack, and then from a different pocket he removed a map of the lower forty-eight. A winding orange line highlighted his route. He put his finger on the line and slowly traced his progress. He had hoped to be at the Grand Canyon by now. Last Friday he had accepted an invitation from a dairy farmer to spend the weekend. Working in the barn, Roger learned more than he ever wanted to know about milk. He didn't need to work his way across the country, he just wanted to see the dairy farm. The journey, not just the destination, was a big part of his planning, so he would get there when he got there, but the canyon remained the main attraction of this trip and he was anxious to see it.

Following the orange line to Vermont, his mood turned melancholy. He missed his family and friends. He allowed his mind to carry him back to the morning he left for this adventure. Millie Morris, Roger's mother, worked out in the garden. Millie spent every morning from Memorial Day to Columbus Day, in the yard gardening. It was an odd shaped yard, almost triangular. Off in a corner separated from the main yard the pool looked almost lonely. A white fence surrounded the house and at its base, flowerbeds exploded in every color, like a scene from Munchkin Land.

Laughter from the house must have grabbed Millie's attention from her garden. She looked up and waved at Roger now standing by the window. With a smile that wasn't completely happy she put her gloves with her gardening tools in a basket at her feet and crossed the yard to the back door.

"Well, it's about time you boys woke up." Millie said walking into the kitchen. "I suppose you're hungry."

"Bacon and eggs sounds good, Ma," Roger replied. He sat at the kitchen table with Ed the morning he left. Ed had been his best friend ever since he could remember.

When she turned to start their breakfast, Ed held his hand up for a high five. She watched their gesture through the corner of her eye, and her lips curled into a knowing smirk. Roger noticed his mother's amusement and gave her a wink, causing that smirk to blossom into a giggle. They played the, "We're just dumb boys" game so many times and they still thought she was clueless.

Roger was startled back to Nebraska when an eighteen-wheeler pulled onto the shoulder of the road in front of him, coming to a stop about fifty yards beyond. The breeze that made the heat tolerable moments before had died off leaving a white dust cloud to linger over the truck, giving it a preternatural eeriness.

He watched the truck, still shrouded in a halo of limestone powder. Cars had little effect on the cloud, but a large red transport hauling a load of cattle passed and the vortex from the big rig speeding by caused the airborne powder to swirl.

A shadow appeared through the dust at the back of the trailer. It came directly toward him. It was a man, his image getting clearer with each step. When the driver emerged from the murk, Roger wondered what the man wanted. It had to be coincidence that this driver picked this spot to stop. Even if the guy could have seen him from the cab of the truck at highway-speed he would've needed a half mile to stop that rig.

When the man got to within ten feet of the bush he began to pull down his fly. Roger decided this was a good time to get up and continue hiking up the road.

The driver jumped and yelled, "Whoa Nellie, you scared the living shit outta me boy." He wiped his brow with the back of his hand and continued. "Been needin' to piss for about an hour now. Saw that bush from about a mile back an figured it's as good a place as any."

Roger just smiled. "Well, I was just about to leave anyway. I'll never get to the Grand Canyon sitting here daydreaming."

"You figure to walk to the canyon from here, kid?"

"Sometimes I walk, sometimes I hitch."

"Well, yer welcome to ride along with me a ways if ya like. I'm gonna stretch my legs a bit but if ya wanna ride, I could use some conversation."

"Sounds good," Roger replied, and then he looked out to the road and watched a red Grand Prix zip by while the trucker urinated behind the bush.

"Name's Pete," the man said emerging from behind the bush holding out a hand to Roger. He faced Roger with his arm extended and offered a smile that was both friendly and disarming.

Roger didn't want to be rude but shaking Pete's hand after what he had just shaken was out of the question. While reaching down for his pack he told Pete his name and thanked him for the ride.

Pete laughed a bit looking at his outstretched hand. In a southern drawl he said, "Can't say as I blame ya there. I wouldn't shake my hand right now either." He reached into his pocket, took out a small plastic bottle and squeezed some waterless hand cleanser into his palm. He rubbed his hands together vigorously, as if he were standing at the sink of the men's room. "Great invention these," he added, holding up the bottle for Roger to see. "Ya never know, with all them stories on the news about SARS and swine flu and bird flu, I always got one of these." He put the small container back in his pocket, "Birds and pigs, damn and shit, eh kid? Who'da thought we'd be catching flu-bugs from critters?"

Pete motioned toward his truck. "Been sittin' in that thing for six hours. My ass is about to go numb."

They both laughed and Roger extended his hand, "Roger Morris. Where are you headed?"

"Salt Lake City. Gotta load of Pringles on board."

Roger looked over at the truck. The dust cloud had moved out over the field. The man with the mustache that adorned every can of Pringles looked back at him. Only this Mr. Pringle was bigger than a horse.

Pete wandered around in the grass, "This heat is something eh, Rog?"

"Sure is."

"I tell ya, son, when this run's over I am gonna take a few days and sit in my chair with the AC blowin' right on me." Pete looked at his new companion, staring at the western horizon with a forlorn expression. "That canyon ain't goin' no place, Rog. You'll be there soon enough."

"It's not that. I like to look at the land. It's so different from Vermont. Have you been to Vermont, Pete?"

"I've been to every state in the nation. Except Hawaii. If I can't drive somewhere, then I ain't goin'. You never catch me in one of those planes, no sir."

The older man talked constantly. When he wasn't talking about himself he pumped Roger for personal information. Roger tried not to be too forthcoming. He had spent enough time in chat rooms on his computer to be cautious about giving too much detail, but Pete had a way of putting him at ease.

Chapter Three

Outside, the din of the city came as a welcome change to the numbing silence of the office tower. The heat however was stifling. Scott struggled with his computer and briefcase while trying to remove his jacket. He slung the garment over his shoulder. His mood soared. He took a deep breath of the stale, Motor City air. Not even the midday Detroit smog could diminish his euphoria. His accomplishment would be unparalleled at Cobra Exotics. Add to that, he could finally take a week or two to relax. Relax and bask in the pleasure of that knowledge.

His eyes followed a blonde wearing tight shorts until she disappeared from sight, then he turned and walked directly into someone. He gave a halfhearted apology, not bothering to see whom he had bumped into, not until the odor registered in his brain. It was the scent of decay, of mold or old newspapers decomposing in a wet basement. It was stink, to an infinite degree.

He looked at the dirtiest human he had ever seen. The man wore soiled jeans that were more charcoal gray than blue, and a gray overcoat. The overcoat in the heat of midsummer looked out of place. His greasy hair hung over his ears and had definitely not seen a comb in ages. His unshaven face had deep creases, hollow cheeks and jaundiced looking eyes.

The bum held out his grimy hand, "Spare some change?"

Scott sidestepped the vagrant without acknowledging him and made to stride by. His progress halted when a hand firmly grasped his arm just above the elbow. His anger boiled over as he spun around and met the piercing stare of the panhandler.

The Nightcrawler

"You were there, I saw you run," the hobo said.

"Get the fuck away from me," Scott muttered jerking his arm free. His anger had abated, replaced by fear. He didn't know why he feared this man. He had no idea what the man meant by his accusation. Nevertheless, Scott saw something in those eyes that scared him.

"You didn't see her face," the bum said, his wide-eyed gaze drilling through the younger man standing before him. "I still see her face."

"Just fuck off," Scott croaked.

"Okie-dokie," the bum replied. He cocked his finger like a gun and clicked his tongue while pulling an imaginary trigger. Without another word or even a second look, the bum walked away and in moments faded into the pedestrian throng.

Scott brushed the sleeve of his shirt where the filthy hand had been as though he could simply whisk the whole encounter away. The man's face, those eyes were burned into the backs of Scott's eyes and he squeezed them shut in an attempt to banish the image. He couldn't fathom a soul beneath that repulsive exterior. He didn't really consider him a person. It was a thing, just street vermin. They should exterminate it with the rest of the creatures prowling the streets and alleys. A few steps along the sidewalk in the opposite direction, he stopped to look back over his shoulder. Scott felt the need to make sure the bum was gone.

He resumed his walk and put the incident out of his mind. This was the beginning of his vacation and he wasn't going to let one unpleasant altercation ruin his day. The only thing he needed to concern himself with was what to do next.

It was much too early in the day to go sit in a hotel room. He couldn't imagine himself watching Oprah, or Ellen, or Jerry Springer. He had no idea what people watched at this time of day. If he were in LA, he would be in the office, or meeting with a client. He wouldn't be watching TV. Before he got to the end of the block his shirt clung to his skin, damp with perspiration. Sweat beaded his face and stung his eyes. He needed to get out of the suit.

In his room, Scott immediately set up his laptop, then changed into shorts and a golf shirt while his computer booted. He sent emails to the office indicating the deal went much better than expected. After checking his voice-mail messages, he hit the street again.

He had lunch on the patio of Antonio's Pasta House, a place plucked right out of a World War II movie. It had small circular tables with red and white checkered tablecloths on the sidewalk in front. The waitress wore a knee-length skirt and a white apron, her long dark hair tied back in a ponytail. She wasn't pretty, but with the right makeup and lighting he thought she could look okay.

Relaxing with a glass of iced tea after lunch, he recognized the same foul smelling bum he'd bumped into earlier, now standing across the street. When the man saw Scott look at him, a yellow smile riddled with gaps noticeable across the fifty-yard separation added to his unsightly appearance. The bum again pointed his finger like a gun, winked, then trundled up the sidewalk and out of sight.

Nevada Bob's was Scott's next stop. He hadn't planned to shop for golf equipment, but his eyes lit up when he walked by and he couldn't resist going in. To reward himself for finalizing the deal of the decade for Cobra Exotics and to cap off the whole trip, he decided to treat himself to a new set of golf clubs. He spent about an hour hitting balls into a net. He tried every brand of clubs in the store. In the end, he went with the King Cobras of course.

He had been in his room just long enough to shower and dress, when the phone rang. The clock radio by the bed showed five fifty-one. He couldn't help being amused by Thomas' punctuality.

He picked up after the second ring. "Hello!"

A woman replied, "Mr. Randall, this is the front desk, you have a visitor in the lobby."

"Tell him I'll be right down."

He made one last check in the mirror. He pulled a loose thread from his pressed taupe Dockers and brushed the sleeves of his navy-blue golf shirt as if to remove lint. Satisfied with his appearance he left the room.

In the lobby, he immediately spotted Sarah.

"Hi Scott."

She still wore the pinstriped suit she had on at the office. The way he ogled her it was obvious he noticed the camisole she wore under the jacket earlier was no longer there. Her heels made her about the same height as Scott. Not that he noticed. He focused on the fabric of the jacket. The way it formed to her breasts.

"Well this is a pleasant surprise. Will you be joining us for dinner?"

Holding her purse to her bosom, Sarah smiled politely, reached into the bag and handed him an envelope. "Thomas asked me to bring this over for you."

When he tore it open two keys fell onto the floor. He picked them up recognizing the Pentastar engraved on them. They were Chrysler keys and had to be for the Charger.

There was also a note in the envelope.

Scott,

Sorry I can't make dinner. Emergency came up. Enjoy the Charger tonight, it's in the hotel parking garage. Call me on my cell if you are interested. If not leave the keys with the hotel front desk. The documentation for the entire restoration is in the glove box. There is a reservation in my name at Pierre's on the Avenue for six-thirty. The desk clerk at the Hotel can give you directions. Have a great meal; the bill is taken care of. If I don't hear from you tonight I'll talk to you next week.

Thomas.

p.s. Sarah volunteered to deliver this. I'm sure she'd be happy to join you for dinner.

Scott folded the letter and put it in his back pocket. He looked at Sarah and said, "So I guess we can get an early start on those drinks."

Frowning, she said "I really can't. Something came up just as I was leaving the office to come here and I have to get home. Enjoy the rest of your stay." She turned and began to walk toward the revolving doors that opened on Woodward Avenue.

More on reflex than actual thought Scott called out, "Sarah." She stopped, turned, but she didn't walk back to him. Scott ate her up with his eyes as he made his way to her, hoping she wouldn't see the eagerness in his gaze.

When he drew near, he saw her demeanor change. A defensive stare replaced her warm smile. She stood with her arms folded in front of her. She clearly wanted to leave.

"Listen," Scott said. "I was supposed to go to dinner with Thomas tonight."

Sarah shifted her weight back on her heels, her eyes not quite meeting his. She had the look of a woman resisting a sales pitch for a used car.

He softened his voice, "He's made reservations at a place called Pierre's on the Avenue. Do you know it?"

"Yes, we have a lot of client dinner meetings there. It's very nice, I'm sure you'll enjoy it." She answered with confident proficiency. Arranging for client dinners must be right in her wheelhouse. She seemed to relax, as though she were back at the office dealing with a mundane task to assist a client.

Scott studied her for a moment trying to get a read. They had an enjoyable lunch yesterday and this morning she seemed open to a late drink. Now she was acting distant.

"Yes, I'm sure it's very nice but it would be infinitely nicer if you would join me."

"I really can't," she said.

Her words left no room for interpretation, but her eyes responded to his compliment. Sensing victory Scott put on his best lost-puppy expression and threw another pitch.

"Listen, I've been eating alone in my room the past two nights. I would really appreciate some company. Besides that, you would get a great dinner on the company's dime. Then if you're not sick of me after we finish dessert we can go out in Thomas' Charger and drive the shit out of it. That'll teach the prick for standing me up. Come on, what do you say?"

"Okay, I guess I could have dinner." Her eyes warmed a bit at hearing the way he referred to Thomas, but it was no more than a glance shared between strangers passing on the street. He could see that her mind was definitely somewhere else.

"Excellent!" Scott said. "Do I need a jacket at Pierre's?"

She nodded.

"Shit, do you want to wait here while I go up and get one?" To his surprise, she started toward the elevator.

They said nothing on the ride up to the seventeenth floor. Just stood there like strangers, Scott thinking things were looking quite good for some after dinner frolics. Sarah stepped out first and he followed, watching her ass while she walked down the hall.

"Just there on the right," he said.

He pulled a jacket from the closet and swung it over his shoulder, "Okay, let's go."

Chapter Four

Before the first hour on the road had passed, Pete knew all about that last morning in Millie's kitchen. Roger told him how Millie tried to talk her son out of this trip. It was too dangerous she kept repeating. Roger had told him about Ed driving him out to the edge of town and Ed giving him the same speech he had heard from Millie.

"He did a little more than drive me to the edge of town," Roger said. "He just kept going. I thought he might come to Arizona with me."

"Sounds to me like he didn't want you to go, you're lucky to have a friend like that."

"Ya, I wish he could have come along, but his dad got him a great summer job.

"He couldn't turn it down." Roger's voice faded, but Pete still managed to pick it up.

They were both silent for a moment, before Roger continued, "Take care, man. You're the only brother I have. That's what Ed told me just before he drove away."

At that point, Roger felt his eyes start to well up with a sudden rush of homesick emotion. He looked into the rearview mirror on the passenger door watching the eastern horizon getting farther away with each revolution of the trucks tires.

Pete turned the radio on and started singing along with Randy Travis.

Roger sat quietly, happy to listen to Pete's rendition. He didn't want to be the topic of conversation, but he was beginning to realize that Pete could give Barbara Walters a run for her money when it came

The Nightcrawler

to getting people to talk about personal things.

"Not your kinda music, is it?" Pete asked.

Roger just shrugged and his grin faded as he turned to look down the road.

"Where's your home, Pete?" Roger asked.

"You're sittin' in it, Rog."

Pete must have seen a look of concern in the boy's eyes, and added, "Not really, I have a little cabin on a lake in Kentucky."

"Is there a Mrs. Pete?"

"Used to be, Rog. Annie passed last year."

Uneasy with how to respond to this news, Roger turned his attention forward. There was a harsh glare, as the sun seemed to be resting directly on the highway in the far distance. Someone who didn't know better might think the rig was on a collision course with the blazing orange orb.

"You didn't mention a girl waitin' for ya back home, Rog."

Again, Roger opened up to Pete. He told him about Paige. How they'd been dating since the eleventh grade. How she had been his first kiss. How they lost their virginity to each other. He couldn't believe he shared that with Pete. Pete just seemed to have a way to keep him talking. He could be a therapist but instead of a couch he had a truck. Roger talked about their breakup. Paige thought he was selfish taking this trip. How she just knew something bad would happen. She claimed she had a dream that he got hurt somewhere in the desert. She said if he wanted to take this stupid trip alone, then he might as well start practicing being alone. She hadn't called him since, and she wouldn't take any of his calls. When he went to her house, she wouldn't come to the door.

There was still a glow on the horizon as Roger returned his gaze to the rearview. The eastern sky had disappeared into darkness.

"You love 'er?" Pete asked with a Dr. Phil, "it ain't over till it's over" tone.

"Ya! I guess I do." Jeez, he thought to himself. I guess I do. That doesn't sound very "happily ever after", does it?

"She love you?"

Roger didn't answer that. He shrugged more for himself than for Pete.

"Well things'll work out if they're meant to, Rog."

He never liked being called Rog, but it sounded okay coming from Pete.

Pete turned the radio back on and they both retreated into their own thoughts for about two hours, while a who's who of country music twanged out of the radio.

"I got a real hunger brewing, Rog. What say we see if we can't find us some food?"

"Sounds great."

The radio continued its Nashville parade. Garth Brooks, Trisha Yearwood, LeAnn Rimes, Clint Black. Roger knew most of the songs. Country is the only music his mother ever listened to. The radio in the kitchen played it all the time. That trip they took to Florida when he was a kid, Dad driving the station wagon and pulling the pop-up trailer, Mom playing the same three tapes over and over again. Even then the tapes were so old they crackled like a bowl of Rice Krispies. If he never heard Kenny Rogers sing "Lucille" again it would be too soon.

Roger woke with a start as Pete jerked the rig to a stop. Rubbing the sleep from his eyes, he looked around confused. For a few seconds he had no idea where he was. The glare of neon and flood lamps of the Coyote Truck Stop caused him to shield his eyes as he looked across a huge parking lot at the sea of tractor-trailers. Two more were coming up the access road. Three were slowly trundling out of the lot, heading in the opposite direction.

"Wasn't sure if I should wake ya er not," Pete said.

"It's cool. I haven't eaten a good meal since breakfast. What is this place?"

"Coyote Truck Stop, kin get gas, diesel and food. There's places just like it all over the country."

"Is the food any good?"

"Ain't eaten at this one. But most will fill the gap in yer belly okay."

Roger climbed down from the cab saying, "As long as it's hot, Pete."

A blue haze of diesel exhaust floated around the overhead lights. Roger recoiled at the combined smell of the exhaust billowing from the dozens of trucks' chrome pipes, fumes from the fuel pumps about a hundred yards away, and the fried food aroma coming from the Coyote Grill. The odors all seemed to meld together into some pungent stink that would've squelched the appetite from all but the hungriest men. Pete broke into a near trot catching up to Roger, who was so used to being on his own that he had just pointed his body toward the restaurant and put his long legs in motion.

Once inside they scanned the place and took a seat in a booth next to the window. They both ordered a burger and fries and ate in silence. Roger gawked around the room like he had just landed on Mars and was stunned by the view.

"What's up, Rog?"

"Nothing, I can't remember ever eating in a place with hardly any women."

"That's life on the road. There's more women drivers every year but it's still mostly men."

"You look out of uniform," Roger said through a giggle.

Pete returned an amused glance and Roger added, "You're not wearing a cap with a MACK logo on it."

Pete returned Roger's snicker. When they got back to the rig, Pete told Roger to sack out in the sleeper for a while. Having spent the last thirteen nights on the hard ground, Roger jumped at the chance to stretch out on something soft so he climbed through the hatch behind the seats and drifted off before Pete got them back to the highway.

Chapter Five

Leaving the elevator, Scott placed his hand lightly on the small of her back. It was hot and damp in the parking garage. The smell of exhaust from dozens of cars that came and went all day hung in the air. A small car squealed around the corner. Startled, Sarah jumped a step back and grabbed Scott's arm. Seeing his peevish grin, she immediately released him and continued searching for Thomas' car.

"Why didn't Thomas just have you drive the Charger here?"

"Please. I don't think he lets his wife drive his precious baby."

"He's one of those, is he?" Scott quipped as they walked, the sound of Sarah's heels echoing off the walls.

Parked directly beneath a set of florescent lights and between two compacts, the Charger looked ominous. Bright red with a black vinyl roof, a black R/T stripe starting at the bottom of the back fenders and up over the top of the trunk lid. Rally wheels and raised white letter Uniroyal tires. The only thing about this car that wasn't perfect was the personalized license plate, *CST VP*.

"Thomas has a bit of a big head?" Scott asked.

Sarah smiled. "You have no idea."

He took the keys from his pocket and walked around to the passenger door.

Almost in one motion, he put the key in, pulled the handle and swung the door open. Sarah glided gracefully in. Seated, her legs seemed much longer, bent slightly at the knee, her pants hiked up enough to expose her ankles. A small tattoo was now visible just below the bottom of her pant cuff, a dragon or maybe some kind of chameleon.

"You take your lizard for a walk every night?" he asked.

"Sorry?"

He pointed to her ankle.

"Long story," she replied.

Sarah had reached across and pushed his door open. She still leaned across the seat when he bent to get in, so the only place he could look was down the front of her jacket. She noticed his gaze, grinned and quickly sat up, flattened her lapels against her breasts and looked out the passenger window.

Behind the wheel, he sat a moment, as if trying to feel the soul of the car. He slid his hands up and down the wheel, surveyed the instrument panel, glanced in the backseat, and then rested his right hand on the gearshift.

"Hmm!"

"What's wrong?" Sarah asked.

"It's an automatic."

She looked puzzled. "And that's bad?"

With a tone that bordered on snarky, Scott explained that most guys who are in the market for muscle cars want to drive a stick. He tried to explain the feeling of becoming part of the car. He considered going into more detail but decided not to; if she had to ask she probably wouldn't understand.

He revved the engine a few times before driving up the circular ramp to street level. Scott swiped his room key and the gate rose to let them exit. The sun was still bright and Scott's eyes had not yet adjusted. Squinting, he was just able to make out the silhouette of a man standing motionless directly in front of the car. He had to brake hard. The car came to a jerking stop on the sidewalk.

Sounding mildly irritated, Sarah asked, "What are you doing?"

"Didn't you see that bum on the sidewalk?"

"What bum?"

Scott looked back, apprehension taking over. There was nobody there. It was the fourth time he had seen that creep and once was more than enough.

"Never mind. Which way to Pierre's?"

"Turn left at the first light and it'll be on the right side about ten blocks down," she answered.

She sat silent, staring out the window. Scott did not notice her aloof demeanor as he watched shops and restaurants on Woodward disappear behind them. The traffic was still heavy with commuters. The sidewalk was teeming with pedestrians, scurrying between the tall buildings like mice through a maze.

"You need to get in the curb lane. It's just past the next light. Do you see it?" Sarah instructed him, pointing.

He nodded and accelerated to get ahead of the neon blue Honda beside them. It had florescent lights that shone on the road illuminating the shadows beneath it, splash decals along the sides, low profile high performance tires, and a whiny sounding motor. The Honda sped up and closed the gap. The driver, who looked to be about eighteen, looked over wearing a smug grin.

With a devious expression Scott looked at Sarah. "So the little prick wants to play, does he?"

It was phrased as a question, but Scott didn't expect an answer and Sarah didn't give one. Both cars stopped at the next red light, the Explorer continued through the intersection and out of sight, leaving the Charger and the Honda waiting side by side. A steady flow of traffic buzzed through the intersection in front of them. Scott craned around Sarah to get a look at the driver.

"Do you believe this? He's barely out of diapers and tonight he wants to race cars."

Scott scanned the intersection and got a very hard look on his face.

"Sarah, this is going to be fun."

"Scott, these kids around here are nuts. What the hell are you

The Nightcrawler

thinking of doing?"

"I'm going to do very little. Junior over there is going to do everything."

With the car in neutral, he depressed the accelerator. It rumbled with the sound of pure, made in Detroit power. Scott taunted the young man, releasing the gas pedal, and then easing it down repeatedly.

Sarah nervously looked into the small car barely more than an arm's length away. The driver's face was full of mischief, but next to him, a frightened girl looked to Sarah as if pleading for her to do something.

"Man, they made great sounding cars back then, didn't they?" Scott said.

Every time the Charger roared, the Honda replied with a screaming whine.

"Look at him," Scott said. "Well he won't be so smug in a minute."

"Just drop it," Sarah said with great urgency in her voice.

The Charger let out another roar, drawing Junior's attention. Immediately Scott put the Charger in gear and the rear tires began to spin, causing billowing blue smoke to fill the wheel-wells. The Honda vaulted forward as the over eager young lad, still looking at Scott, popped the clutch and darted into the intersection. Almost as quick as the Charger lurched forward, Scott released the accelerator and slammed the brakes hard, stopping the car dead. The light hadn't changed. A loud crash filled the air, vibrating windows in adjacent shops. A red Dakota pickup met the Honda with the force of two tons of steel at forty miles per hour. Pieces of Japanese engineering flew in all directions as the truck spun one hundred and eighty degrees then came to rest against a parked car. The Honda was no longer recognizable, at least from the front. The left fender, bumper and hood were on the road. Broken pieces of plastic and glass were scattered over the pavement throughout the intersection. The left front wheel was at an extreme angle to the other three and the tire was as flat as day old beer. Steam swirled in the breeze as it oozed from the ruptured radiator of the battered Honda.

"You did that on purpose, didn't you?" Sarah yelled. "They could have been killed. And the guy in the truck, what did he do to deserve that?"

"He's fine and so are those kids," Scott said.

The driver of the truck had gotten out and was surveying the damage to his vehicle. Junior was banging on the steering wheel and arguing with the teenage girl in the passenger seat. On the sidewalk, several pedestrians began to gather, chatting to each other and pointing at the Honda, then over to the Dakota.

Scott drove up alongside of the Dakota and handed his card to the owner, a young man of about thirty give or take.

"I saw the whole thing. We can't wait for the authorities to come but if they need a statement, have them call the cell number on my card," Scott told him, smirking like a child just pulling a gag on his little sister.

Before the guy could reply, the Charger, glowing red and pristine was heading up the road to Pierre's. In the parking lot, Scott guided the car to a stop beside a light post. Sarah remained seated as Scott walked to the passenger side and opened her door. He held out his hand but she didn't take it.

"What's wrong?" He was completely oblivious to the cause of her soured mood.

"They were just kids having some fun. They could have been seriously hurt. Shit they could have been killed." She was already three steps toward the front door to Pierre's before Scott closed the car door and turned to join her.

The entrance was old and stunning. Large wooden double doors curved to a peak at the top where they met. Big bronze handles gave the patrons a sense of entering a European castle. The doors were sheltered by a long burgundy awning, "Pierre's" in large white cursive text emblazoned on the side.

As they approached a doorman greeted them, "Welcome to Pierre's."

"Thank you," Sarah said.

They stopped in front of the maitre'd. "Hello my name is Serge, welcome to Pierre's. Do you have reservations?"

"Scott Randall," Scott announced.

Serge looked on his sheet. "I'm sorry, we have no Scott Randall booked this evening. Would you like to put your name in for a stand-by table?"

Scott chuckled to himself, "Stand-by, what is this Delta Airlines?"

Sarah stepped to the front. "Try Thomas Andrews."

"Ah yes, now I recognize you, miss. Mr. Andrews will not be joining us this evening?"

"No." she said. "He wasn't available tonight."

"Yes, yes." Serge said. He led them to a table in the very back corner of the room. "Will this be suitable?"

"This will be perfect, Serge." Scott said. Who knows, maybe with some luck and some good wine he could get this train back on track. He really didn't want to go back to his room alone tonight.

They didn't talk much before dinner, but as he hoped, both loosened up after a couple glasses of wine. Scott gave his best effort at being remorseful about screwing Junior over. They both had a few laughs at Thomas' expense. Sarah had tapped his hand once while making a point about Thomas, and Scott felt sure she let it linger just long enough to be suggestive.

Soon, they relaxed into the casual banter of two people on a first date. They discussed movies, music, favorite books and TV shows.

"So, do you have anyone special back in LA?" she asked.

"Does my dog count?"

A nervous giggle escaped her lips. "Come on, there must be someone back home."

Scott gave her a history of his relationships. How he lived with someone for four years but it didn't work out. How she couldn't get used to him spending so much time at work. How she often accused him of cheating, so they ended it. How they are still friends. How she has moved on, now married to a nice nine-to-fiver, they have a baby boy now. How this, how that...blah, blah, blah.

Sarah gave him a similar tale. Scott had a good idea that Thomas Andrews figured into her story, but she didn't let on.

"So you have a dog?"

"Sure do. She's the closest family I have."

"What kind of dog is he?"

"*She* is a Doberman. She's two and a half and her name is Max."

"A girl named Max?"

"Well her real name is Equinox Dark Angel, from the TV show. I got her from a nice old lady in Vancouver. She knows everything there is about dogs."

"What do you do with Max when you're on the road?"

"Well, the first time I had to leave her in a kennel. She wasn't the same for a month. It was a good kennel. I checked them out and they were the best in the area. I guess it just wasn't home. Now one of the girls from the office stays at my place when I'm away. She isn't allowed dogs in her building so she looks forward to my trips."

"One of the girls," Sarah repeated with one eyebrow raised.

"What?"

"Girls?"

"Okay, one of the women," he said, adding, "And she's just a friend."

"I wasn't going to ask."

The waiter arrived at the table, "Will you be having dessert or cocktails? Tonight's dessert special is New York style cheesecake with cherries or blueberries. But quite frankly all the desserts are special here at Pierre's." The waiter's name was Bob. A tall, thin man who enunciated more clearly than any man Scott had ever met.

"Bob, dinner was great and I couldn't eat another bite. Sarah, would you like anything else?"

She looked directly into Bob's eyes saying, "No thank you."

"Very well," Bob said. "Then if you'll just sign here. Mr. Andrews has left instructions to forward the bill to his office, so I will say good night and thank you."

Scott signed the bill and handed it back.

He got up from his chair and as Sarah retrieved her purse from the floor beneath her, he walked to her left to help her up. She smiled and told him she needed to use the ladies room before they left. She disappeared behind a swinging door, with the word "Mesdemoiselles" written in the same script as the awning out front. He leaned against the wall as nonchalantly as he could, waiting for her return.

He was checking his watch when she came out. It was nine thirty-nine.

"I wasn't that long, was I?" she asked.

She looked beautiful. He was once again aware of the way her jacket cradled her breasts. The V-shape made by her lapels seemed to be saying "look here" and he found it hard not to listen. The slender cut of her slacks, hemmed to accommodate her heels, combined with the vertical pinstripes made her legs look five feet long.

"Not at all." He put his hand gently on her shoulder and motioned her toward the exit.

They walked quietly across the parking lot to the Charger, parked strategically under a light. Scott crouched down looking along the lines of the car. He scoured it from the hood to the trunk lid.

"What are you looking for?" Sarah asked.

"Sometimes tiny dents stand out better in artificial light."

Returning to the front of the car, he reached his hand into the grille and released the hood latch. He lifted the hood and began to inspect the machinery within.

"Is something wrong?" Sarah asked.

"Not a thing," he said. "Everything looks great."

Sarah stood beside him as he admired the source of the Charger's power. It was spotless. Black hoses glistened as though polished. Red wires fanned out from the distributor. Large letters on the breather spelled SIX PACK.

"What's a six pack?" she asked, pointing.

"It has three two barrel carburetors," he answered without looking up. "It wasn't available in the 69 but it is a fine engine." He reached into his pocket, and pulled out the keys. Holding them out he asked her to start it up. She took the keys and got in.

Scott was leaning on the car with both hands when it started. He closed his eyes and listened as Sarah depressed the gas pedal and the engine rumbled like rolling thunder in the distant sky. The way Scott stood over the 440, his eyes closed, he could have been listening to a violin solo. He shut the hood and saw through the windshield that Sarah had shifted across the gap between the seats to the passenger side and was playing with the radio. Once again, his eyes were drawn to her breasts while she reached for the volume control. This time he was more than enjoying the view, he was getting aroused.

Back in the drivers seat, his eyes were locked on her every movement as she finished adjusting the radio and sat back.

"So where should I take you?" he asked.

"My car is in the garage at the office," she said and turned to look toward the street. Not what he was hoping to hear, but he didn't hear any fat lady singing yet.

"How did you get to the hotel?"

"I walked. Thomas didn't want to pay for parking." She grinned sheepishly. "You're not supposed to know that."

The drive to Sarah's car started out a bit edgy, their conversation forced. They spoke of one neutral topic after another, the weather, sports, Thomas Andrews. As they neared the office, Scott threw out a few subtle innuendos.

"I'm wide awake. I know I won't be able get to sleep tonight."

"I know what you mean. A big meal like that this late isn't a good idea."

"Do you want to grab a nightcap? There's a cozy piano bar in the hotel."

"That sounds nice, Scott, but I have to be at work early tomorrow. I really shouldn't have come to dinner."

"What was it you were supposed to do tonight? Back at the hotel you said you had something to do."

"Nothing really. Just something with my sister. Nothing I can't do tomorrow."

So it went, until they pulled up to the parking garage entrance. Scott looked at her. The door was closed and he didn't have the key.

"Oh yeah!" she said grinning. Her purse was between the two front seats, she turned toward him and he looked directly into her eyes. Sarah averted her gaze and Scott noticed her hands were a bit unsteady as she fumbled through her purse. He took her passkey making sure to stroke her hand as he retrieved it.

"Nice ride," he said motioning to a candy apple red Miata. It was the only car left in the garage, and he pulled the Charger in beside it.

He walked around to open her door. Standing beside the car, his right hand holding the open door, Scott extended his left and this time she allowed him to assist her.

He watched as she raised herself out of the car. Standing, she released his hand as they came face to face. He put his left hand on the roof blocking her escape and looked deep into her eyes. She held his gaze and they moved toward each other until their lips met.

He guided her away from the car door and closed it. Scott pressed his body against hers and forced her against the side of the car. With each breath, their lust for each other grew, overriding any inhibitions. Sarah's earlier reluctance to continue their evening with a drink was now forgotten as she surrendered to her desire. This wasn't dating or courting, it was desire, lascivious hot passion. She wrapped her arms around him, pulling him closer.

He slipped his hand between them and unbuttoned her jacket. She willingly allowed him to maneuver her to the front of the car. Their hands twisted buttons and pulled at belts and zippers as they moved. Her jacket had slid down her arms to her elbows. His hands were all over her. She reclined on the hood of the car, Scott following her, his lips moving from her neck to her breasts. He slid her bra under her breasts, not bothering with hooks or clips. Completely given into the sexuality Sarah reached over her head and clung to the edge of the hood along the windshield. Her back arched as his lips traced the lines of her abs until he reached the line of her lace panties. Scott gently guided the lacy garment to her slacks, which were already down around her knees. She moaned when her completely bare ass made contact with the warm steel of the hood.

They were beyond turning back as he rose up to meet her, their bodies slick with sweat in the hot humid air. They moved with a rhythm that quickened as they drove each other closer to climax.

They did it right there on the car. It was exciting, fast animal lust and it was exactly what they both wanted. When they finished, he collapsed on her, both gasping for air.

Scott didn't get back into the Charger until Sarah was out of sight. When he did, he was in no mood to go back to his room. He left the garage and began driving. By twelve-fifty, he found himself on the 696 heading east. The throaty drone of the Charger, and the wind coming in the open window were the only sounds. Ninety-five miles per hour and she has lots more. One hundred, one ten.

Very nice he thought.

Chapter Six

Roger woke to a loud banging noise on the side of Pete's rig. He cried out at the suddenness of the thumping. His clothes were damp with perspiration and he could feel his heart pounding inside his chest. The absolute dark inside the sleeper had the boy a bit confused at first.

The familiar sound of Pete's voice cleared that up, "Damn, Rog, you gonna sleep all day?"

In spite of the smell of sweat, stale air and his damp clothes, Roger felt recharged by a good nights sleep. He scrambled around in the dark for a way out of the truck. The early morning light struck him in the face with the force of a camera flash and he winced while holding his hands up to shield his eyes. The passenger door of the truck hung open and he climbed down to see Pete grinning like a dad waiting to take his boy to his first NHL game.

"Like I said last night, I hate sleepin' in that thing. Don't seem to bother you none though, do it? Anyway, I dropped in on a friend last night and slept in the house there. She got some breakfast started if you're hungry." Pete's endearing Kentucky twang came across with added enthusiasm.

"What time is it?" Roger asked rubbing the sleep from his eyes and still squinting from the harshness of the sunshine.

"'Bout six, maybe a little after. You been sleepin' since nine or so." Pete studied Roger and added, "You look like crap, boy. Ya feelin' okay?"

Roger ran his fingers through his hair then brought his hands down across his face. "I'm good. I was just dreaming."

A look of fear seemed to seep into his expression. "There was a car. It was big and old but new too. A red noisy car. A guy standing over me. He seemed pissed. Pissed at me."

Roger stopped and looked at Pete. There was a genuine look of concern in Pete's eyes.

"He was mad at me but I was hurt, lying on the ground bleeding and bent into weird contorted angles. It seemed so real."

"Sometimes dreams don't make sense but they feel like real life. Funny huh?" Pete put his hand on Roger's shoulder and guided him toward the front steps.

It was a small white frame cottage with green shutters and a white picket fence. The paint on the house and fence needed some attention but the yard was well-kept and the flowerbed in front was full of color reminding Roger of his mother. The front porch spanned the full width of the house. Potted geraniums bloomed bright red on both sides of each step. A two-seat swing sat empty in the shade of the porch overhang, swaying slightly in the early morning breeze. The only sounds were their foot falls on the wooden stairs and the birds enthusiastically welcoming the day.

The screen door creaked when Pete pulled it open and he nudged Roger inside. Roger looked around the front room with adoration. It was just like his Gran's. The furniture looked old but clean and solid. The dark wood end tables were covered with framed snapshots and bric-a-brac. Everything on them sat on lace doilies. A large coffee table in the center of the room was adorned with a big purple molded glass bowl filled with pink and yellow M&M's. Roger thought they had probably been there since Easter. Maybe not even this past Easter.

Pete stepped around him and headed through a door in the back right corner of the room. "Come on, Rog, Jenny ain't gonna bite cha."

Roger followed Pete into the kitchen, surprisingly modern compared to the room he just left. Ceramic tile covered the counter and backsplash, and perfectly matched the floor. Stainless steel appliances glistened as the morning sun streamed through the bow window. The plants on the window shelf cast oddly shaped shadows across the floor. A small round oak table with three mismatched place settings on frilly floral print placemats filled the room.

Without realizing it, Roger inhaled deeply. The smell of bacon invaded his sinuses. Jenny stood at the counter next to the stove cracking eggs into a bowl. She turned to Roger and smiled. She had the kind of smile that could make anyone feel welcome. Wearing jeans and a T-shirt covered by an apron that could be from Minnie Pearl's own clothing line, Roger thought she looked like a cast member from *Hee Haw*, another of Millie's favorite forms of syndicated entertainment when he was little.

"Roger, I make the best cheese omelet in these parts. Can I interest you in tryin' one?"

"Sounds awesome, Miss ..."

"Just call me Jenny. Okay, Roger?"

"Okay, Jenny it is."

Pete had made his way to the table and sat with his back to the wall. He motioned to Roger who followed suit and sat in the next chair, both watching Jenny as she poured some of the whipped eggs into a skillet, filling the room with a loud sizzle.

"Don't cha just love that sound, Rog?" Pete said. "Nothing sounds better than a batch of eggs hittin' a hot griddle." He began rubbing his hands together as if in anxious anticipation of something phenomenal.

"Here's the secret to a great cheese omelet, Roger. After you fold it put it on a plate and put it in a warm oven." Jenny slid one plate into the oven and removed two others. One was piled high with what looked like a whole loaf of toasted bread. The other was covered with cooked bacon.

Continuing she said, "Just for a minute or so to give the cheese a chance to melt into the eggs." Putting the bacon and toast on the table she winked at Roger and added, "But don't go telling everyone my secrets you hear."

"No ma'am," Roger replied, grinning back at her.

"Rog is plannin' to hike the Grand Canyon," Pete said as if trying to find a way into the conversation.

"That so, Roger? Well you be careful when you get down to the canyon floor, it's terrible hot down there this time of year." Jenny's face took on a look of mild concern. "And you make sure you get a guide and if you can't find a guide you make sure you let someone know what part of the canyon your gonna be in, okay? That is one place you don't wanna get lost. By the time the rangers see the buzzards circlin' it's too late." She took the plate with the eggs out of the oven and shoveled them onto the three plates. Roger and Pete started on their omelets and Jenny poured them each a glass of OJ and sat down.

"Now Jenny, don't go scarin' the boy. He'll be just fine, eh Rog?" Pete said through a mouthful of eggs.

Roger was nibbling on a piece of toast and didn't answer. He just nodded and with a warm grin did his best to ease Jenny's mind. The dream that Pete woke him out of had slipped away until Jenny's advice brought it right back.

"So listen, Rog, I don't know if yer in a hurry to get to the canyon but Jenny tells me there's a rodeo at the Buffalo Bill State Park nearby if yer interested."

"Sounds cool. Either of you going?"

"Not me," Pete answered clearing off his plate. "I gotta get this load into Salt Lake City." He wiped his hands with a red and white checkered napkin, and then began rubbing his belly with great satisfaction.

"I'm takin' the Greyhound to visit my sister in Lincoln," Jenny said. "She ain't been feelin' too good these days. You should go though, Roger. It is a nice place to visit. You can camp there for a while too."

Jenny finished her omelet, took a strip of bacon in her fingers and nibbled at it. She looked across at Roger. He smiled at her in a way he hoped said thanks for the breakfast.

Returning his smile she said, "I put out a fresh towel in the bathroom if you wanna take a shower. Old Pete there used up most of my hot water but I bet by now the tank should be back up to temp. I could wash your clothes for you if you like. I bet it would feel good after bein' on the road for a while."

"I can't think of anything I'd like more." This time, his smile emanated from pure joy. Roger couldn't remember ever going this long between showers.

"The bathroom's just at the end of the hall, hon," Jenny said, patting him on the hand.

Roger got up and began to pick up his dishes.

"You just leave them, dear. I'll take care of it later."

Jenny had also got up and reached for Roger's plate. Pete remained seated, sipped his juice, and chuckled quietly at the sight of Jenny exercising her mother instincts. Her boy had left town for college eight years ago and she only saw him a few times a year now. She was relishing the feeling of youth in the house again.

Two hours later Roger had showered, shaved and dressed in freshly laundered clothes. Pete left while he was in the shower. Jenny told him that Pete hated goodbyes. She also said that Pete had really formed an attachment to him and wished him all the best in the future. Roger was disappointed that he didn't get to say goodbye to Pete but he hoped they would meet again.

"Well dear," Jenny said as Roger stood at the front window looking out at the glorious day. "Have you got a plan for the next part of your journey?"

"I think I'm going to check out that rodeo."

"Good for you, hon. When you get there try to get back and meet some of the competitors. They really are a colorful bunch."

"I'll do that. I should get out of your way so you can pack for your trip. I hope your sister is doing better."

It wasn't until that moment that Roger noticed Jenny was holding his backpack. Hugging it would be a better description. He stepped toward her and she handed it to him. As he took it she held out her arms to draw him in.

Mick Ridgewell

"I put lunch and some treats in your pack. Pete left his card for you. It has his cell number on it. He said to call him anytime, I wrote my number on the back. I hope you will call once in a while. You know, just to say hi."

With Jenny still clinging to him, Roger asked for directions to the rodeo. She released him and explained in detail how to get to Buffalo Bill Park.

Chapter Seven

Scott rolled over and rubbed the sleep out of his eyes. The digital clock on the bedside table glowed 8:17 am.

"Shit," he said in a half whisper. His plane was somewhere over the Dakotas, give or take. He flipped the covers off his naked body and sat up on the edge of the bed. His feet rested on the pile of clothes he had worn the previous night. He turned on the radio and the sultry voice of a woman said, "Hello boys, it's eight-eighteen and you're listening to Classic Rock on WCSX. This one is going out to all of our boys overseas. They're putting theirs on the line for us." Bob Seger began to sing.

Scott sat, wondering what to do with his day. It was too early to phone anyone back home. Max wouldn't be rousing Tina to take her morning walk for another hour at least.

He walked over to the window, slid the curtain over just far enough to look down onto the street. The sunlight came crashing through the gap like a passenger train through a dark tunnel. Scott stood his ground squinting down at the carpet until his eyes had adjusted. The bustle of rush hour was well underway.

It looked like the start of a beautiful day. The sun's glow was brilliant, the sky was clear and blue, a few thin white clouds barely noticeable high up in the atmosphere floated along adding just the right amount of contrast to be beautiful. He looked over his shoulder at his new golf clubs and smiled. Maybe he could do nine somewhere on the road.

At nine fifteen, he picked up the phone, dialed C.S. and T.'s main line. After two rings, "C.S. and T., Sarah speaking. How may I help you?"

"Good morning. And how are you today?"

"Are you back in LA already?" Her tone became hushed. Scott thought she sounded much the same as his assistant when she was talking to her boyfriend during working hours.

"No. I missed the plane. I'm still in the hotel. Is Thomas in yet?" His voice carried no hint of having been intimate with her just hours ago.

"One moment and I'll transfer you," and with a sharp click he was listening to a weak instrumental rendition of "Me and Bobby McGee".

Scott could picture Thomas at his large L-shaped desk, with the cherry wood top. There'd be no clutter on it, just an in-tray, a picture of his wife and a flat screen computer monitor.

Scott heard one ring then, "Thomas Andrews."

"Good morning, Thomas, it's Scott."

"Are you calling from the plane?"

"Still in the hotel. Slept in."

"Well I guess it was a good night then." That comment had them both chuckling a bit. "So, what do you think of the Charger?"

"It's a great machine. I may have a buyer for it. He really wants a Hemi but I may be able to hook him if he drives yours. I thought I'd take a couple of weeks off and drive her to LA. Maybe hit the links here and there along the way. If this guy doesn't buy the car I might buy her myself."

"Sounds good to me, I'm sure all the paperwork you need is in the glove compartment. Do you think you can get thirty for it?"

"It'll be close but let's wait and see. I'm going to head out soon; thanks for dinner last night. It couldn't have gone better. I'll call you next week about the car."

Thomas wished him a safe trip and Scott hung up the phone.

After a quick breakfast in his room, he packed his bags. He

traveled light, a small carry-on bag, his laptop and a small suitcase. He called guest services and requested a bellhop to bring his things down.

At 10:37, there was a knock at the door. Scott opened it.

"Good morning, Mr. Randall. My name is Jimmy," said a skinny, pimple faced kid who looked about nineteen. "I'm here to get your luggage."

Scott didn't say a word. He just held up a finger, and then sat on the bed to make another call. The bellhop worked slowly putting the bags on his trolley unable to avoid hearing Scott's side of the conversation.

"Tina. Scott."

"Are you at LAX?" Tina asked.

"No I'm still in Detroit. Missed the plane."

"When's the next flight, can I pick you up?"

"I'm driving. I'm going to bring a car back. It's a 69 Charger."

"From Detroit?"

"Ya, gonna take some time to see the country. Play some golf."

"Did you bring your clubs?"

"Not a problem, I bought some new ones here. Can you stay there until I get back?"

"Sure, they're renovating the pool in my building, so I can use yours for now."

"Great. How's Max?"

"As sweet as ever."

"Good. Don't feed her too much. I don't want a fat dog when I get there."

"You're such a worrier."

"Thanks again, Tina, and let them know at the office that I'm not coming back right away. I'll call you again when I get to Vegas. Bye."

Jimmy said he was ready to go down and Scott followed him out of the room, as though the bellhop knew a shortcut to the lobby.

"Where ya from?" Jimmy asked.

"LA" Scott replied, annoyed that this pimple faced, little pissant was talking to him.

"Nice clubs, Mr. Randall. Where did you play while you were here?"

"Didn't. Just bought them yesterday."

The elevator door opened. Scott was relieved that the Q & A with Jimmy was over. He approached the front desk where a cheerful woman asked, "Checking out?"

He just nodded and said, "Scott Randall."

She typed his name into her computer and inquired, "Was everything satisfactory, Mr. Randall?"

He smiled and nodded without saying anything.

"Your bill has been taken care of by a Mr. Thomas Andrews. If you'll just sign here." He scribbled an illegible signature. "Thank you, please come back and stay with us again."

Scott smiled again. "Thank you. I will."

A few steps behind him Jimmy was waiting with Scott's bags neatly placed on the trolley.

"Can I get you a cab, Mr. Randall?"

"No, I have a car in the garage."

Jimmy pushed the cart inside the first available elevator and Scott stepped in behind him not bothering to say a word.

"Did you park on level one or two, Mr. Randall?" Scott held up two fingers.

The door slid open, the garage was near empty.

"Which one's yours, Mr. Randall?"

"The red Charger just ahead on the right."

The young lad stopped behind the Charger. "Whoa! Bitchin ride."

A smile crossed Scott's lips briefly.

While Jimmy stowed the luggage in the trunk, Scott looked at his watch, 11:15. "Jimmy, I need to pick up a road atlas. Any idea where I can get one?"

"Sure, Mr. Randall. There's a bookstore across the street. I'm sure they would have one."

You couldn't figure that out, Scott thought to himself. You were just there yesterday. Jimmy pointed him in the direction of the stairwell.

"The stairs are the quickest way, Mr. Randall," he said. Scott thanked him, handed him a twenty then walked up the stairs.

Stepping out onto the sidewalk he took a deep breath, exhaled and felt energized by the improved air quality compared with the dank garage. Then two steps toward the street, a familiar pungent odor made him feel nauseated.

"Say man, can ya spare some change?"

It was him, the same bum that spoiled his walk yesterday. So much for the rejuvenated feeling he got from the morning air. The stink on this guy was worse than yesterday. Who would have thought that possible? Scott was as angered by the intrusion as he was repulsed by the smell.

"I told you no yesterday, now fuck off."

The bum just grinned, cocked his finger like a kid playing cops and robbers. He pointed at Scott, made that same clicking sound with his tongue and said "Okie-dokie."

Scott crossed the street and when he looked back the bum was gone.

Inside the bookstore, the same clerk who rang in his purchase the previous day was working the cash register.

"I need a road atlas," Scott announced.

Just then the phone rang and she answered it. "Books and More, can you please hold?" She looked at Scott and pointed him to the travel section. He quickly found the atlas and returned to the checkout, putting the atlas on the counter.

"Hold on," the clerk said into the phone, and then rung in Scott's purchase. "Will there be anything else today, sir?"

He looked out the window, no sign of the smelly man.

"That'll be all," he said.

She smiled that same smile that must be part of the training in retail. "$11.75," she said. She took his money, made change and said, "Please come again." Then she continued her phone conversation.

He put the change in his pocket without counting it and headed back to the hotel garage.

In the driver's seat, Scott opened the road atlas and planned the first leg of his journey. He needed to get to the westbound I-94. Confident that he could get there, he closed the atlas and put the keys in the ignition. The 440 started with a roar that vibrated through the entire garage and then backed out smoothly. He smiled as the tires squawked from the slightest pressure on the gas pedal.

When he got to the sidewalk, a fine mist of water on the windshield blurred his vision. A man reached across the hood and removed the water with a squeegee. The guy leaned up close to the open driver side window with an outstretched hand.

"Jesus Christ," Scott blurted out.

Scott didn't expect to see him again. Yet there he was inches from his face, smiling. The teeth that were there were a decaying yellowish color. Scott's sinuses were now flooded by the bum's breath, the smell turning his stomach.

Offended and a bit shaken, Scott yelled, "Get the fuck away from me!"

The guy's smile never waned. He backed up a step. Then made the same finger gun gesture and clicking sound with his tongue.

Scott squealed the Uniroyals as the back end of the Charger fishtailed a bit, and narrowly missed an oncoming car.

"Fucking freak. Smelly fucking freak." he said to no one in particular.

He drove in silence for fifteen or twenty minutes, more than a little creeped out by too many encounters with the bum. Gradually his mood returned to where it was when the morning air first hit his face. He got to the I-94 with no traffic headaches. The sun was brilliant. The sky was as blue as he could ever remember it being. The wind rushing through the open windows of the car was exhilarating. The familiar drone of the Charger's V-8 was very calming. He reached for the radio.

"Well that isn't original equipment Thomas," he said, not caring that he was alone in the car. AM/FM, four-disc CD changer. He turned it on and pressed the scan button. He stopped when he heard "You're listening to Karen Savelly on 94.7 WCSX and here is Fleetwood Mac." Then Stevie Nicks started to sing "Gold Dust Woman." What rock and roll loving American male doesn't turn up the volume when Stevie starts singing? Thomas' stereo was up to the challenge. Stevie came through loud and clear.

Chapter Eight

It took Roger about five hours to get to the rodeo grounds. He had spent the last hour riding with Bill Hicks. Now there's a man who can talk. From the time he picked Roger up until the time they got to the rodeo he rambled about everything from the weather to the thrush in his favorite horse's front feet. Roger made a sympathetic sigh at that news having no idea what thrush was. He just assumed by the tone of Bill's voice that it wasn't good. One bonus to catching a ride with Bill was his pass to the rodeo. In addition to getting Roger in free, he also offered to show him around after his calf-roping event. With his horse being lame, Bill didn't expect to make the second round.

After Roger adjusted to the smell of livestock, he had a good time wandering around the rodeo. Everywhere the aroma of cotton candy and farm animals hung in the air. The announcer's voice rang out with enthusiasm from cone shaped speakers mounted high on weather beaten wooden poles. Roger enjoyed the bull riding. He hung on the fence like the real cowboys, some of them with large paper numbers pinned to their backs. They all had a sense of purpose in their gaze, studying how the other riders handled each bull and how the bulls reacted.

Roger had just heard the bell indicating the release of the next competitor when he heard the voice of a young woman.

"Hey, you a cowboy?"

Everyone on Roger's section of fence turned to see the source of that inquiry. They all looked down on two girls. Neither girl looked a day over twenty. Both had long dark hair that glistened in the sun.

The Nightcrawler

They were gorgeous, their tight jeans hugging their hips and thighs then disappearing into cowboy boots. The one on Roger's left was wearing a white T-shirt that fit like a second skin, the one on the right a denim shirt rolled up in the middle and tied in a bow exposing her flat midriff. They were both smiling and their twinkling green eyes were locked on Roger. Everyone but Roger had returned to watch the end of the current ride.

Trying to look in control while thinking of a comeback, Roger released one hand from the fence and down he went. His foot had slipped off the metal rung of the fence and he found himself in the dust at their feet.

Just then, there was a loud rattling bang behind him, followed by four cowboys joining Roger on the ground. The bull in the ring had thrown its rider, lost its footing and crashed into the fence with two thousand pounds of force.

The girls giggled at the sight of five men floundering in the dirt and walked off, their jabbering interrupted only by the occasional chortle. The cowboys got right back up and dusted off. Roger sat there watching the girls trundle off toward the barrel racing ring.

"You're real lucky you fell off the fence when you did. That bull's head hit right where you was standing. You'da been stuck for sure," one of the competitors said in a Texas drawl.

Roger looked up to see the source of the voice. A young man, dressed like the competitors, hat, jeans, denim shirt, boots, and a big number 51 on his back stood over him. Roger recognized him as the kid about his own age standing next to him on the fence. The kid turned and joined the other three cowboys who had already got back up on the fence.

Roger looked back to see where the girls went. Apparently they had saved him from serious injury, maybe even death. He had to find them to say thank you. The bull riding was entertaining but those two were the best sightseeing he had done so far on this vacation. He doubted the Grand Canyon would be as awe-inspiring. So he got up, dusted himself off and with an urgency in his stride, he headed in the direction he had last seen them.

"Fella, yer outta yer league." Roger looked back to see number 51 looking down from the fence. He gave the cowboy a wave and walked away.

Roger walked the length of the bull riding ring, circled the calf roping enclosure and scanned the grandstand of both events. All the while the announcer's voice echoed through the grounds. "Let's have a hand for Tommy" or "That should get the newcomer to the next round." Roger barely heard any of it. He had a mission, but there was no sign of those girls. He turned toward the concession stand, the line was long. If they were getting anything to eat or drink they would still be in line. Slowly he made his way along the line. Nothing. There were hundreds of people wandering the rodeo. Finding his rescuers would be a needle in a haystack effort.

After three or four laps around the grounds Roger found himself back at Bill's truck. He decided it was a sign to get back on the road and opened Bill's horse trailer to retrieve his backpack. What he saw inside made him weak in the knees. He'd left his pack hanging on a hook at the front where the horses head would be. Now, the pack lay open on the floor of the trailer, his belongings strewn around it. He leaped inside, and began to inventory his things. Everything remained but his money. What he now had in his pocket would definitely not be enough to get him home so the canyon was out of the question. He had no choice; he would have to phone home for money. There would be some "I told you so's". He knew his parents struggled hard to get their money and he hated asking for more. What choice did he have?

Roger repacked his stuff, and then counted the cash in his pocket. He had less than thirty dollars. He would grab a bite at the concession stand then try to hitch a ride into town. He needed to find a phone.

The line for food looked like it stretched all the way back to Vermont and Roger just didn't have the heart to join the queue. He leaned against one of those wooden poles with the loud speakers at the top and slid down to the ground.

He had been there for just minutes, staring at the tops of his shoes

The Nightcrawler

listening to the commentator announcing a new record for calf roping at this venue when he heard it again.

"Why the long face?"

Roger looked up to see the girl in the white T-shirt. The sun still high in the sky gave her a luminescent glow. He shrugged without speaking. The girl returned his shrug and walked away.

"I got robbed," he said.

She stopped and turned to face him. "Well that sucks."

When Roger didn't offer a response she walked back and prodded him for details. He told her how he got to the rodeo, and what he found when he got back to Bill's trailer. She reached out to the dejected boy. Roger took the offered hand and she tugged to help him to his feet.

"What are you going to do now?"

"I guess I'm going to have to start heading home," he said, picking up his pack.

"And where is home?"

"Vermont."

"Vermont, I knew you were no cowboy."

"And why would you say that?" He asked the question like it wasn't obvious to every rancher and competitor at the rodeo.

"Well, for one thing I've never seen a cowboy wearing shorts and hiking boots." She stepped toe to toe with him. Placed her hands on his shoulders, put her cheek against his and inhaled deeply. Gently pushing him away she added, "Besides, you don't smell like a cowboy."

Roger could feel his ears burning and he knew his cheeks had just gone a deep shade of crimson.

Undaunted he held out his hand, "Roger Morris. You may have saved my life."

"Is that a fact?"

"Yes, it is a fact. Had you not come along when you did I wouldn't have fallen off the fence."

53

She paused for a moment, pondering his assertion.

"How did falling off a fence save your life?"

He explained the bull crashing the fence story to her, then he added, "Well, you got me. What is the punishment for a non-cowboy attending a rodeo?"

"For starters you're going to have to take me to dinner."

"An hour ago that would have been my pleasure, but I have about thirty dollars to my name and I'm about fifteen-hundred miles from home."

"Well then, Vermont, I guess I'm going to have to buy you dinner."

Roger looked toward the line at the concessions, then back to her. She was shaking her head as if to say "You have got to be kidding". They both laughed and Roger asked her name.

"My name is Bethany. My friends call me Beth."

She then grabbed him by the arm and led him away from the crowd.

"There's a barbecue and corn roast at Buffalo Bill's house. Would you like to go?"

"That sounds great, Beth, but I need to get to a town and see if I can get my mom to wire me some money to get home."

The way she was pulling him through the crowd, it didn't appear that she heard him or that he had a choice but to follow.

Finally she said, "That's no problem," looking back over her shoulder in his direction. "I'll give you a lift to town after dinner. But we don't need a ride to the cookout. There are covered wagons that shuttle people back and forth during the rodeo."

"Covered wagons? Like circle the wagons?"

"Yes, just like that, Vermont. So what do you say?" She had stopped and turned to wait for his reply.

"I don't feel right, letting you spend your money on me," he said looking down at his feet.

"We won't need any money. The meal and drinks are included with the entry ticket; my sister gave me her ticket. She hooked up with a cowboy. He's taking her to some hoe-down."

"What's your hurry?" Roger asked. He didn't really care but she did seem to be itching to get away from there as if she were in some kind of trouble.

"What's wrong, Vermont, can't you keep up with a little girl?" She stopped and stood hands on her hips and smiled innocently.

"I had a sausage about an hour ago and I'm not all that hungry."

"Well shit, Vermont, why didn't you say so? What do you say about going for a swim? The dinner can wait; they will be there until eleven or twelve."

"Now that sounds awesome. But where do we swim around here?"

"You leave that to me." She took his arm again and dragged him toward the exit.

The cheering of the crowds and the narration from the speakers faded with each step. Beth led them through the gate and into a large temporary parking lot. They walked down aisles of pickups and livestock trailers parked on grass that had turned brown in the hot, dry summer, then beaten into submission by the abuse of hundreds of heavy vehicles pounding it down.

Beth stopped next to a Hemi-orange Challenger. It seemed so small and out of place surrounded by all the trucks and trailers. She took a single key out of her pocket and handed it to Roger.

"Here, Vermont, you drive."

Roger just stood anchored to the ground, staring at the car.

"You do know how to drive, don't you?" Beth was now standing at the passenger door waiting. Roger walked around to her, pushed a button on the key then opened the door and Beth slid into the car.

He popped the trunk, stowed his pack closing the lid gently, then settled into the driver's seat and turned to Beth. "Whose car?"

"Mine. Daddy gave it to me for graduating high school." Noticing the look of amazement on his face she added. "It's just a car. Now if you're going to see me in my new bikini you're going to have to start the engine and get us the hell out of here."

Eagerly Roger started the car and left the rodeo behind in a cloud of dust. The announcer's commentary faded to garbled noise then it was gone.

Several lefts and rights and an hour later Roger was thoroughly lost. A sudden gloom had come over him. Could this be a practical joke or maybe something much worse? A girl like Beth isn't going to pick him up out of the blue. She was leading him out into the middle of nothing. Her sister hadn't hooked up with a cowboy. She recruited a bunch of friends, they were going to turn him loose out here and hunt him down like it was a rich kid's game reserve, and he was the game.

Letting his imagination, or was it paranoia get the better of him he looked over at her. His anxiety must have been visible because she put her hand on his thigh and asked if he was okay.

"I'm good," he said. "I just get a little nervous when I have no clue where I am."

"Well shit. You're in Nebraska." And she giggled in an innocent way that made him feel more at ease. "See that gate about a quarter mile up on the left? Turn in there."

Not realizing how fast he was going, he had to brake hard when he got to the gate and the tires moaned their disapproval as he turned into the driveway of the Three B's Cattle Ranch still going thirty-five. An ironwork gate that looked like something from a John Wayne movie marked the entrance.

"I'm guessing you are one of the B's. What do the other two mean?"

"My sister Bobbie, you sort of met her at the rodeo, and my brother Billy. Can you believe it? Bobbie, Billy and Bethany, how lame sounding is that?"

Roger had been captivated by this girl. He was so rapt by the sound of her voice and the way she tilted her head when she was trying to be flirtatious that he failed to be impressed by the biggest house he

The Nightcrawler

had ever seen. He was imprisoned by emotion and he didn't want to be let out. He turned to her and she motioned for him to drive around back. Just as they cleared the side of the three-story stucco mansion, a white garage sporting six bays and a green hip roof with three dormers came into view.

"Just park over there." Beth motioned to the side of the garage.

Roger parked the car and quipped. "So does your dad supply the whole country with beef?

"Well not Alaska and Hawaii." Giggling again, she got out of the car and Roger followed. "I changed my mind, Vermont. I'm not going to show you my new bikini." She turned and walked around back of the garage.

"Hey. Wait up." Roger called as he double-timed after her. When he caught up to Beth, she was standing at the edge of the pool. It was a big pool. Olympic-size, Roger figured. The sun reflected off the water like a barrage of sparkling jewels rising out of the blue depth. It was surrounded by white columns topped with lamps. Several stone statues of naked men and women guarded the perimeter. In the far corner a hot tub was being tended by another statue of a nude woman holding a large decanter. The decanter was tilted and water poured endlessly into the hot tub. The pool area looked more like a scene from Greece than a backyard pool in Nebraska. Ivy climbed up many of the columns adding a splash of green to the picture. As impressed as he was with the scene, it all paled in his eyes when he shifted his gaze to Beth. She stood motionless on the cut stone deck surrounding the pool. Her hair framed her face and hung over her shoulders. Her eyes seemed to be smiling although her lips were not. Roger would have never thought anyone could be so completely captivating. If she looked this good in a T-shirt and jeans, could he hold it together when she changed into a swimsuit? He approached her slowly and she held up her hands motioning him to stay where he was. He stopped his advance without removing his eyes from the vision in front of him.

Beth smirked at him as if to dare him to move without permission. Almost like he were a dog being tempted out of a stay command. He didn't move. Mostly because he had no idea what the rules of this game were, or what game he was playing for that matter. She was beautiful, confident and definitely in charge of this encounter. Without warning, she bolted toward the side of the garage. A steel staircase painted the same green as the roof lead to a loft above.

When she reached the base of the stairs she called back, "Well Vermont, are you coming?" She had about a twenty-yard head start on him but he climbed the stairs three at a time and gently bumped into her at the top before she could open the door.

They entered the loft and Roger couldn't believe what he saw. He expected some old farm equipment and maybe a small change room. This was a lavish apartment, bigger than his parent's house. The furniture was contemporary. A huge TV mounted on the wall came to life. It was loud, and the channel was set to MTV. Beth seemed to notice Roger's confusion.

"We had it connected to the motion sensor. When we walk in the room the TV comes on. Isn't it cool?"

"You do have a swimsuit in that pack, don't you?"

He looked over his shoulder toward the door. His pack was still stowed in the back of the car. She pointed toward the last room on the right at the end of the hall. "You can change in there."

He stood, watching her saunter down the hall, unable to believe this was happening to him. His eyes followed her every curve gliding away from him. If an expression could define happiness, it was the one on Roger Morris' face as he gawked at Beth's retreat.

"You better haul ass, Vermont, you don't want me to change my mind about treating you to dinner, do you?"

He turned and bolted from the room taking the stairs three at a time to retrieve his pack and two at a time on the return trip. A quick look around told him he had entered a guest room. An oak four poster covered with a patchwork quilt, a matching oak bureau and some paintings on the walls, all depicting some old west cattle drive. Two doors on the wall opposite the window opened to a full bathroom and a

The Nightcrawler

small closet. He tossed the backpack onto the bed and explored the room. Closet empty, bureau empty, a cabinet behind the bathroom mirror empty. Roger walked over to the window and looked down on the pool. He began to wonder if Beth's dad owned all of Nebraska. Just then his thoughts were interrupted by Beth's voice through the door.

"What the hell, Vermont, did you fall asleep in there?"

"Sorry, I'll be right out."

When he opened the door, Beth stood leaning on the opposite wall. Roger was stunned. *Sports Illustrated* would not be able to print a better cover for the swimsuit edition than what he was looking at.

She held her arms out in a runway model pose and said. "Well, what do you think?"

Roger searched for an answer but all he could muster was a boyish grin. She returned the smile and he followed her to the pool.

Roger looked up the road. It was dark, but for the streetlights illuminating the black pavement. Turning in the opposite direction the scene was the same. A fog seemed to hover just above the tops of the light standards. In the distance the two rows of lights merged. A brightness different from the street lamps blossomed, causing Roger a sense of unease. As it got closer he realized headlights were headed his way. Closer and closer they came, now two distinct orbs. Squinting, Roger struggled to see the oncoming demon. The rumble of the laboring motor indicated a high rate of speed. The lights were close enough to make out now. That car. The same car, the same dream. A big red noisy car. New but not new. Or was it old but not old? It didn't make sense. Speeding straight at him. Each streetlight extinguished as it passed. The headlights bright and blinding, freezing him to the spot. Then darkness. He saw himself lying on his back looking at the stars. His body in the same grotesque position as the dream he had in old Pete's truck. Roger knew what would come next but he was helpless not to look. That same guy. *Why did he look so angry, staring down at the twisted, bleeding body? Close your eyes, Roger, and he'll go away.* When he opened them again the guy was gone. Somebody else stood over him. *Come closer. Help me.* Roger fought the confusion that

59

pushed him toward panic. He seemed to be communicating to this person without speaking. It was a girl. She came closer and held out her hand. Big sister Lisa had come to his rescue. He wanted to reach for her but couldn't. Then she began to back away. Not walking, more like floating. Her legs weren't moving. He screamed her name. LISAAAA!

Roger woke confused and terrified. His breathing came in heavy gulps and sweat dripped from his face, as he sat bolt upright in the dark.

Beth rushed in, flicking on the light.

"Hey Vermont, are you okay?"

They both blinked and looked to the floor until their eyes adjusted and he saw Beth standing in the doorway. "What the hell? I thought you were being murdered in here."

He told her about the dream. About the car and the guy. The angry guy.

She was sitting next to him on the bed hoping to offer some comfort, her hand on his leg. He just stared blankly at the wall.

"Who's Lisa?" she asked.

Without looking at her he answered in a monotone almost trembling voice, "My sister."

"She died when I was ten. She was twelve, almost thirteen. We were tobogganing near the pond at the park. She wasn't supposed to use that side of the hill. She slid right out on the ice. All the way to the middle of the pond. She got halfway back then she was gone."

"As far back as I can remember Mom called her my guardian angel. She saved my life when I was two and after that she was my protector. Then she was gone."

He looked at Beth and she wiped a tear from his cheek.

"Sounds like she is still your guardian angel," Beth said, then leaned over and kissed his cheek where the tear had been. "It's the middle of the night. I'm going back to bed."

She staggered back to the door, yawning while she walked. She stopped at the door, turned to look at Roger, like a mother looking in on a child who had just had a bad dream.

"Good night, Roger," she said and turned out the light.

Roger's dream was a vague memory, replaced by the vision of Beth, standing at the door in her little nightie. It took all his control, combined with a huge fear of rejection to keep him from following her across the hall.

It took hours for him to get back to sleep, but when he did, he had no more visits from demon cars or dead sisters.

Chapter Nine

Around one o'clock Scott took the I-69 exit to Ft. Wayne. He got off the highway minutes later at W. Michigan Ave. feeling hungry and needing gas. He pulled into a full service Mobil station. A scruffy man in blue overalls approached the car. The patch on his right breast pocket indicated his name was Sam. He looked older than he probably was and very familiar. His shoulders slumped, he appeared beaten down by the knowledge that unless his lotto numbers come in, this is as good as it gets.

"Filler up, mister?"

"Ya. And check the oil and coolant," Scott instructed him dismissively.

There was a small confectionary and Scott went inside. He picked up a small Coleman cooler. A bag of ice and two six packs of Dr. Pepper, some chips and a bag of M&M's.

"That all?" said the woman by the cash register.

"And gas," he answered pointing to the car.

She checked the LED display behind her. Scanned the bar codes on the items in front of her and said, "Fifty-nine dollars."

Scott gave her three twenties and she handed him a single without looking up. Service with a smile, he thought.

"Can you recommend a place for lunch close by?"

Still not looking up she replied, "Charlie's, across the street."

When he got back to the car, Sam was leaning against the pump. Scott walked past him and opened the door.

"Nice car, mister," Sam said. "Oil's down about half a quart, maybe less. You want me to top it up?"

Scott just waved him off. He wondered, was it just his luck today or did all the lowlifes in Michigan smell this bad? Back inside the car he heard what sounded like "okie-dokie" and that tongue clicking sound. A chill ran down his spine and the hairs on the back of his neck bristled up against the collar of his shirt. With a flurry of movement, Scott started the car, put it in gear and drove to the edge of the road. Framed in the rear-view Sam leaned against the storefront.

"For Christ's sake, Scott," he scolded himself. "Get that bum out of your head. He's at least a hundred miles behind you."

This worked like a pep talk. Scott considered himself a realist. In his mind, there were no monsters, no ghosts or goblins. Bigfoot is an old Indian myth, perpetuated by tourist centers of the north-west. If you can't see it, or feel it, then it isn't real. That is what Scott Randall believed and it's worked out for him so far. Since it was not possible for a panhandler from Detroit to follow him, then it only made sense to forget about the fucker and enjoy his road trip.

He took his foot off the brake pedal and began to cross the street. The loud scream of a car horn brought his concentration back to the road. A light blue, maybe grey blur streaked by, missing the front of the Charger by inches. Panic and instinct took over and he pounded his foot back on the brake with all the force he had.

The car stopped with the nose jutting out onto the road. Scott took a deep breath. He could feel his heart pounding in his chest. So, this is what junior in the Honda felt like when the front end of his car was scattered all over the road. Well maybe Junior felt worse. Scott checked for traffic, and then proceeded to Charlie's.

It didn't look like much. The neon sign by the road definitely lacked inspiration. "Charlie's" in big red print. Below that, printed in blue, "Good Food". The building was a small wood frame structure with a second level over the restaurant. There was probably an apartment, maybe two on the second floor. Clean looking, and nicely painted white, with green trim. The door looked like something from an old farmhouse. Panels on the bottom, and windows at the top divided into nine sections. An Open sign hung on the inside of the door.

It looked even smaller from inside. The front wall along the windows was lined with booths. The tabletops were all reddish brown Formica. A narrow aisle separated the booths from circular bar stools along the length of a bar with the same surface as the tables. The bar reminded him of the soda shop he used to go to when he was a kid. Behind the bar was a woman dressed in a sleeveless denim shirt. The lines on her face were deep but it was obvious that there was a time when she could take her pick of the boys. A time before life etched out its map on her features.

"Sit wherever you like, hon," she said. Her voice had a deep sexy quality and her expression was warm and friendly.

He sat at a booth beside the window. There were paper place mats on the tables with the menu printed on them. Scott picked one up and began to scan the selections.

How ya doin'?" He got a start as he turned to see the woman from behind the bar standing next to him. "I'm sorry, didn't mean to scare ya. My name's Grace."

Scott just smiled and said, "What's good here?"

"I saw ya talkin' with Sam across the street. Now if you was to ask him he'd tell ya to get the chili." She looked across the street at the Mobil station. "He comes in every Monday for the chili. It's on special on Mondays. He sure is a sweet boy. Always smells like Aqua Velva. Just a sweet boy."

"Sam. Sam standing at those pumps across the street?" Scott looked over to see a young man in blue overalls.

"Well the other Sam isn't so sweet is he?"

"Other Sam?" Grace asked.

Scott could see confusion on her face.

"The Sam who filled my tank wasn't a kid. He was a lot older than you are. Scruffy and he smelled worse than the men's locker room after a big game. And, I tell you something. There's a guy panhandling in

The Nightcrawler

Detroit right now who has to be his brother."

"Ain't anyone over there like that, mister."

"The name's Scott."

"Like I said, Scott, ain't but one Sam over there. There he is. Ya see 'im? Such a sweet boy."

Scott looked across the street. Even from this distance, he could tell that that wasn't who he saw fill his tank. He was just a kid. His blond hair was shining in the sunlight. He stood in front of the store right where the old Sam had been when Scott drove away.

Scott started to feel something in the pit of his stomach. Sweat began to bead from his forehead. The lift his pep talk had given him minutes earlier had melted away, leaving a puddle of doubt. He looked up at Grace standing there. She was looking through the window at Sam. She had a look of adoration on her face. She looked like a mother watching her boy climb into the school bus for the first time. Turning her gaze to Scott, the look of fondness for Sam changed to concern. He was looking right through her, his hands still holding the paper placemat. They were trembling. The paper fluttered as though a stiff breeze were blowing across the room.

"You feelin' okay, mister?"

"What? Oh, sorry I'm fine. Just a bit hungry." He forced a smile onto his face. "Grace, I'm going to have a turkey club," he said with a jovial tone, trying to put himself in a better mood.

"Good choice, mister," Grace said jotting it down on her pad. "Anything to drink? Made a fresh jug of lemonade this morning, squeezed the lemons myself."

"Lemonade sounds great. And please call me Scott."

"All righty, comin' right up, Scott."

Scott watched her walk away. Her denim shirt was tucked neatly into tight jeans. He stared as she crossed the room to the kitchen. Her long ponytail hung to the middle of her back, shiny and dark. It was a stark contrast to the faded denim. His mood had brightened as he watched her ass until she disappeared through the swinging door to the kitchen. Alone in the dining area, he stared across the street.

The Mobil station looked deserted. He saw no sign of any Sam, young or old. He looked over at the Charger. The sun glared off the glass and chrome. The red paint almost glowed. He concentrated on the hood. Thinking about Sarah, her hot naked ass had been buffing that hood just hours ago; he began to feel aroused.

A slight thud brought him back to the present. Grace had returned and set his lemonade on the table. The tall glass garnished with a piece of lemon wedged on the rim already dripped with condensation.

"There ya go. That'll pick up your spirits."

She leaned on the table to look at the sky. "The guy on the radio said we might get a storm today. Sure don't look like it. Does it?"

Scott agreed, not that he could tell anything about the weather. While she was leaning on the table looking toward the sky, he was gaping at her breasts thinking "Amazing Grace". She noticed but didn't seem to care. She just stood up and grinned.

"Your club will be ready in a minute," she said and returned to the kitchen.

Again, he watched her until she was out of sight, and then looked back to the pumps across the street. Sam was cleaning the windshield of a blue minivan. He looked like the Sam that Grace had described. Letting go of his paranoia, Scott looked around Charlie's. He hadn't noticed until now that he was the sole diner. The only sounds were the muffled sounds of the traffic passing by outside and Shania Twain coming from a radio behind the bar.

"There ya go," Grace said setting his plate down. "You ain't touched the lemonade. I can get you something else if you like."

"It's fine. So is it always this slow in here?" he asked as he sprinkled salt on his fries.

"We do okay for lunch. Business really dropped when the McDonald's went in just up the road."

"Grace, I really hate eating alone. Would you like to join me?"

"Well, I could use a coffee break," she replied with a mischievous grin. She walked away and returned moments later with a glass of lemonade. "Decided it was too hot in here to be drinkin' coffee."

Scott ate almost without speaking. Grace didn't really need anyone's help carrying a conversation. Scott would smile or nod at the appropriate moments and she would go off again. How she's owned Charlie's for seven years. That she was married once. It didn't last as long as her marriage with Charlie's. Scott thought she probably used that line more than once but he laughed just the same. Her look turned somewhat somber when she told him about her daughter. She called her Sandie. Grace had given Sandie up for adoption a month after she was born. Kids shouldn't raise kids, she said.

"She's twenty-seven now," Grace said with pride in her eyes. "I bet she'll be finishing med school next year."

"I bet she will," Scott said.

Then he caught her wiping a tear from the corner of her eye. "Sun sure is bright, isn't it?" She mused, gazing across the street.

When she looked back Scott was checking out her breasts again.

"Not bad eh?" She cupped her hands under them. Her voice had regained the jovial tone she had when she first sat down. "They cost me a pretty penny. Money well spent, don't ya think?"

Scott flushed a bit. He could feel his ears turning red. He looked at her chest again as if by invitation, and then looked into her eyes. She was smiling like a teenage girl, just asked to the prom. She sat up as straight as she could. Her shoulders pushed back. Her chest seemed to be crossing the table toward him. He had an urge to reach over to meet them. He had only ever been with younger women, no older than twenty-seven, maybe thirty. Nevertheless, as he sat across from Grace, forty-five years old, maybe fifty, he was aroused. He wondered if she knew how turned on he was.

The door opened and a woman walked in. She was about thirty, tall with short dark hair, small on the top, and big on the bottom. Scott thought she looked like a walking pear. She was wearing a white T-shirt that was loose on her shoulders and tight around the hips.

"Hey Annie," Grace called out, waving.

Annie walked over to the table.

"Scott, this is Annie."

"Hi Annie, it's a pleasure."

Annie nodded but didn't say anything. Grace excused herself and walked with Annie into the kitchen.

Scott took a twenty out of his pocket and put in on the table. The price on the menu was $6.99. He felt somehow ashamed. She was a nice lady. Not old enough to be his mother, but maybe his mother's little sister, and he checked her out like a butcher eyeing a side of beef. He stood up and left, not wanting to wait until she got back.

He opened the car door, but before getting in, he heard a familiar voice. "You forgot your change."

Grace was standing a few yards away. She looked younger out here. The sun's rays put a glow on her face that seemed to erase the lines he'd noticed inside.

He just raised his hand up in front of him as if to keep her at arms length.

"That's okay, Grace. Keep it."

"Listen, Scott," she said coming closer. "I live up top of Charlie's. Would you like to come up and chat? It does get lonely up there."

He could feel an erection coming on. His wish to sneak away before she got back to the table had been replaced by a lust that over took him with a fury. He closed the car door and stepped toward her. With a pleased look on her face, she turned and he followed her to the stairs at the side of the building.

Scott spent most of the afternoon up in Grace's place. He had never known sex like that. She was like a piano teacher placing a child's hands on the correct keys. Only her body was the piano and he was the child. She was setting the pace. At first, she slowed him down. If he moved too slowly, she would shift gears and he would follow. He felt like he was doing it for the first time. He was tempted to stay the night when she invited him, but decided against it.

"You better stop in next time you're in Michigan," Grace insisted.

He just nodded politely and went out to the car.

Scott Randall would never see Grace or Charlie's again.

Chapter Ten

Forest Glenn, Indiana, is a quaint little hollow not quite half way between Fort Wayne and Indianapolis. It's mostly a residential community, home to commuters who make the daily trip to nearby Muncie, or Anderson.

It's Mayberry living at its best. With a population of less than two thousand, everyone knows everyone else's business. The only commerce in town is on Main Street. Standing on the corner of Main and First is the Mercantile Trust, a classy looking building with a stone facade and columns framing the main entrance. A large white-faced clock with Roman numerals keeps time over the door. It's been the only banking in town since Forest Glenn became a town. Looking out from the bank you can see Gordon's Pharmacy, a sign in the window advertising Coca Cola, $5.99 a case. Opposite Gordon's stands a newer two story brick building, The Forest Glenn Medical Center, a list of doctors and dentists displayed in brass on the marquee in front. Across from the bank, Amy's Deli, in the window a poster promoting adopt-a-dog week at the Forest Glenn Shelter.

Looking in either direction down Main Street, it isn't the bowling alley, or the shops that catch your eye. Not the gas station or the high school. It is the clean tree-lined streets. Almost too clean, like they were actually on a Hollywood set and Gene Kelly was going to come dancing down the middle of the road any minute. There are no concrete light poles standing twenty feet above the road. These are the old-fashioned black iron light poles, the kind with the frosted white spheres on top.

One block north or south of First, Main turns residential, with

The Nightcrawler

grand old houses from days gone by. No two alike on the full length of the street.

On the corner of Main Street and Maple sits a stately Georgian two and a half story. It is a brown brick colonial with a row of windows on the second floor and a bay window on each side of the beautifully framed front entrance. The front yard is small and surrounded by a knee-high hedge, trimmed with geometric precision. In front a sign, "Shady Glenn B&B". In the driveway next to the hedge, a red 69 Dodge Charger with Michigan plates dripped with dew left by a cool humid night.

Scott Randall walked out onto the porch. He was dressed like a man on his way to the links. Tan shorts and a dark-blue shirt. He turned as the door squeaked open and a kindly looking woman, who Scott thought had to be a sister to Alice from the Brady Bunch stood in the opening. She wore her hair in a bun, a floral print dress that went just past her knees and a white apron.

"Would you like to have breakfast in the gazebo, Mr. Randall?" she asked him.

"Just a coffee and maybe a Danish if you have any." He didn't bother to look at her. His mind was on the road. He hoped to make up some time today.

"Well, that's no kind of breakfast. I'll bring you some eggs and toast. You just come right in and sit down at the table and let Lizzie take care of things."

Scott turned to look at her now. He was smiling and thoughts of his grandmother trying to get him to eat breakfast came rushing through his head. Whenever he stayed at Gran's she always tried to get him to eat. *Have another sausage, Scottie, eat all your pasta, it will put hair on your chest, have some cake, Scottie, you're too skinny.* Lizzie stood holding the door open with a look that said, *come in and eat, or you can't go out to play with your friends.* He went back inside and Lizzie followed.

Scott didn't have much time to read *The Indianapolis Star* that

71

Lizzie had left on the table. She returned in minutes and put a plate with eggs, bacon and hash browns down in front of him. She left without a word and returned moments later with a pitcher of orange juice and four slices of toast.

"I just started a fresh pot of coffee, Mr. Randall. Can I get you anything else?"

"Well Lizzie, you can start by calling me Scott and I think I'll pass on the coffee after all."

Lizzie went back into the kitchen and returned with a small mug in her hand. She put it down on the table opposite Scott and sat down. She sipped the coffee then asked, "So Mr. Ran..., I mean Scott. Do you plan on being in the area for a while?"

Slightly amused by her questioning, Scott explained that he was passing through on his way back to LA. Being a true ambassador to her community, Lizzie tried to interest him in some local attractions. Forest Glenn Country Club, it was private she explained, but her nephew worked there and could get him a tee time. The wineries just about forty miles from Muncie were beautiful and she felt the Heritage Car Museum might interest him considering the old Dodge in her driveway.

Scott finished eating while she gushed on about the local charm that was Forest Glenn. He had put his bag out on the front porch earlier and when he got a break in Lizzie's sales pitch he stood, thanked her for the hospitality and walked to the front door. There was no hustle and bustle of daily life out on Main. The only sounds were birds, a barking dog in the distance and a lawn mower next door. He stepped out onto the porch, bid Lizzie goodbye, descended the steps and walked along a small garden path that crossed the front of the house leading to the driveway. Snapdragons and marigolds bordered each side of the walk. He passed through a small gap in the hedge, tossed his bag in the backseat, got into Thomas' car, opened his road atlas and planned the day's route.

He wasn't happy with the progress he had made yesterday. Now Sarah and Grace were just fond memories. He would make up a little

The Nightcrawler

time today, and tomorrow he would be in better shape. He closed the atlas and left it on the passenger seat. He would head toward Indianapolis then take I-70 across the heartland to Utah. He had been skiing there many times, but had never seen the mountains in the summer.

Scott started the car and began to back out of the driveway. Lizzie remained on the porch, He looked back and gave her a wave. When his attention returned to driving, a man stood on the sidewalk directly behind the car. He jammed the brake pedal and stopped inches from the man's legs.

Scott looked up to see an emotionless grin on a face that haunted his mind. It was the bum from Detroit. It had to be, no two people could look that much alike. Scott's breakfast began to churn in his stomach. He didn't recognize the emotion he was experiencing. Was it fear, anger, anxiety? He had a strong urge to punch the accelerator and put the rank smelling fucker out of his misery.

His fugue state was broken however by the sound of Lizzie's voice. "Archie you old coot get the hell out of the way before you get killed."

Scott spun toward the porch and when he looked back the bum was gone and in his place stood Archie, a gangly white haired old man with blue denim overalls and a big straw hat. Archie waved Lizzie off with a swipe of his hand and walked on.

Scott backed the car to the edge of the road, stopped and watched the senior gent saunter along. The Charger entered the roadway and headed in the same direction as old Archie. Scott drove slowly past glancing over at him, checking to make sure it wasn't the bum. When he got alongside him, Archie looked into the car with a big yellow smirk, cocked his finger like a gun and pointed it at Scott just like the bum had yesterday. Thoroughly creeped out, Scott punched the gas pedal. With the smell of burning rubber and the sound of squealing tires, Archie was but a speck in the rearview.

Heading through Forest Glenn, the red Charger slowed down only for stop signs and the solitary red light at First and Main. A slight squawk emanated from the rear tires each time it pulled away from a stop.

Scott drove out of town taking little notice of the quaint architecture. His head was beginning to ache and the bright sun seemed to be drilling through his eyes to the center of his brain. It seemed that each car he passed had a grubby looking driver grinning at him with yellow teeth. They were all pointing their fingers and winking. He thought he could actually hear them making that fucking clicking sound. He wondered if it might be some kind of mid-west salutation, but he had been in this area several times and hadn't noticed it before. He blamed the gesture for his pounding head. The damn gesture was a vice and each time he saw it the vice tightened another turn increasing the pressure between his ears. So, he didn't pass any cars and didn't let any pass him unless he couldn't help it. If they did pass he stared straight ahead.

Chapter Eleven

By midmorning, Roger wished he had denied ever having ridden a horse. Sure, he and Ed had gone riding a couple of times, but only for an hour each time. Beth rousted him from the guest room at 6:00 am and had him in the saddle by 7:30. After three hours his ass was killing him.

Not even the ache in his rear end however could dampen Roger's awe at the vastness of the landscape. The bleakness of central Nebraska had turned quite stunning here. The trees, hills and outcropping rocks were things that together could inspire artists. He hadn't seen a sign of human habitation in over an hour, not a power line, road, or even a fence post. Back in Vermont there was forest and wilderness, but this seemed endless.

"Beth, don't the people around here mind you riding through their property?"

"I don't know. I have never ridden off Daddy's land."

"Man, your backyard must be as big as the state of Vermont."

She shrugged, then without warning, kicked her heels into the side of her mount, and hollered, "YAAH."

The bay filly beneath her bolted, leaving Roger literally in the dust. He watched her ride off, her hair whipping out behind her. It occurred to him that if he lost her out here he might never find his way back. With a kick and a, "Yeehaw!" his black horse galloped after her. He knew he wasn't catching up but at least he could still see her. No amount of urging got him closer, but at least he maintained his distance. He would rejoin her when she decided to let him. He knew it, and contented himself with the belief that she would indeed let him. In a few minutes she pulled her horse up and moments later Roger came to a stop beside her. Both horses were damp with sweat and beneath the reins lather streaked their necks. Their chests heaved and nostrils flared as they drew in much needed air.

Beth made a great tour guide. She spoke with enthusiastic pride as she pointed out trees and rocks. She walked him through an archeological dig site. A group of students gathered artifacts the previous summer from what they believe was an Arapaho camp. He loved the sound of her voice and he couldn't keep his eyes off her. At first, the riding was fun. Roger thought seeing the countryside from horseback could not be equaled, but by 11:00 am he was glad to see Beth climb down from her horse. Happily, he followed suit only to find his legs had gone to sleep. When he swung his right leg over to dismount, his numb left leg buckled and he fell to the ground. Beth burst into a fit of laughter as Roger tried in vain to salvage some dignity by not letting her know that he may be injured.

"Is that how you Easterners get off a horse?" she said through her giggles.

"Well, why climb down when gravity is perfectly capable of doing it for you?"

Beth wrapped the reins of her horse around a tree branch, and then walked over to where Roger's mount stood grazing. The big black horse trotted a few steps away after his rider fell to the ground at his hooves. Beth secured the second animal then plopped on the ground next to her fallen companion.

"My legs went to sleep," Roger said. His voice sounded a bit shaky and his heart rate was still a bit elevated from the fall. Add to that the pins and needles in his legs had begun, as the circulation returned to his lower extremities.

"I guess I should have remembered, you're not a cowboy," she said through another wave of guffaws.

He shoved her, a bit harder than he had intended causing her to tumble on her side but she continued to laugh. Roger joined in on the laughter, while rubbing and massaging his thighs.

"How about some lunch, Vermont?"

"Sounds great, can we get a pizza delivered?"

Beth didn't answer that question. She stood and extended a hand, "Can you walk yet?"

He accepted the hand offered, not that he needed it, and stood.

"I think I can manage."

"Then go get the saddle bag from your horse," she said pointing.

He managed, none too gracefully to his horse. Pulled at the saddlebag a couple of times, then noticed the straps. He undid the ties, flung the leather bag over his shoulder like he had seen in many a western. He turned back to Beth seated on a blanket in the shade of the tree where her horse was tethered.

Roger joined her on the blanket, handing her the pack. She tossed him a bottle of water and a sandwich in a Ziploc bag. "I hope you're not allergic to peanut butter."

Biting into his sandwich he said, "Mmmmm, Peevee thay." Another round of giggles followed his peanut butter induced speech impediment.

"Jiffy and Smucker's, nothing but the best," she replied.

She pointed out a colony of prairie dogs, which they watched while they ate their picnic lunch. They even saw one take flight in the talons of a bald eagle. After lunch they walked around, Beth schooling him on the flora and fauna as they went. She showed him some elk, wild turkeys, and even a rattlesnake sunning itself on a rock.

Roger was in heaven. He hadn't even known this girl yesterday and today he couldn't imagine not knowing her. Yet sadness came with that feeling. He had a mission. The canyon was his goal and he always followed through. Quitters never win and winners never quit. Roger Morris was no quitter. He would have to say goodbye soon. The canyon was waiting. He would not lose sight of the goal.

To Roger it felt like they had traveled three hours in a straight line away from the ranch. If it took half the day to get out here, it would logically take half a day to get back. With the lunch break and the walk through the hills, he was sure it would be well past dark when they returned.

"Should we be getting back soon?" he asked.

"Sure, I like to have a swim after riding."

Together they shook the blanket clean and folded it. They packed the baggies and bottles in the saddlebags and Roger followed Beth in what he felt sure was the wrong direction, but to his surprise, an hour later they were back at the ranch.

Chapter Twelve

By late afternoon Scott was on I-70 just past St. Louis. His headache had subsided to a dull throb. With an empty stomach and nature calling, it was time for a pitstop. A sign displaying the symbols for food, lodging, restrooms and gas at exit 36 was all the invitation he needed to get off the highway. He hadn't even noticed that he was on empty until he pulled into a Mobil station. He filled the tank and paid at the window.

"You have a restroom I can use?"

The clerk was watching a small TV and didn't look up. He put a key attached to a long chain on the counter and pointed to the left side of the building. Bright blue doors with the men and women restroom symbols broke the dreariness of the solid cement block wall.

Surveying the road Scott decided the Wendy's across the street would fill the void that was his stomach. He could use the drive thru and wouldn't have to interact with anybody shooting off their fingers.

With heavy traffic it might have been a bit of a challenge crossing the road, but with the 440's torque it wasn't too much of a problem. At the menu board a crackling voice inquired, "Welcome to Wendy's drive thru. Can I help you?"

"I'll have a Classic combo with a Coke, please."

"Would you like to make that a large for forty-nine cents, sir?"

"That would be great, thanks."

"$6.89. Please drive up to the first window."

A minute later a teenage boy handed him a cup of Coke the size of a child's beach pail. Scott set the cup on the passenger seat and balanced it with his right hand. A much more cumbersome task than the pop cans he'd been used to up to this point. A few seconds later the lad returned and handed him a yellow bag.

"Wendy's Classic combo, large?"

"Thanks" Scott said. He parked in the Wendy's lot overlooking the road and took a drink from the bucket-o-Coke. He watched the traffic in silence while he ate his burger and fries. When he finished he carried the empty bag and other trash to the garbage can at the corner of the parking lot. It felt good to be on his feet. Scott decided to walk a while to get some blood back to his legs so he got his Coke from the car and walked in the opposite direction he had driven in from the highway.

About a hundred yards from the corner the concrete sidewalk gave way to a paved shoulder. Scott was the lone pedestrian, which suited him fine. No people meant nobody making gun motions with their fingers. It also meant no smelly vagrants. He watched with some interest as two teenaged boys on a single bicycle passed him on the opposite side of the road. The bike looked much too small. The boy on the seat pedaled with great effort while the passenger stood on posts extending from the rear axel. He saw nothing unusual about these boys. It was a scene that could play out in every town across the nation but Scott watched them until they turned into a driveway and disappeared.

Crosby Park was what had drawn the boys on the bike. With nothing else of interest within sight, Scott crossed the road. The main attraction in the park was a skateboard area. The cement ramps and hills captivated at least a dozen kids doing their best to find a way to the emergency room. Scott leaned on the fence watching with some admiration as boys with bleeding knees and elbows, flipped and twisted, zipped and grinded with some degree of skill.

"Higher, Mommy, go higher," a small child's voice called out.

Scott looked to the source of the child's plea to find a young woman pushing her son on a swing. The boy's expression was joy, plain and simple. It would have been hard to imagine anything could thrill the child more than what he was doing right then. His mother seemed to share his fun until she noticed Scott watching. Her smile faded somewhat and Scott sent her an awkward smile before walking away.

An hour had passed when he returned to his car. Maybe it was two hours he didn't know for sure and didn't really care. He felt better than he had since getting up from the table at Lizzie's. He went back into Wendy's to use the facilities. Picked up another Coke for the road and walked out to the car. The sun was getting quite low in the western sky. It would be dark in a couple of hours and he wanted to get a little more distance in before stopping for the night.

Across the road next to the Mobil station, a large tractor-trailer pulled up and stopped. He waited for the rig to clear the intersection so he could proceed but it didn't move. Scott grew impatient as he watched the truck but it remained parked and nobody got out. The sun reflected off the driver's side window making it impossible to see the inside. The side of the trailer had an orange glow. He could hear a slight clanking of the diesel engine and a hue of blue exhaust rose from the stacks just above the top of the trailer. The traffic disappeared with the arrival of the truck, replaced with a freakish quiet.

Curious, he squinted at the truck trying to get a view of the driver but his gaze couldn't penetrate the glare. He began to feel an uneasy presence and convinced himself the source of the anxiety was inside that truck. He backed up parallel to the truck trying to get a better vantage, but the glare off the truck didn't diminish.

Scott drove out onto the street slowly moving alongside the rig. When the two front bumpers were even, someone darted out in front of him and stopped directly in Scott's path. He jammed both feet on the brake pedal and the tires screeched to a halt. It was a girl, or young woman. She stood there for a few seconds, eyes wide with fright. The sun's reflection gave her a celestial glow.

Her trance-like stare was broken by some noise from behind the rig. She ran to the passenger side door of the Charger, swung it open and climbed in before Scott could object.

She screamed, "Get the hell out of here!"

Scott hit the gas pedal and blue smoke from the burning rubber of the rear tires spewed out from the wheel wells. He stopped at the corner and looked in his rearview. A large man carrying a baseball bat was running up the road yelling something that to Scott was just gibberish. Gibberish that was without a doubt, fueled by anger.

The girl hugged her backpack and looked back over her left shoulder. "Go." Her tone and volume made it quite clear that whoever that was back there was dangerous. The tires squawked a bit as the Charger made the right turn and accelerated back up the road to the interstate.

With the angry batter no longer in view Scott looked over at his passenger. She was very young and pretty in a girl-next-door sort of way. Scott's best guess had her at eighteen, twenty tops. She wore denim shorts that were tight around her thighs, a white sleeveless T-shirt that seemed a size too small and a Detroit Tiger's cap. A long blonde ponytail trailed out of the cap and her blue-green eyes stared unblinking into the rearview mirror on the door.

"What the hell was that all about?" Scott asked. She didn't answer. She continued to stare out the window as if the guy from the truck would be giving chase any minute. Scott pulled off the road.

"Look, either you get out of the car or answer the question. What the hell was that?"

"Like, okay. I'll tell you, just drive."

She looked at him while wiping a tear from the corner of her eye. "He picked me up near Toledo. I'm hitching to LA to get a job. He seemed nice enough. When I started to fall asleep, he told me to climb in the back. Said I'd be more comfy. I'm like, it's better than waking with a stiff neck. So I did."

She paused and shrugged her shoulders as if to say, "Stupid me."

"So anyway, I'm in the back sleeping and I get woken up by a hand squeezing my ti…, my breast."

She paused again but this time she seemed resolute, not shaken at all.

"Creeped me out. Well I pepper-sprayed the fucker. Didn't get him clean or he wouldn't have chased us down the road with that bat, but he'll think twice the next time he tries that. Like, what a perv."

"No doubt he will," Scott replied grinning like she was his little sister who had just chased off an overly amorous suitor.

"I tell you, he seemed nice but he sure was gross. He smelled worse than a football team after a game. Had a real mangy looking face and the yellowest teeth you ever saw." She shuddered as if a cold draft had just slinked down her back. "And he was trying to be Mr. Cool. I climb in the truck and he says, 'How far ya goin' babe?' then he shoots his finger at me like it's a gun and clicks his tongue." She paused again shaking her head. "What a geek."

She didn't notice that she had lost Scott somewhere. He was now staring through the windshield, his left hand on the wheel and his right massaging his temple, the speedometer climbing. The needle was past one twenty and still going up, the scenery a blur through the side windows. The Charger began to whine in protest.

"Hey mister, slow down!"

Scott turned toward her with a start then looked at the instrument panel. He released the gas pedal and the whining engine resumed its throaty drone as it coasted along the highway. When it got below fifty Scott guided the car onto the gravel shoulder sending a huge cloud of white dust into the air. The Charger fishtailed a bit before coming to a stop on the shoulder.

He sat silent and motionless staring into nothingness as deep and black as outer space. Sweat beaded his forehead. His respiration was fast and deep. He could feel a throbbing deep inside his head. He just sat there staring.

A tiny voice broke his trance. "Mister, are you okay? Like you were way out there."

Slowly he turned to face her. He had forgotten there was someone in the car. "Who are you?"

"Ashley. You picked me up after I got out of the truck. You know, across from the Wendy's."

"How old are you, Ashley?"

"Nineteen, almost twenty, I'll be twenty next month. You think I look twenty?" She turned to face him smiling as though he were about to take her school picture. "Some people think I look much older than I am. I've been getting into bars since I was sixteen. Once a doorman was fired because he let me in and somehow they found out how old I was. I..."

Scott put his hand up between them and she got the hint and stopped talking. "Ashley, I've got a headache the size of Texas." Both his hands were rubbing circular indents into the side of his head.

"You shouldn't be driving then, should you?" She grabbed his right wrist and pulled his arm toward her. She squeezed her thumb and index finger into the skin between his thumb and index finger. "It's a pressure point." She said. "My mom taught me this. It really works."

"Ashley, can you drive?"

"I've been diving since I was like eleven. Daddy used to let me drive the pickup when we were out in the country. He said some day I might need to drive him home if he got hurt. I was always like, I'm sure."

"Good. Then you drive. Stay at or below the speed limit. Take the next exit that has some kind of lodging. Okay?"

"Like, no probs."

Scott looked at her, raised eyebrow, as if he were an English teacher. "Ashley, please do not use 'Like' anymore. You seem to be a bright girl and it makes you sound like an idiot. And besides that I hate it." She nodded.

They both got out of the car and traded places. Before Scott had his seatbelt fastened, the rear wheels were spinning in the gravel and the Charger fishtailed onto the road in a billowing cloud of white dust.

"Jesus Christ, Ashley! You can't drive this car like Daddy's old pickup."

"Like relax. I'm just getting used to it. I'll be fine."

Scott put his head back against the headrest and closed his eyes.

Chapter Thirteen

Scott had fallen asleep in the car while Ashley drove and wasn't sure where she'd stopped. He knew when he checked in that they were at a Best Western somewhere in Missouri and that was good enough. He got two keys for a room with two beds. You're welcome to the other bed he told her handing her the second key. He paid no attention to the *you dirty old man* look of disdain the desk clerk gave him when Ashley took the key. The headache had exhausted him and all he wanted was a bed.

While sitting at the desk in room 218 he estimated that between the car and the room he had slept for about twelve hours. He hadn't slept twelve hours in a single day since high school.

The room was dark but for the luminescent glow from his laptop screen and a dull hue from a desk lamp. Scott was dressed only in black boxers, he had a towel around his shoulders, and his hair was still damp from the shower. Ashley slept while he checked his e-mails, which were all non-issues. Most were congratulatory praise from his boss and co-workers. A note to say his dog Max seemed to be missing him. Thomas checked to see what he thought of the Charger. A few thank-you notes from clients and the last a potential client inquiring about a Lamborghini.

He spent most of the time just staring at the screen. His mind was going over the previous two days. That smelly fuck from Detroit, just a homeless guy, that's all he is. He wasn't pumping gas, or walking through the streets of Forest Glenn. He wasn't driving the truck Ashley jumped out of and he definitely wasn't chasing us down the road swinging a baseball bat. He was still in Detroit panhandling for change.

Maybe he would hit up that pompous ass Thomas for change today. Funny thing, Thomas hadn't really done anything to offend Scott but Scott didn't like him much just the same.

About to do some online research on a new contact in the UK. Scott heard a rustling sound to his left. He turned to see Ashley get out of bed and walk into the bathroom. The light in the room was very dim but she appeared to be wearing nothing but a T-shirt. The loose fitting garment hung almost to her knees. It was much too big to be hers; maybe it belonged to her father or a boyfriend. The fabric seemed well-worn and draped her every curve in a provocative fashion. Scott's conscious mind was telling him she was much too young, but some inherent animal tendency deep inside prevented him from breaking his gaze until she closed the bathroom door.

The sight of the cotton fabric clinging to her curves woke all his senses. The AC sent a chill down his exposed torso, the air smelled faintly of tobacco, and he realized he hadn't eaten for thirteen hours. When the girl came out of the bathroom he said, "I'm going to get some breakfast, are you hungry?"

"Huh! Oh. Shit, is it even morning yet?" She was squinting at the laptop then yawned. She didn't notice the way Scott's eyes seemed to be locked on her body. She stretched her arms out, arching her back and standing up on her toes reaching for the ceiling to shake off the sleep. The cotton hem of the T-shirt climbed enticingly high on her thighs. When she settled back into an "at ease" stance, she grinned and asked, "Sounds cool. Do I have time for a shower?"

"Sure take your time."

Her youthful exuberance and tone had extinguished his erotic interest and his attention returned to the computer. Ashley turned back toward the shower then stopped and looked back over her shoulder.

"Hey mister, you were in such a crap mood in the car last night, you didn't tell me your name."

"Sorry I guess between the mad batter and the killer headache my manners took a break. The name's Scott."

She beamed like a child being offered ice cream, "Pleased to meet you Scott," then she disappeared behind the bathroom door.

When Scott heard the water running in the shower he put on a pair of pleated shorts and a slightly wrinkled shirt. He pulled on ankle length white socks and a pair of white runners. He repacked his small suitcase excluding his carry-on bag and laptop and took them out to the car.

It had rained overnight and the wet pavement surrounding the Best Western sparkled in the floodlights mounted on the side of the building. The air was refreshing compared to the heat of the previous day. It smelled of nightcrawlers and the damp decaying mulch piled high around the landscaped grounds of the hotel. A particularly large worm had caught Scott's eye. It slithered across the parking lot just behind the Charger. Nearly a foot long, it left a trail of mucous that ran all the way back to where the lamp light faded into the night. Scott stood watching, wondering why they always came up on the pavement when it rained. If they didn't get underground before the sun got too warm they would dry up and die. If the birds got them, the end would be quicker. Yet there they were, all over the parking lot heading for what?

His wonderings about the worms came to an abrupt end with the sudden bang of a car-trunk being shut. About thirty feet to his right a man stood behind a black Lincoln. He was just standing there, looking at Scott. Scott could only make out a silhouette against the streetlight behind him. The posture was eerily familiar. He began to make his way toward the Charger. His gait was unmistakable. It was him, Scott was sure of it; it was the bum from Detroit. He must have stolen a car. God knows he couldn't afford a Lincoln. Scott locked his stare on the man's eyes. When he stepped under the full glow of the mercury-vapor lamp overhead the light revealed his face.

"That's a real nice car you got there, son." His friendly voice had an undertone of envy.

Scott looked at him with relief. It wasn't the bum. A tall and

The Nightcrawler

slender man between fifty and sixty ogled the Charger like a child in a toy store. The top of his head was completely bald and the hair on the sides mostly gray. The gentleman was well-dressed, clean-shaven, and he had a smooth gliding stride. As he approached, Scott got a thick whiff of English Leather that overpowered the smells brought on by the rain.

Scott didn't reply. His pulse had spiked at the sight of the man's approach, and he was feeling a bit jittery. While he took a moment to settle his nerves, the stranger continued.

"Yes sir. My first car out of college was just like this one. It was a 68 though. If I'd waited six more months I could've gotten the 69. This one's the same color mine was."

He walked around the car. He didn't seem to care whether Scott had no interest in his rambling or that he was there at all.

"Would you like to look under the hood?" Scott asked, fully recovered from his jitters.

"Would you mind?"

"Not at all," Scott said reaching under the hood. He pulled the latch to release it. With a clunk the hood popped up and he raised it as far as it would open. Beneath the light overhead and the two bulbs Thomas had installed in the hood, the engine gleamed like it might have in a showroom forty plus years ago. Scott thought he could sell the car to this guy right now and get on a plane to LA where things would make sense.

"My name's Scott," he said extending his hand.

The man took his hand and shook it firmly, the kind of handshake that oozed confidence and leadership. "Wayne Roberts. It's a pleasure, Scott." Wayne was now leaning both hands on the fender of the Charger admiring the big shiny V-8 under the hood.

Scott had satisfaction on his face and with his best used-car salesman voice he asked, "Would you like to hear her purr?"

"I sure would, Scott."

Before Wayne even finished, Scott had settled himself into the driver's seat and was putting the key in the ignition switch.

"Wait till you hear this, Wayne," he called out.

Wayne stood back from the car as it started up with a rumble that echoed off the walls of the Best Western like pit lane at Indianapolis. The fabric of his shirt fluttered in the breeze from the big motor's fan.

Wayne resumed his place at the side of the car, staring into the engine compartment in a trance. Scott joined him and noticed that old Wayne didn't appear to be with him. He looked like he drifted off to another world, or another time. Could it be, Scott wondered, that Wayne was cruising his hometown strip, all his hair intact and down to his shoulders? Imagining himself driving fast with his left elbow resting out of the open window, his best girl in the passenger seat and the Beatles crackling from the AM radio.

"What do you think, Wayne?" Scott stood directly in front of the Charger now, his arms crossed in front of his chest, and sporting a smile he hoped would be sincere and friendly. Wayne looked up with a bit of a start and Scott asked, "Would you like to take a quick spin? You can drive."

Wayne looked down at his watch and reached out for Scott's hand. "Thanks for showing me the car, Scott, but I have to get back inside. The wife is likely already wondering what happened to me."

Before Scott could even begin his sales pitch the old man was steps toward the hotel. He stopped once, turning to get another look at the car, and then waved at Scott still standing at the front bumper. Scott closed the hood and walked around to kill the engine.

Without getting in the car, he shut the 440 down and removed the keys. Wayne was just getting to the side door of the Best Western when Scott slammed the door, the noise echoed loudly through the still morning. Scott watched Wayne enter the building, amused at the way the light over the door reflected off the top of his shiny head. It wasn't until Wayne was out of sight that he noticed the orange glow of the rising sun silhouetting the hotel.

He looked down at the pavement and followed what he thought

was the slime trail left behind by the worm he was watching before Wayne's arrival. He couldn't be sure it was the same one. The parking lot was crisscrossed with glistening lines that headed in every direction but didn't seem to go anywhere.

He didn't know why the gooey trails held his attention but his eyes followed one after another. He amused himself imagining the lines as a map of the LA freeways. This one's the Harbor freeway, that one's the Santa Ana and the one over there's the Hollywood Freeway. He was about to start naming the surface streets when he heard it. That sound, the clicking sound the bum made with his tongue. He could feel his heartbeat quicken and had to force himself to breath.

He fought back the fright taking over his conscious mind and slowly looked in the direction of the noise. It wasn't him. It wasn't even human. Twenty feet away a huge crow stood on the curb with a foot long worm dangling from his beak. He felt a bit of rage thinking that was his worm, the one he watched earlier. How stupid was that, getting mad at a bird for eating a worm. The bird was staring at Scott. It had no fear in its eyes. It was defying Scott to come closer.

The crow flipped its head back and the worm disappeared down its throat. Then Scott noticed a shadow beneath a tree on the lawn about twenty yards from the Best Western sign. The shadow was moving. He squinted hard trying to focus on the shadow.

"What the hell is that?"

The sound of his own voice gave him a start. He took a step toward the crow, trying to make out the moving shadow.

"Holy shit."

Two steps closer. The ground was moving. It wasn't a shadow moving, it was the ground, dark brown wet soil moving in a wave like a mudslide after a heavy rain on a deforested hillside. The wave moved over the crow, engulfing it. The mud seemed to collect on the crow. The pile was getting taller and taller but it didn't advance onto the parking lot. It was four feet high as Scott stepped closer. His curiosity temporarily overwhelmed his fear. He had to figure out how mud could form a pile on its own. He was in horror when he realized it wasn't mud. It was worms. Thousands of thick brown nightcrawlers, squirming higher atop the now buried crow.

The pile grew to over five feet tall and began to ooze and gyrate; making a hideous wet sticky sound. It continued to get taller and thinner and formed into the shape of a man. Scott wanted to run, needed to run. Run as fast as he could, but his legs were paralyzed with terror. The worms pulled tighter and the shape began to look familiar. It was him, the bum from Detroit. The yellow light from the Best Western sign and orange sunlight cresting the horizon behind the building gave the abomination a devilish color. A slimy reddish arm extended and cocked a finger like a gun, pointing at Scott. Like gawkers passing a car wreck, Scott found he was unable to avert his eyes. He wanted to look away. He wanted to turn and run, but he stood immobile and stared right at it.

A sound came from deep inside the thing. That same clicking sound and the worms fell into a puddle on the grass. The crow emerged from the pile, picked up a six-inch nightcrawler and flew off cawing repeatedly almost as if he were laughing. As if he laughed at Scott.

He watched the bird fly off then returned his gaze to the grass. Thousands of worms crawled around. Not going away, just squirming around on top of each other. Scott felt his knees weaken and his stomach twisted into a knot so tight he was sure he would vomit right there. He staggered back inside, with every step back to room 218 he tried to rationalize what he just saw. He hadn't eaten, it was a hallucination brought on by extreme hunger, worms can't sculpt themselves into people. He'd been under a lot of stress and it was getting to him now that the pressure had abated. That's all it was, his mind playing tricks. He'd check out of the hotel, have a good breakfast and laugh about what he thought he saw.

Scott returned to his room without experiencing the passage of time it took to get there. He didn't notice the neatly folded newspapers on the carpet in front of each door. The smell of Pine-Sol on the freshly washed stairs still damp and slippery didn't register in his brain. He didn't acknowledge the lady from housekeeping who said good morning as he entered the second floor corridor from the stairwell. He didn't even notice the local weather coming from the TV as he opened the door to the room. "Last night's rainfall is going to bring in a day of high humidity and we have a real possibility of scattered thunder storms this afternoon. The five day forecast coming up right after this."

He stepped into the bathroom, closed the door then fumbled in the dark for the switch. The bathroom lights flickered on with a harsh flash causing Scott to wince. His breathing was quick and shallow as he stared at his reflection in the mirror. His face was wet with perspiration and his eyes looked back with unease. He turned the water on, cupped his hands and leaned over the sink splashing water on his face. Each handful washed away a little of the image that had shaken him to his core. After several rinses, the worms were like a bad dream that faded almost immediately after waking.

Eyes closed, he scrambled around for a towel. The next thing he saw caused him to stagger back until he banged into the wall. The reflection in the mirror was no longer his own. It was the fucking bum. The bastard was standing behind the glass, his yellow teeth grinning with malevolence. For the second time in ten minutes, Scott lost his ability to look away. He closed his eyes jamming the heels of his hands against them as if to punish them for their betrayal. The man in the mirror replaced first with total blackness and then as Scott applied more and more pressure to his corneas his optic nerves began to send visions of exploding stars to his brain. Then the pain, Scott was putting so much force on his eyes that he was close to passing out from the pain. Dropping his hands, he slid down the wall to a seated position and rested his head between his knees.

A light tapping brought him out of the trance. Confused, he looked around the bathroom. His vision was unclear and streaked with odd floating shapes as his eyes recovered from the abuse. He started to think. Why was he sitting on the floor? The damn headache was back. Why were his eyes hurting? What the hell was happening to him? He had always been in control. He had never been into drugs. He didn't hallucinate, so why now? It couldn't be stress. He'd been working his ass off for five years with Cobra. He'd worked harder than this. Then the tapping came again. Was that real or just another figment of his imagination? He was scared. He couldn't remember feeling fear before; not since childhood anyway. More tapping, a little louder this time.

"Are you okay?" Ashley's voice came through the door, mousey and barely audible.

Scott pushed himself up the wall, and stared into the mirror at his own reflection. He regained some composure and Ashley called through the door again.

"I'm fine, I'll be right out." His voice was tattered and old sounding. He continued to stand there watching his own chest rise and fall with each breath. He was trying to psychoanalyze himself. Was he cracking up? He was in the middle of Missouri, in a hotel with a girl he didn't know, preparing to finish his cross country trek in a car that wasn't his, being stalked by a man who could not possibly have left Detroit let alone made it half way to the Pacific coast. Then there were the worms. Shit, looking back, the beer he drank in college didn't get those kinds of results. Whatever this was, if he could put it in a pill he could make a fortune.

He took one last deep breath, exhaled and opened the door. Ashley was sitting cross-legged against the wall staring up at him.

"Are you okay? It sounded like you fell down in there." Her face had lost all the confidence she had displayed when she climbed into the car. Ashley was scared. She looked more like a six-year-old who lost her mommy at the mall. For the first time since she left the note on her pillow and snuck out at five in the morning three days ago, she was homesick. She needed her mom. She had been positive that the only way she was ever going to make something of herself was to get out and do it and to do it she had to go to Hollywood. Ashley always felt a movie star inside her, and she wanted to let it out. Mom, however, was certain that the only thing in Ashley's near future was college and a career. In the middle of the night, Ashley packed some things and took a city bus to the end of town where she stuck out her thumb. The first one to pass by was the batter, and climbing into the truck, she was sure it would be easy to get to Hollywood. Now she felt defeated. Her first ride was a perv and this guy looked sick, crazy, or maybe something worse.

In a very timid whisper she asked again, "Are you okay?"

He looked down at her with unsympathetic eyes. He just had the shit scared out of him twice in fifteen minutes. His skin felt clammy, and a jackhammer had begun banging out a drum solo in his head, and he could feel his heart pounding in his chest. *So what was this kid's problem?*

"I'm fine."

He walked over to the desk and began to pack his computer. Crossing the room, he grabbed his carry-on from the closet floor and went back to the bathroom to pack his toiletries.

Ashley didn't get up from the floor. From across the room Scott looked down on her. Two weeks before her twentieth birthday and to him, she looked beaten down by life, like a young woman with the eyes of a little girl. It saddened him a bit. He liked the spark she had showed him yesterday and now she was beginning to ooze self-doubt. Maybe she wasn't ready for this trip after all.

Putting whatever Ashley's problems might be from his mind, his carry-on hanging off his shoulder and his computer case in hand, he asked, "Well, are you coming or not?"

She looked up at him as if hoping for some encouragement but all she got was, "Look, you don't have to ride with me but you do have to get out of the room because I'm checking out. So what's it gonna be?"

She got up, walked over to the first bed and picked up her pack. "I'm coming." She had regained some of the attitude and swagger she showed in the car. Scott knew it was an act, but he admired her grit just the same.

"Okay, I have to check out then we'll get some breakfast. Maybe some food will get rid of this headache."

It was 7:38 according to the clock behind the front desk. The hotel lobby was empty but for the desk clerk. He looked up and smiled warmly.

"Good morning. Checking out?"

Scott nodded, "218."

The desk clerk scanned the keycard into the computer and still smiling asked, "Was everything satisfactory, Mr. Randall?" Scott nodded again. "Would you like all the charges on your Visa, sir?"

Scott was so out of it when he checked in that he barely remembered giving his Visa. "That would be great," he said. The clerk looked up at the sound of someone's voice other than his own, this time he nodded, then printed out the bill and put it down on the counter.

"Thank you for staying at Best Western and we hope to see you again, Mr. Randall."

Scott took the invoice off the counter and put it in the side pocket of his carry-on. He looked at the nametag on the clerk's breast pocket. "Bill, is there an IHOP, or a Denny's, or something similar around here? I am really in the mood for some pancakes."

Bill just pointed out the front window of the lobby. Right across the street sparkling in the bright morning sun were the windows of IHOP.

"Okay then," Scott said with a "stupid me for asking" tone, then with an almost airy quality he turned to Ashley, "Pancakes sound good to you, Ashley?"

She giggled and headed for the door. Scott followed her out to the car. He stood for a moment looking at the spot where the worm-man had been. The grass was green and lush. There was no sign of anything that would indicate a pile of worms had been there less than an hour ago. He opened the trunk and threw his things in.

"You want to put your pack in?"

"I'll carry it. It's all I have. If someone steals the car while we're eating I'll be screwed."

He was sure what she really meant was, "I'm not going to lose my pack if you crack up, dude."

Just as Scott opened the driver's side door, he heard that clicking sound again. Looking toward the source, he saw a crow on the top of the lamppost. It had a long worm dangling from its beak. The crow flipped its head back just like it had earlier and the worm disappeared. Then it flew away making the same caw-cawing cackle as before. His gaze returned to the grass; a single shiny black feather lay exactly where the worm-man had stood. Correction Scott thought, where he imagined the worm-man had stood. It was a hallucination, caused by hunger or stress, or maybe it was post stress. Scott was sure some shrink must have put some syndrome or disorder name to it in order to publish a paper in the trades.

He took one last glance at the crow as it flew off in the distance then got in the car. Reaching across the seat, he unlocked the passenger door and Ashley climbed in settling her pack on the floor between her feet. Scott had an odd look on his face that made Ashley a little uncomfortable.

Inside, the IHOP waitress told them to sit anywhere. It was still early and the place was empty with the exception of one other table. He hadn't noticed the Lincoln in the parking lot but there sat Wayne and his wife. Scott thought immediately that it was no wonder the old man rushed back in to his wife. She was a small woman, her hair pulled back into a bun so tight it made the skin on her face shine like polished ivory. She wore little oval shaped glasses that sat on the end of her pointy nose, but what Scott noticed most were her eyes. They looked like cold deep holes of despair. She appeared to Scott to be completely void of fun. He doubted that she had experienced fun since before Jesus was a baby. If anyone could use a good laugh it was this woman.

Wayne had looked over his shoulder to see who else was in the restaurant and gave a nod when he saw it was Scott. His wife instantly started in on him, probably about why he was acknowledging those people. He just looked down at the table and ate his eggs like a little boy cowering from an overbearing mother.

"Divorce has got to be better than that."

He didn't realize he was speaking aloud and Ashley turned to see what he was talking about. Wayne's wife sneered at her and she turned back to Scott and began to giggle.

It wasn't until that moment that Scott noticed how truly stunning Ashley was. Her smile was warm, framed by the sweetest dimples he could remember ever seeing. She had big blue eyes, the kind that you usually saw in toddlers. She had perfect features, flawless skin, and the blondest hair this side of the Alps. He didn't consider himself an expert but he believed it was her natural color.

She suddenly became aware that he was looking at her for the first time. "What?" She said smiling uncomfortably.

With the same level of discomfort Scott said, "Sorry, it's nothing." He opened his menu and said, "I don't know about you, but I'm having pancakes." He found himself looking over the menu at her again.

She didn't notice this time, "Pancakes sounds good."

The waitress, a pale skinned older woman with salt and pepper hair and a body that was as wide as it was high stepped up to their table with a coffee pot. She wore a uniform that was clean and pressed but well-worn. Scott waved off the coffee and Ashley shook her head.

"We'd both like pancakes and some orange juice," Scott said handing his menu to her.

She winked at him, "Okie-dokie! Well my name's Jean and if you need anything you just holler." Then she scooped up Ashley's menu and walked away.

The color drained from his face and he stared out with a blank expression. If it wasn't hand gestures, winking, or clicking tongues it was that stupid fucking phrase. Okie-dokie. *What the hell does that mean anyway? Okie-dokie my ass.*

Ashley noticed that Scott seemed to have left the building and cautiously asked, "Are you okay?"

He gave a forced smile and nodded.

She wasn't sure if this was a good time, but at this point she wasn't sure if getting back in the car after breakfast was a good idea. She didn't think Scott would hurt her but she was beginning to wonder if he might be unstable.

"I hope you didn't mind that I called my mom from the room last night. I left without telling her and I wanted her to know I'm okay."

"I'm sorry, what?"

"I was just saying I called my mom from the room. It should have been on the hotel bill."

"Don't worry about it. I'm going to expense it anyway."

Before Scott knew it, they had finished eating. He now knew Ashley's life story. It seemed that once she started talking she couldn't stop. She broke up with her boyfriend last week. His name was Harold. He was a great guy but she felt he was willing to settle for less than she was. He got a job at the steel mill. He would be like his daddy and Ashley sure didn't want that. Her cat died this summer. Oh how she cried. Her best friend Marcie got herself knocked up by Billy Johnson, yuck. Ashley had been accepted to two colleges, and her mom was so excited. She would be the first in the family to go to college. But that was also not for her. At least not right now.

Jean came over with the bill and Scott almost jumped out of his chair to pay it. He left a twenty on the table for a thirteen dollar tab and headed for the door unsure whether Ashley would follow. Almost at the car he saw her trotting out, her head bobbing with each step.

Again he reached across from the driver's seat reluctantly unlocking the door. She threw her pack in the backseat climbed in and showed him the way back to the interstate.

Chapter Fourteen

About the same time Scott and Ashley were heading for the highway, leaving the worms and taunting crows behind, Roger was beginning to stir in Beth's guest room. It had been a great couple of days but if he didn't leave now he may not get to the Grand Canyon. Thanks to his mother wiring him some cash and Beth driving him into town, the trip was back on. He would tell Beth during breakfast that he was hitting the road. He hadn't tried to turn their budding friendship into an all out summer romance because he had a plan and he still had strong feelings for Paige. The plan was to hike the Grand Canyon. If he gave in to his attraction, the plan would be history and so would Paige. He couldn't see Beth backpacking through the desert anyway. The canyon was still a long way off. Would she be standing on the road hitching? More likely Daddy had a fifty-foot motor home with a hot tub and satellite TV that she would no doubt suggest they bring. No, that wouldn't do at all. He wanted to rough it across the country. Today he would thank her and hope she would invite him to get in touch with her when he got back to school.

Roger dragged himself out of bed and walked across the room to the window. Looking down at the pool, he decided a morning swim would be a great way to end his stay.

He felt like the only person on earth. Birds chirped, and a dog barked, but otherwise he heard nothing. It was so quiet, too quiet for daytime. There were no sounds of air conditioners humming, or traffic from a nearby street. From what he remembered of the drive in there weren't any nearby streets. The driveway must have been a mile long and he didn't remember there being any neighbors.

The Nightcrawler

When he got down to the pool he stood at the edge hypnotized by the silence.

"You going in?"

He turned with a start to see Beth's sister. She was wearing a large white fleece robe that hung to her knees.

"Jesus Christ, you scared the shit out of me," he said. He checked her out the same way he did both her and Beth at the rodeo and a pang of guilt made him look away. He wondered how two sisters could both be so beautiful.

"You're the guy who fell off the fence, aren't you?" she asked with a smirk.

Roger's ears began to turn pink. "And you must be Bobbie." His eyes were again studying her. She obviously noticed, and gave him the once over, smiled and shot him an animated wink.

Her face lit up as she dropped the robe on the ground, leaving Roger stunned. Bobbie stood on the cut stone deck surrounding the pool. The robe was bundled around her feet. Bobbie's feet were the only part of her that was covered. Her grin turned naughty as she reached provocatively behind her neck and tied her hair back in a ponytail. Roger stared unblinking as her naked body glistened in the morning sun. She took a step toward him then asked again, "You going in?" She walked to the edge of the pool and jumped in.

She swam underwater to the far side of the pool. Roger stared at the perfect human form gliding through the water. He began to feel as though he were intruding, or worse like a peeping Tom. He was transported back to a time when he was eleven. He was playing in the backyard with Ed when they heard splashing next door. They hustled over to a loose board in the fence that they used as a gate to the neighbor's yard to retrieve errant balls and Frisbees. They slid the board aside expecting to see Lois Stork and her friends in the pool. Lois was old, at least seventeen they figured and she always had friends over. Roger and Ed never missed an opportunity to sneak a peek at Lois and her friends in their bikinis. This day was different. Lois was alone and she was skinny-dipping. They watched her for just moments but to Roger it seemed like much longer. He suddenly became very embarrassed and told Ed he had to go in.

Inside the house he ran straight to his room. He barely heard his mother ask if he had an argument with Ed. He just answered no and closed his bedroom door behind him. It was the first time he had gotten an erection, the first time in the middle of the day at least. He didn't count the ones he woke up with every morning. They just meant he had to pee really bad. This was the middle of the day and he didn't need to pee. His window overlooked the Stork's yard. Lois was done swimming. She lay naked on her towel beside the pool, drops of water sparkling all over her body. He learned how to masturbate that day and he spent a lot of time watching Lois swim from his bedroom window that summer.

Roger felt the same way looking at Bobbie gliding below the surface of the water that he did when watched Lois from his bedroom window.

"Hey Vermont, you goin' in?" Beth said from behind him.

Startled and a bit embarrassed he looked at her trying to be nonchalant. Roger doubted he was very convincing. It felt like he just got caught watching Lois Stork skinny-dipping. His face and ears were hot and he was blushing furiously. He hoped his deep tan from being on the road masked what would normally be a red glow. Not likely, but maybe.

Roger looked back at Bobbie then back to Beth. He didn't know what to do.

"Well?" she quipped looking over at the pool. She wore an orange Body Glove bikini. Like the day before, Beth looked like a swimsuit model.

Suddenly Roger was glad he had the oversized beach towel hanging over his shoulder. It hung down well past what he now realized was an obvious pup tent in his swim trunks.

Beth seemed to have figured this out. She sauntered over and began tugging at the towel saying, "Come on, Vermont, let's go swimming." She didn't care that her naked sister was in the pool.

"Don't fret about her," Beth said. "Daddy won't even come down to the pool anymore because he's afraid of seeing his daughter naked. Even if everyone else in Nebraska has." With that, Beth pulled the towel away, threw it on the ground. She ran screaming across the deck and landed a cannon ball right next to Bobbie. When the wave subsided they began to splash each other, laughing and shrieking like a couple of ten-year-olds. Roger laughed to himself, and then with a Tarzan holler did an even bigger cannonball on Bobbie's other side.

The shock value gone, Bobbie got out of the pool. Roger watched her walk across the deck and Beth got his attention back by bouncing a lime-green volleyball off the side of his head.

"You are so dead," he said swimming toward her.

She headed away from him with a giddy shriek and he realized at once that she was a much better swimmer than he was, but he could throw so instead of chasing what he couldn't catch, he got the volleyball and launched it at her wake. The wet ball sailed wildly over her head, ricocheted off one of the Greek statues, and splashed down in the corner of the pool.

Bobbie returned wearing a one-piece black swimsuit with a red Nike swish just above the point of her right hip. The suit was cut high on her hips, dipped low in front exposing most of her breasts and the back plunged almost down to her tailbone.

"You all done with the nakie game sis?" Beth said with a disapproving sister look.

Bobbie produced an orange volleyball from behind her back and spiked it down on Roger, "Can I play too?" She dove back in and began to swim laps with the form of an Olympic swimmer while Roger and Beth continued to play a little courting game in the shallow end, splashing and dunking each other. When Beth climbed up on Roger's back trying to pull him under with the skill of a calf roper, Bobbie stopped swimming and said, "For Christ sake, Beth, why don't you take him inside and jump his bones."

Beth picked up the green ball that was floating by and tossed it at her missing by six feet. Bobbie giggled and resumed her laps. Roger and Beth both retrieved a ball and fired them at Bobbie in tandem. Neither ball struck its target. Bobbie however assumed it was game on and made a B-line for the nearest ball; it was a free for all. Both girls scrambled out of the pool and headed for benches at opposite sides of the pool. The seats opened and assorted water weapons came flying out. Pool noodles, Super Soakers and beach balls.

They splashed around hurling one projectile after another at each other until the game changed to boy against girls. Roger was able to block most of the incoming attacks while being deadly accurate with his counters. The girls retreated to the hot tub and Roger did a victory dance beside the pool then joined them.

"So Roger, how long are you going to stay?" Bobbie asked.

"Are you tired of me already? Maybe you can't stand getting beat in the pool by an easterner and you want me gone."

Both girls sprang like cats and Roger found himself submerged with both girls holding him under. They let him up and between coughing up hot chlorinated water and laughing uncontrollably he surrendered. From his knees, the steaming water agitating around his neck, his hands folded in mock prayer he begged forgiveness.

"We'll let you off this time, Vermont, but you best remember your place in the future."

"Yes ma'am," he replied through his laughter. Then as quick as the girls moved on him he grabbed them both by an ankle and with a sharp tug pulled them off their seats and it was their turn to come up spitting hot tub water.

"You kids want something to eat?"

A woman was standing over them with a huge smile on her face. "It looks like you girls may have found someone who is up to the task." Her smile didn't fade while she spoke. "I'm Nora, mother of these two bobcats." She was looking directly at Roger, her smile unwavering and warm. About the same size as her daughters and stunning, Roger immediately saw where Bobbie and Beth got their beauty. She looked young enough to be an older sister. She wore white pleated shorts and a red sleeveless blouse that had pockets over each breast. Her long dark hair was as shiny as she was impressive. She had the collar on her blouse turned up and a wide brimmed hat shaded her neck and face.

Roger got out of the hot tub and did a quick job of drying himself. He reached out his hand and said, "Roger Morris, ma'am. It's a pleasure to meet you."

Roger put a T-shirt on, the girls grabbed matching terrycloth robes and they all followed Nora up to a large gazebo behind the main house. There was an assortment of muffins, bagels, and fruit put out on a circular table. They ate and talked and laughed. Roger sat between the girls, while Nora sat across the table. Roger was struggling with his plan to see the canyon. He was having the time of his life, he hadn't been truly happy since Paige refused to see him when he went to her house. Now he was drowning in glee and it felt good, it felt right.

"So Vermont, you didn't answer Bobbie's question." Beth looked directly at him and didn't look like she would let him off the hook this time.

Roger was just about to tell Beth that he planned to leave right away when they were interrupted by a voice from behind. This time it was a deep, almost menacing, male voice.

"What's going on out here?"

Roger heard in stereo, "Hi Daddy."

Behind him there stood a mountain of a man, clean-shaven, wearing pressed jeans and a denim shirt. His sleeves were turned up exposing muscular forearms. Roger's mind began to race. Here he is sitting at this man's table, eating his food and the last two nights sleeping in his guest room. The big man probably thinks Roger is banging one of his daughters. At least ten farmer's daughter's jokes came into Roger's head and the punch-line never favored the guy banging the farmer's daughter.

"How you doin' son, I'm Jackson Walker. Who the hell are you?"

"Daddy," Beth said looking sternly into the giant's eyes.

Roger stood up and extended his hand, "Roger Morris sir. It's a pleasure meeting you." He noticed that Mr. Walker wasn't so much a giant now that he was standing. In fact, they were about the same height. Roger however, was outweighed by at least eighty pounds of muscle.

"One of you two want to explain who this scrawny feller here is?"

"Daddy, he's my guest and you better be nice." Beth stood beside Roger, and hooked her arm in his.

His face softened a bit with Beth's gesture of solidarity with Roger.

"So where you from, Roland?"

"It's Roger sir, and I'm from Vermont."

"No kiddin' kid. I ain't met anyone from Vermont before. Whatcha doin' in Nebraska?" Mr. Walker's words came out sounding hick but his eyes were anything but. Roger saw dominance and confidence in the big man's gaze.

Before Roger could answer they were joined by another man. This one younger, about Roger's age and build. He also wore jeans and a denim shirt. He took no notice of Roger, "Daddy, we have a problem. Davey Johnson went to Wheeler Saloon last night, got sauced and got in a bar fight. He broke his wrist and he won't be able to play tonight."

"Shit. This is the first time I really felt we would kick Tom Dinkle's ass and that dummy gets his arm broke." He looked back at the table then his eyes brightened as if a light just went on.

"Robert, do you play ball?"

"The name is still Roger, sir, and I play a little."

"Well, we have this annual slow pitch game 'ginst Tom Dinkle over at the Double D ranch. One of our boys got his arm broke last night. Now we're short a man. Whadaya say?"

"Mr. Walker, if you're asking me to play ball I'd be glad to. But I don't have a glove or shoes or ..."

"Bethy, you take this boy down to see Ray, get him a glove, some shoes and fit him with a uniform and anything else he needs. You tell Ray to put it on my tab. Then you get him to the ballpark at four. Billy you round up the rest of the boys and get 'em to the park at four."

"Four, damn Daddy that won't be easy."

"Just get it done, Billy."

Billy didn't say a word, he just did an about-face and went back the way he came. It was obvious to Roger that when Jackson Walker gave orders they were obeyed.

"Randy, you sure you can play ball?"

"Yes, Mr. Winter, I play a little ball."

"You a smart ass, Roger?" Jackson said.

"Yes sir, sometimes I am." Roger replied with the confidence he developed once he realized Mr. Jackson Walker needed him to fill his squad. If there was one thing Roger had confidence in, it was his prowess between the foul lines.

Jackson turned and headed back to the house. He looked back and said, "Bethy, you make sure you get to the park by four and kid, you can call me Jack." He turned and resumed his walk up to the house. His head was shaking and he chuckled a bit saying, "Mr. Winter, well I'll be dipped in shit."

"You got some big balls, Roger," Bobbie said looking at him in amazement. "Daddy does the wrong name thing with all of our friends. Nobody has ever corrected him. Then you throw it right back at him. Huge ones, Roger, huge."

Beth had been standing with her mouth open not believing what just happened. Daddy had never told any of their friends to call him Jack or Jackson for that matter. He was Mr. Walker or Sir and all the kids visiting at the Three B's Ranch knew it. Roger gave her a nudge and suggested that they go see this Ray guy. She nudged him back and grabbed his arm dragging him away.

"Thanks for breakfast, Mrs. Walker," he called back over his shoulder.

Beth yelled a giggling goodbye to her mother as she dragged Roger across the lawn toward the car.

Chapter Fifteen

"So Ginny's dad buys a condo in Toronto so she can go to fashion school at some place called Ryerson. I think that's what it's called. I'm sure, right? Why does she have to go to Canada? Anyway, her condo is like five minutes walk from this huge mall. And he gives her a new car and her own Visa card. Can you believe it? Like, she goes to school a couple of hours a day then she spends the day at the mall. Like, I'm sure. Last week I asked my mom if we could go to the Frosty Freeze for an ice cream and she says 'Ashley, for the cost of one cone there, we can get a gallon of ice cream at the supermarket.' I mean, I wasn't asking for a car or a condo, was I?"

Scott just nodded once in a while but he didn't really care to participate in a conversation that chronicled Ashley's life. He sat quiet letting her carry on, while he thought to himself, *if she was a good representation of today's youth then look out, world.* He wondered how anyone could talk so much, yet say so little. She didn't even seem to breathe when she spoke. It was just an endless whirr like driving next to one of those crotch rockets the kid's race around the LA freeways. Scott was beginning to like her but that feeling began to fade every time she began another onslaught of "Ashley, this is your life." What he liked most about her was that she liked to drive and it gave him an opportunity to do some work on his laptop and make some phone calls. He just wished he had internet access in the car.

"So I told Kimmie there is no way that I'm going to hang out in some bar so she can meet Johnny. You should totally see this guy. He …"

Scott held his hand up between them as if to shield himself from the barrage of senseless nattering.

"I have to make a call. Can you hold that story for a bit?" Not waiting for her to answer he dialed. As he held the phone to his ear he was thinking to himself, "Thomas, you had better be there. I need a break from the fireside chat with the valley girl".

A familiar adult voice was music to Scott's ear. "C.S. and T. How may I direct your call?"

"Hi Sarah, it's Scott. How is everything today?"

Scott deliberately tried to be distant with Ashley, but he was getting the feeling that she was beginning to develop a crush. She didn't look like she thought much of him calling another woman. She had the hurt look of a school girl who just heard that the boy of her dreams had just asked someone else to the prom.

Sarah gave him a courteous "all's well here" response and asked how she could direct his call.

"Is Thomas there?" he asked.

Hearing that, Ashley inserted the ear-buds of her iPod and added a smile. Happy again, her head began to bop to the music.

Scott explained some of the issues about the website mentioned in an email he had read while at the Best Western. He told Thomas that the car was running great and that he was somewhere between St. Louis and Kansas City. Scott left out Ashley who was barely old enough to drive, tooling down I-70 in Thomas' prize Charger. After Thomas, he called to check on Max. He called the office to fill the boss in on his conversation with Thomas. Not able to think of any more excuses to stall the never-ending onslaught of Ashley-ism's, he put his phone down between the seats. Ashley still bobbed, her eyes bright and alert, gave her a grownup look that was a stark contrast to her giddy happiness.

While her attention was on the road and her music, Scott took the opportunity to rest. He reclined his seat as far as it would go. Silently he thanked Thomas for replacing the original seats, which would not have been nearly as comfortable.

The fluffy white clouds that dotted the morning sky when they left the IHOP had become heavy and considerably darker as the day progressed. Now in the early evening it looked like they were heading into some serious weather. The surroundings, which may have been vibrant on a sunny day, looked muted by the gray sky. Scott stared off into the distant storm, his eyes fixed on the darkest part of the sky. Flashes of lightning streaked toward the ground with regularity. He looked at the scrub on the side of the road. The air was still but it felt alive with electricity causing the hair on his neck to stand. A shiver went up his arm to the base of his skull. He told Ashley to take the next exit that might have a place to eat then resumed his fixation with the distant lightning.

It was completely dark now. There was no visibility. Or, there was just nothing to see. The headlights didn't illuminate lines on the road. There was no shoulder, or wild grass to mark the edge of the blacktop. The only images his eyes could make out were the instrument panel in the car and the yellow glow of the headlights dissipating into total blackness.

Scott was driving, the needle on the speedometer buried, but the engine made no sound. The window was open but there was no wind noise. At one hundred plus miles per hour there should be some wind, lots of wind. It wasn't silent, though. George Thorogood screamed out "Bad to the Bone". The Charger appeared to be cresting the top of a steep incline. Then from out of nowhere, he was there; standing in front of the car. How could a panhandler from Detroit be in the middle of a road in Missouri? If there was a road? Scott wasn't sure. He jammed on the brake pedal and the car came to a stop inches from a man Scott was sure he would never see again. He just stood there, wearing the same shabby clothes he had worn in Detroit. Standing in the glow of the only visible light, grinning that hideous yellow grin. Scott stared through the windshield into the darkest night he had ever seen. There were no stars in the sky, no lights from a distant town, no headlights in the rearview mirror or taillights up ahead. He didn't see any cars going in the other direction either. Yet with no traffic on the road but for Thomas Andrews Charger, there was a man standing in the middle of the road. How did he get there?

Scott decided the time had come to put an end to this shit. He got out of the car slamming the door. The door made no sound. There should have been a bang audible from a quarter mile but Scott didn't hear it from inches away. Through the open window George still boomed.

Scott looked to the front of the car. The bum was gone. Scott stood staring at the exact spot yet there was nobody there. In fact, there was no sign of anything. No weeds, trees or fences were visible to mark the roadside. No roadside that he could see. No cars or trucks approached in either direction. He saw no moon and no stars in the sky. Just the Charger. If it weren't for the solid ground beneath his feet Scott could have been convinced he was floating in space. Then the smell, that terrible, unmistakable smell hit him. The same rank odor that repulsed him in front of C.S. and T. Squinting into the blackness, he began to pan around. He was alone. The air was neither hot or cold, it wasn't anything. It didn't move or feel dry or humid. Goose bumps began to rise at the nape of his neck and suddenly he was glad the bum had disappeared.

Scott turned to get back in the car and there he was. As ugly and noxious as any creature had ever been and he was standing inches away. Scott felt a scream of terror escape from his throat just before his throat collapsed in a spasm of fright. He staggered back and fell landing hard on his ass, the flesh of his hands were scraped from their impact on the rough surface of the pavement as they sprung back to brace his fall.

The foul smelling vagrant advanced and Scott pistoned his legs in retreat until he pressed against the front tire of the car. Standing directly over him, the bum reached out and pointed his finger like a gun the same way he did in Detroit. He just stood over Scott pointing that make-believe revolver. Scott sat against the car trembling, unaware that he had wet his pants.

"Who the fuck are you?" His voice was shaky but otherwise loud

The Nightcrawler

and clear. "Let's say you just call me the Nightcrawler. Okay, Scott?" Then something began to extend from the pointed finger, almost like the digit was elongating toward Scott. It stretched about a foot, and as thin as bootlace. Extending until it fell off in Scott's wet lap.

Not wanting to look but unable to stop himself, Scott saw a huge earth worm squirming around on his wet lap. Scott brushed the nightcrawler off his pants and noticed the wet fabric. He wanted to cry like a baby but he held it back. Then the clicking sound rose above George Thorogood. Scott looked up just in time to see the Nightcrawler collapse into a pile of worms that buried him to his waist. He scrambled away from the writhing mass screaming; this time he heard his own scream.

The darkness was gone. He was sitting in the passenger seat and Ashley was driving. The sky was an angry charcoal color and lightning was dancing violently across the horizon. Ashley turned to him and said in a Darth Vader sounding mechanical voice, "Welcome back." She smiled, showing sickeningly black teeth. Then she started to laugh loudly and eerily and worms began to spew out of her mouth, filling the car.

He woke himself with a wail, pressed against the passenger side door. He stared at Ashley, his eyes wide and filled with terror and confusion. He woke from the blackness of the dream to the early evening twilight. Startled by his scream, Ashley swerved toward the edge of the pavement. The right front tire caught the gravel shoulder and she lost control. The loose gravel on the road's edge pulled the car over and she began to fight the Charger's desire to fishtail into the ditch. Scott managed to overcome the nightmare, his gaze darted from Ashley to the terrain ahead, and then back to Ashley. He began to bark instructions "slow down, get back on the road…" She ignored him and with the skill of a NASCAR champion, she managed to regain control then gently applied the brakes, coming to a stop in the deep grass just beyond the gravel. The menacing sky temporarily blotted out by the dust cloud kicked up by the tires.

"Jesus Christ, what the hell was that?" Scott's voice was shaky and sweat beaded on his face.

"Well first thing, what did you go screaming for? You scared the shit out of me. And second, if you're going to sleep and make me do all the driving then shut the hell up when I'm trying to regain control, you asshole." She paused for a moment, then beamed with devilish mischief and added, "Like, was that a wicked cool ride or what?"

He calmed down knowing everything she said was bang on. "Cool ride. We could have been killed." The smirk on her face had overcome him and they both burst into spasms of laughter.

"We all gotta go sometime, Scottie," she said through the guffaws as though she had just ridden the best amusement ride in the country. "That musta been some dream. You were moanin' and groanin' then you screamed something. I couldn't make it out but it sounded like you were getting murdered or something. Scared the crap outta me. Can't imagine what you were going through."

She released the brake pedal and guided the dusty car back onto the road. The surrounding landscape seemed featureless; the color was bleached out of the grass by a midsummer drought. They drove past a billboard inviting travelers to stop in on Ronald McDonald just ten miles ahead.

"A Big Mac and fries sounds good, Scottie."

Scott jumped a bit at the sudden break in the silence. "It's Scott, and I guess that'd be fine." He resumed his blank gaze at the storm that seemed to be rushing at them like a charging bull though neither Scott nor Ashley had given it much concern. He was embarrassed. He had woken in fear. First, it was fear of the events in the dream. Then he began to think he was losing his mind, which scared him more than any dream or stalking vagrant.

He couldn't remember being this scared since he was six and wandered away from his dad at the fishing expo in Toledo. He had meandered around amongst hundreds of people, crying to himself. His daddy didn't like cry babies and Scott didn't want his daddy to not like him, so he wouldn't cry. No sir, Scottie Randall wasn't going to cry. He just walked around looking down so nobody could see the tears in his eyes. Six years old, scared to death, but he was not going to let anyone see him cry, especially not Daddy.

Little Scottie heard someone shout his name through the din of the crowd. When he looked in the direction of the voice he saw his dad standing on the bow of a bass boat waving. Across the sea of men in denim and plaid, Scottie saw his father standing on that boat waving to his little boy. Scottie ran to that boat and his dad pulled him up and held him tight.

"I didn't cry, Daddy," he said. Then the well opened and he sobbed uncontrollably for what felt like hours. When he stopped, he looked up at his daddy, "I didn't mean to cry, Daddy. Do you still like me?" That was when he noticed that his dad had tears on his own cheeks.

"Daddy, why are you crying?"

His dad pulled him close again and told him he would always like him. Now here he was, a grown man at the peak of his professional life, scared shitless and wishing he had his daddy and thinking, "I didn't cry, Daddy."

A crack of thunder brought his attention back to the here and now. That was when they saw it. A huge funnel had descended from the black clouds. The sky all around had turned an ominous shade of green. Golf ball sized hailstones pelted down on the Charger. Scott and Ashley cranked the windows up as fast as they could, but both took hits from the ice cold projectiles. The noise in the car was thunderous, like being trapped inside a kettle drum during a percussion solo.

Ahead there was an overpass, barely visible through the rain that rushed in torrents horizontally at them. Parked near the embankment, a Chevy Suburban rocked violently in the wind. Ashley guided the Charger to a stop behind the Suburban.

"Come on," she yelled.

They both struggled to get the doors open. The wind was pushing against the doors like sails on a schooner. Scott managed to get out and ran around to help Ashley. Just as he rounded the front of the car, a gust hit her door hard knocking her to the ground. The same gust blew Scott over and he landed hard on one knee. The gale was beginning to barrel roll Ashley away from the shelter of the overpass and into the open. Scott crawled toward her, the wet pavement abrasive on his hands and knees. He managed to grab her by the wrists, stopping her from rolling away. They helped each other crawl past the Charger and the Suburban.

The green sky was now blotted out by deep blackness. It was as though Satan himself had stolen the sun from the sky. The frequent flashes of lightning were the only break from the unnatural dark. A warp speed parade of paper cups, cigarette packs, old newspapers and a host of other discarded waste whizzed past them as they slowly made their way on hands and knees to the overpass they hoped would provide shelter. Parked under the bridge just in front of the Suburban was a red Caravan and in front of that an old Winnebago. Next to the Caravan, a concrete pillar rose to the underside of the bridge. Scott motioned Ashley to it. They wrapped their arms tightly around a support pillar. Ashley sat directly against the pillar and Scott behind her, his arms around her and the upright. Their backs were to the wind, oblivious to what might be coming their way.

When the twister reached the bridge it sent debris through the tunnel-like enclosure at seventy, maybe eighty miles per hour, or could it have been one-fifty. Scott watched the objects fly by at blinding speed while Ashley buried her face against his arm.

The debris was not all paper. He could make out some of the items that whizzed by careening off the bridge supports and the vehicles. He saw tree limbs, hubcaps and all manner of unidentifiable objects flying by in a blur. A destination sign reading, "Salina 75 Miles" wedged into the windshield of the Caravan for a moment and then continued through the van and came out of the rear window slightly altered. Now it read "lina 75 mil". The sound of the rushing wind was a high constant roar unlike anything Scott had ever heard or would ever forget.

A metallic scraping sound caused Scott and Ashley to turn in horror as the Winnebago's front wheels lifted off the ground and began grazing the roof of the tunnel. The RV began moving slowly toward the upright they clung to. If they let go, they'd be swept away by the wind. If they stayed put they would surely be crushed by the runaway camper. The roof of the Winnebago struck the underside of the bridge again, breaking off chunks of concrete, which were hurled through the air like Nolan Ryan fastballs, disintegrating the windshield of the Suburban. Without a windshield, the SUV became a two-ton kite. It left the ground and disappeared into the dark sky. The RV crashed back to the ground and stayed there wounded, but no longer threatening. The roar of the rushing air through the underpass was relentless and horrific. Scott and Ashley were soaked to the skin and shivered from cold and fear.

As fast as the tornado whipped through the tunnel, it was gone. The subsequent silence was both welcome and eerie. The monster had passed. Scott hadn't released his grip on the pillar. He sat relieved and collected himself.

Then he said, "That was a close call, eh kiddo?"

When he looked at Ashley her head was slumped on her left shoulder. The shivering he'd felt was his alone, Ashley felt cold and lifeless against his chest. A stream of blood coursed down the side of her face and dripped to her shoulder where it collected in the fabric of her shirt. Scott lowered her to the ground and looked for the source of the bleeding. She had a large gash on the side of her head. Struck by debris or maybe a piece of the bridge broke off by the motor-home. He looked up and saw people shuffling down from a small wedge-shaped enclosure at the top of the embankment beneath the overpass. They had to be the owners of the camper, the van and the SUV. They had all crawled up, crammed against the underside of the bridge hoping for shelter from the monster. They were cautiously making their way down.

Scott yelled at them, panic evident in his eyes.

"She's hurt. We need help."

Chapter Sixteen

Beth turned into the parking lot of the ballpark at just after 4:30, the Challenger's rear end fishtailing in the loose gravel, kicking up a billowing cloud of white dust that drifted over the infield reducing visibility to zero. When the dust finally cleared, Roger and Beth were already sitting on the hood of the car.

Jackson Walker made his way through the dust. He was standing ten feet from the car, when the cloud drifted off. "God damn, Bethy. D'you know what time it is? Where you been?"

"Daddy, you know what that idiot Ray is like. He wouldn't give us a uniform without putting a nickname on the back. It took him twenty minutes because he spelled Vermont wrong twice."

"Well, as long as you're here. You can get dressed over there, kid. Let's see what you got."

Roger picked up the new leather bag at his feet and went to the dugout. He was very impressed with the stadium. When he agreed to this gig he pictured himself playing with Shoeless Joe Jackson in a ballpark cut out of a corn field. This field was anything but. The infield was green and plush. The base paths were smooth and chalked to perfection. The expanse of the outfield was a sea of green that didn't fit in with the mid-summer burnt yellow of the surrounding landscape. Inside the dugouts the walls were freshly painted and there was a set of stairs leading down a tunnel to the locker room. Roger stopped at the top of the steps and turned to look at the scene just to make sure it wasn't a mirage.

"Well kid, you gonna play or watch?"

The Nightcrawler

"Sorry, Jack. I'll be right out"

When Roger got back to the dugout, the whole team was standing at the on-deck circle looking at him.

"So." Jack said. "What position do you play, kid?"

"I usually play middle infield but I'll go where ever you need me."

"Give him Billy's spot at short, Daddy," Beth chimed in with a giggle.

"Bethy, you hush now. Kid you can start in Davey's spot out in left.

"Daddy, shouldn't we see if this guy can play before we pencil him in?" Billy said. He was talking to Jack but he was looking at Beth.

Roger walked over to Billy and offered his hand. "Hi Billy. Roger Morris. I tell you what. I'll go out to left and you hit five fly balls out to me. If you make it to first more than once, I'll sit on the bench or up in the stands with Beth, if that's what you'd like. And by the way, your fly is down."

"Hot damn, he's a pistol," Jack chirped.

Before Billy could zip up and respond Roger was trotting out to left and settled into the middle of left field. Billy dug into the batter's box and turned his attention to the team still gathered around the on-deck circle.

"Well Jimmy, get out there and pitch me some."

Jimmy was about thirty with dark hair and eyes and a friendly face. On his back in capital letters was CAT. Roger thought of all the men in uniform on the field Jimmy looked less like a cat than anyone. He was stout with a slight belly hanging over his belt and his legs were as thick as telephone poles.

Jimmy looked out at Roger standing casually all alone in the outfield. "You ready out there?" Jimmy called in a squeaky little voice that didn't seem to fit his appearance. Roger just waved his glove at Jimmy and settled his hands on his knees in a semi crouched position.

Jimmy looped the first pitch to the plate and Billy fouled it back to the fence then walked back to retrieve the ball. He tossed it at the crowd announcing, "Jeb, how 'bout doing some catching here."

Jack told him if he hit the ball in the other direction he wouldn't need a catcher.

Jeb, a muscular kid about eighteen grabbed a ball and threw it to the mound. Jimmy looped another in and Billy launched a shot directly at Roger but deep. Roger turned on his heel but that one caught him by surprise and bounced off the left field fence. Roger picked up the ball and threw it feebly back to Jimmy who had to walk over and pick it up on the base-path between second and third.

Roger resumed his position and Billy launched another one to the same spot. This time Roger was ready and pulled it down with his back to the infield. He made two more running catches. One was a diving grab that would have impressed the outfield coaches at Yankee Stadium.

The last fly ball was a gork that may or may not have made it over the head of the short stop. Billy was trotting toward first base glancing over at Jack with a superior look on his face. He had just beaten the smartass. Roger on the other hand charged the ball with unequalled determination. He caught the ball on one hop and fired it at first base. The ball sailed across first on a rope. It crossed the center of the bag two steps before Billy's foot touched down.

Roger joined Billy and the team at first where Billy was getting ribbed by the team for lollygagging his way up the base line. Billy offered his hand to Roger and welcomed him to the team.

By the time Roger's fielding clinic had ended, the Double-D boys had started to trickle in. Dan Mandville was the first to greet Billy and the rest.

"You ready for another lickin' this year, Walker?"

Dan was tall and thin. He was a fairly good looking guy in a down on the farm sort of way and spoke with just a hint of hick. "How you doin', Beth? You wanna sit on the winner's side like last year or are you gonna hang with your brother's losers?"

The Nightcrawler

Beth flashed him a hand gesture that she would normally not use in the presence of her daddy, then walked over and sat beside Bobbie and Nora who had already taken seats in the first row behind the Three-B's dugout.

Billy passed possession of the field to Double-D and his team took seats. The Double-D's began taking batting practice. Roger stared at them with every swing, studying the way they moved and where they hit the ball. Then he noticed that his teammates were chatting and heckling. Not wanting to step on anybody's toes he quietly made his way over to Billy and suggested he try to get his guys to study the hitting patterns of the other team, since they appeared to be so willing to show everything they had. By the time Billy had made his way across the bench the heckling was replaced with whispers and finger pointing with each crack of the bat.

The game started just before six. Beth had run down to the dugout before Roger took the field and kissed him, making sure Dan was watching. Roger figured she had dumped him some time between last year's game and this year's rodeo. Not that he cared. If she wanted to use him to make Dan jealous that was fine by him. Dan appeared to be an ass anyway and kissing Beth was definitely a bonus. He watched the gentle sway of Beth's butt as she made her way to the seats behind the dugout, when his gaze was broken by Jack's accusatory voice, "Get your head in the game Ronald."

"Whatever you say, Jake." Roger didn't look to see what Jack's reply would be. The umpire, if that's what you could call him, had called the teams to the field. He was wearing a black Harley Davidson ball cap and a black Coors T-shirt with a cigarette pack rolled up in his left sleeve. He had untidy gray hair that matched the stubble on his face.

"Okay, you punks. Most of y'all know me but for those of you who don't, my name's Joe Purdy and I'll be officiatin' this shindig today. Dan, Billy, git yer asses over here and let's git this coin toss done."

The team captains stepped up and Joe Purdy flipped the coin in the air to what seemed to be a dozen feet and Dan yelled tails. It was

Mick Ridgewell

tails and he opted to take the field first. While the Double-D's ambled to their positions Billy set the batting order. Roger would be batting last. Billy apologized but he would have to work with these guys after Roger had hit the road. Roger sat on the bench and watched his team take some awkward swings. The first guy, Mikey, was all arms and no body rotation, but managed to connect and beat out a weak throw from third. The next guy, Todd, was hitting with all his weight on the front foot and dribbled a soft grounder to first moving Mikey to second on a fielder's choice. CAT batted third and sent one to the gap. It would have been a triple at least for Mikey, but CAT got into second just in time. Mikey was safely home to start the scoring. Billy batted cleanup and was the cream of this crop as far as Roger could tell. He had a smooth swing and ripped a line shot to left center that was brought down by a lanky guy they called Slinky. Slinky had surprised CAT by catching that one and CAT was doubled up before he could get back to tag up.

Slinky had the leadoff spot for the Double-D's and sent Roger back to the track making a snow-cone grab over his shoulder. He then returned the ball to the infield on a bounce to Billy who had come out from short to cut off the throw. By the end of the first they had answered the one and tallied two more for good measure.

Roger had cranked out the first round tripper of the game with two out and two on in the second and they took the field three batters later with a two run lead.

The score had see-sawed all night and there was never more than a three run difference. Roger wasn't accustomed to slow pitch and had never been in a game since t-ball that had this high a score. What made things worse was watching both teams record more errors than runs. By the time they got to the bottom of the ninth the Three-B's were up by one. This was the first time they ever led in the last inning, and they all looked nervous. Jack sat shifting in his seat with Beth and Bobbi sitting to his right, Nora on his left. Between the heat and the nerve-wracking ninth inning lead he was sweating like a plow horse. The girls seem to be enjoying the fact that their dad, the strongest most self-confident man they new, was currently as nervous as all their dates seemed to be around him. He had been keeping a close watch on Tom Dinkle who also had free flowing sweat on his face.

In the stands there were about a hundred people, friends and family of the players and employees from both ranches. Coolers of every color sat perched between them, and cold beer cans on the seats sparkled in the sun, which by the ninth was getting low in the sky but still shone bright and hot. Jack and Tom were the only people present who didn't seem to be enjoying the game. These men had no money riding on this game. Bragging rights for the next year were the only thing at stake and the score had been much too close all game for either to relax. It started out years before as a friendly game between neighboring ranches, but as the Double-D's winning streak extended year after year, the friendliness was replaced with animosity. This was bigger than the World Series to these two men and it was game seven.

Roger had been quite bored playing left most of night. The Double-D's had sent a parade of lefties up who were all pull hitters. Since Slinky's liner in the first he had fielded a few routine flies and a couple of ground balls that got through the infield but mostly he watched in frustration, as a bunch of hayseeds on both sides of the field booted one easy play after another resulting in a 19 - 18 score to this point. He did enjoy the batting. In addition to the homer in the second, he had two doubles, a triple and an RBI sac fly and he scored three times. All totaled he had contributed to seven of the nineteen runs.

Now they were on the field for what he hoped was the final out. With two out and Slinky at third, Dan stepped to the first base side of the plate with a look of hard determination on his face. All he needed was a single and this thing would be all tied up. CAT lobbed one in and Dan watched it drop for strike one. Roger felt Dan's eyes burning through him and he expected Dan would be swinging at the next pitch. Roger hoped the lefty was going to the opposite field. He grinned at this, thinking "you bring it on, hayseed." The pitcher looped one in lower than the last one and Dan scorched a ground ball dead center between Billy and Jeb, who was playing close to third to prevent one going up the line for extra bases.

Roger broke at the crack of the bat and was fielding the ball in seconds. Tom Dinkle was hopping up and down talking smack over in Jack's direction and Dan was hopping up and down and skipping toward first base blowing a kiss in Beth's direction as he passed. He was only half way to first when he noticed that Roger had the ball in his hand in shallow left and was coming up throwing.

Nobody in the park but Roger seemed to think this play was possible until they all heard Dan choke out, "Oh shit."

Sammy over at first scrambled to the bag and everyone else watched as Roger unleashed a throw from a cannon attached to his right shoulder. Dan had hit his stride with a vengeance but the ball got to Sam's glove a full step before Dan got to the bag.

Joe Purdy punched Dan out with exaggerated animation and the Triple-B's had won for the first time in this game's history.

Roger hadn't really felt like a part of this team all night but within seconds of Joe calling that third out the whole team had jumped on him in celebration. That was when he almost wished he wasn't part of the team. Being buried under twelve sweaty cattle ranchers was not the way he had planned to spend his summer vacation. They hoisted him up onto their shoulders and carried him back to the infield. He could see Tom Dinkle reluctantly congratulating Jack while Dan was shoved and poked by his team for his base running blunder. Someone had knocked his cap to the ground and another of his fair weather friends had nailed him in the back of the head with his ball mitt.

Then he saw Beth. He saw Beth standing on the roof of the dugout. Beth looking as beautiful as any woman ever had. Beth pointing at Roger and smiling. That was all it took. He knew that tonight, his efforts to steer clear of an all out summer romance would end. Paige was a memory that happened in another lifetime. Beth was this lifetime and he wanted to live in the present.

Chapter Seventeen

Scott Randall always hated hospitals. When he was a boy his grandfather had had a stroke and his mom would visit every day. She couldn't afford to get a babysitter so Scott had to go too. He had spent the better part of his summer vacation when he was ten being dragged to the hospital to see Gramps.

He was very close to his grandfather but he didn't want to see him in there. Before the stroke, Scottie was always the first to the car when it was time to visit Gramps. The hospital however was no place to be for little boys with unlimited energy and very little patience. Little Scottie would be okay for the first ten minutes. The eleventh seemed longer than the first ten combined, and the twelfth longer still. By the time Scottie and his mom had been in that place for fifteen minutes he began to ask the question, "Is it time to go yet?" Before another five minutes had passed, his mother would be losing her own patience.

"Scottie, shush," she would say. A bit later Mom would announce, "Scottie, we will leave when we leave, now please be quiet." That would inevitably be followed by, "Scottie, can't you just sit still for five minutes?"

He never got his Gramps back. His grandfather recovered enough to go home but he was never Gramps again. He was an old man who never spoke or laughed. Before the stroke, Gramps always told stories and laughed and laughed. In Scott's mind the hospital with all the shushes had taken the fun from his grandfather. All that, "don't bother the sick and dying" quiet had taken the fun out of Gramps.

So here he was all grown up and still hating hospitals and the quiet in them. The white walls and cheap watercolor paintings. The antiseptic smell. The staff in their white uniforms or green scrubs all hustling around importantly not seeming to notice the people they passed in the halls. But what he hated most of all was the quiet. It was that *don't disturb the sick and dying* kind of quiet. A silence that appeared to be annoyed by interruptions. Interruptions like an occasional page: "Dr. Nobody, please report to Radiology" or "Dr. Anonymous to the ER stat". Christ, what he wanted to hear was "Scott Randall, please report to the fucking Charger and get the hell out of here." Now that would be a welcome interruption to the quiet. Whether the "hospital-quiet" thought so or not, Scott Randall would love to hear that.

That page would not come. Scott paced the floor in the waiting room of the Salina Surgical Hospital wanting to be just about anywhere else. He listened to the "Dr. Nobody Cares, please report to wherever" pages and the sound of soft-soled shoes on the shiny tile floor. To the chimes of the elevator down the hall just before it clanged open casting out its cargo of more clip clopping shoes and whispering voices. Most of all, the quiet, the "do not disturb the sick and dying" quiet.

Just when Scott considered making a run for the exit Fred Webster came up and tapped him on the shoulder causing him to jump. "Sorry pal," Fred said in a half whisper. Fred had been the unfortunate owner of the Suburban that took flight back on the highway. As luck would have it he was also a retired doctor. He was a big man, both tall and wide. He had a kind face that was younger looking than the full head of white hair made him appear. He still wore a shirt and tie, more out of habit than anything. His white shirt was damp and soiled but it looked as though it had been neatly pressed when he put it on.

"Scott, I have never traveled that fast in a car before and I sure hope I never have the pleasure again." Fred's expression was a mix of mild amusement and admiration. Scott was in no mood for pleasant chit-chat. He was worried about Ashley. Moreover, he wanted to get out of this hospital as soon as he got word that she would be okay. "Forty-five minutes from there to here has got to be some kind of record. That's a hell of a car you got there."

Scott nodded politely, "It actually belongs to a business associate back in Detroit." It would have been easier to say a friend but Thomas was a pompous ass and Scott didn't want to call him a friend even in conversation with a man he would probably never see again. "He's hoping I can find a buyer for it when I get back to LA. I think his wife is making him sell it, probably to get some SUV the size of Rhode Island."

"My truck might have flown to Rhode Island. Did you see it take off? It flew right over your friend's car like it had wings and that Charger stayed put." Fred shook his head, an incredulous look on his face. "Not a scratch on it. When the storm passed and the sun hit it, she sat there shining, red like the devil."

Fred had come bounding down the embankment to Ashley's aid with the dexterity of a twenty-five-year-old fire and rescue worker. Scott admired the way Fred took charge. He called over to the old couple who were examining their crippled Winnebago. Fred sent them into their broken home on wheels to get clean towels and a first aid kit. The old doctor dressed Ashley's wound and fashioned a collar out of a hand towel to secure her neck. The Charger was the only road-worthy vehicle left so they got Ashley in the backseat as carefully as possible, where Fred secured her head with a couple of the old folk's beach towels, then climbed into the passenger seat barking at Scott to get moving.

The old couple and a young woman whose minivan the sign had passed through, stood watching the Charger as it disappeared into the haze left behind by the storm. The same storm that would lay waste to the town of Sherwood just minutes later.

Sherwood, Kansas, a farming community, was about twenty miles west of where Fred's Suburban landed in a field of corn. Four people had died in Sherwood and Rosie Sanchez; a two-year-old girl had been torn from her mother's arms and was presumed dead.

Now Scott stood nodding at Fred's banter, his mind wandering. His gaze fell on the Charger sitting in the ER parking lot glistening in the sun. *Shining red like the devil.*

"Scott. Scott, are you okay?"

Scott looked back to Fred and nodded with a confused, blank look in his eyes.

"I'm going to check on Ashley. The attending is an old friend and he'll be straight with me," Fred said. Scott nodded once and Fred disappeared behind the sliding doors to the ER.

A TV mounted on the wall was now showing an on-the-scene report from Sherwood. A pretty young reporter in a stylish yellow rain slicker gave her best effort to appear grief stricken at the devastation surrounding her. The shot started as a close-up and panned out showing a backdrop of ruination. A bleeding woman in a shabby housecoat holding the limp body of what was once her beloved toy poodle wandered aimlessly behind the reporter looking lost and alone.

That was the kind of footage that often made national coverage, but it didn't. What did reach the National News from Sherwood was Pete, an old trucker with a friendly smile and a little girl named Rosie Sanchez. Pete had just delivered a load of Pringles to Salt Lake City and was now on his way to Toledo with a load of some kind of health food snack he hadn't heard of. He had just got moving again after waiting out the storm on the shoulder of the road when he saw her. "Damndest thing I ever saw", he would tell the reporters. "She was walking down the side of the highway a mile and a half from where she had left her mommy. At least that's what the officer told me," Pete said. The reporter said she was scared and cold but otherwise unhurt. Pete was being called a hero but he said that all he did was bring a little girl to the police so they could find her mommy. Pete said, "it was little Rosie who was the hero."

The people in the waiting room cheered when they saw little Rosie reunited with her mother. The "don't bother the sick and dying" quiet didn't seem to be offended by this interruption. It was a respectful, polite cheer that was stifled by another page that nobody in the waiting room heard. The page just made them aware that they were interrupting the quiet. There was a brief buzz in the waiting room as the occupants discussed the news report. The buzz faded to a low hum and then the quiet came again.

Scott felt cold as an air-conditioned blast from overhead blew down on his wet clothes raising goose bumps over the exposed skin of his arms and neck. He decided to go to the car and get a change of clothes. Stepping out into the sun was liberating. He felt warm and free. He didn't want to go back in there. He was out. He could just get in the car and leave. Then he remembered, he had put Ashley's pack in the trunk to make more room for her to lie in the backseat. He couldn't leave with her pack. He picked it up and looked at it. A name tag on the zipper filled in with pink ink. Ashley Troop. He hadn't even known her last name until now. All he had to do was leave it with the front desk and he was gone.

"Nice car, son."

Scott turned with a start and saw a state trooper standing beside him.

"Funny thing about this car, son, I was heading west after the storm went through and I see this red blur streak past me faster than I ever seen a car go on that highway. And I seen plenty of speeding on that stretch."

He wasn't looking at Scott. He was looking into the trunk, craning his neck to look inside the car. "I figured anyone driving that fast must be in trouble or on drugs. You on drugs, son?"

Scott was beginning to look a little nervous.

"As I live and breathe. Wayne Tucker, is that you?" Fred was approaching the car dressed in clean scrubs and sporting an ear to ear grin.

Scott looked at the two of them. Fred the old doctor and Trooper Wayne Tucker and thought, *of course Fred knows him. He probably knows everybody around here.*

"Well shit, Doc. You back in the saddle?"

Fred looked down at the scrubs and explained the events back on the highway. Then he asked Wayne how his boy was doing. Fred had set his leg after a tree climbing incident some years back. Wayne's boy was now in his second year at college and his boy this and his boy that. Scott tuned out and was now looking at the name tag. Ashley Troop. Had they got in touch with her parents? Had she regained consciousness? Hell if she hadn't then they sure as hell hadn't called her family. Nobody even knew her last name around here until now.

"Isn't that right, Scott?" Fred said unaware that Scott hadn't heard a word.

"I'm sorry. What was that?"

"I was just telling Wayne how you and that car there may have saved that girl's life."

"Is she going to be all right?"

"Her x-rays are clear. She's awake now. Boy, can that girl talk." Scott couldn't help but smile at that. There were a few times in the car when he feigned sleep so she would shut up for a few minutes. "They got in touch with her mother," Fred continued, "All looks okay for now, should be out of here in a day or two."

"That's great," Scott said looking at the officer and still feeling uneasy. "I'll just leave her pack at the nurses' desk and get going."

"She asked about you, asked if you had been hurt. I think it would help if you went in and said goodbye," Fred said, his eyes less friendly than they had been. "I know you've only known her for a couple of days but you're the closest she has to a friend for a thousand miles."

"Well, I'm not going to get back on the road tonight anyway." He threw her pack over his shoulder and grabbed his own bag out of the trunk. "Is there a place in there I can get out of these wet clothes?" He looked over at trooper Wayne and asked, "Is there anything else you need from me, officer?"

"If the Doc thinks you're okay then I'm done here. Mind you don't race outta town the same way you came in, okay, son?"

"You can count on that," Scott said and headed back inside.

"Hold up Scott, I'll show you where to get cleaned up," Fred called out, shaking Wayne's hand and telling him to say hi to his boy. He trotted up to where Scott stood and put an arm on his shoulder leading him back inside.

Scott crept into Ashley's room with the stealth of a cat burglar. He slowly peered around the corner hoping she had gone back to sleep so he could leave her pack and get out. Maybe even leave a note wishing her well. But he wouldn't be so lucky. When his head rounded the corner Ashley called him in, beaming like she was reuniting with her long lost brother.

"So they say you're going to be okay."

"Yep, Dr. Fred says you and that car are genuine heroes, he also says he doesn't ever want to ride in that car again." They both laughed. Ashley's chuckle was tempered by a grimace of pain in her head. Scott thought she looked like something out of an old civil war flick, lying in bed with the top of her head bandaged.

"I brought your pack in," he said, holding it up to show her. "Fred says they got in touch with your mom. Are you going to go home until you heal up?"

"Naw, Mom just took care of the paperwork with the hospital over the phone. She tried to get me to come home but I have to keep going. If I don't I may spend the rest of my life thinking 'What if?'"

Scott hadn't really recognized her as an adult until this moment. She yawned and apologized saying it must be the drugs. He set her pack beside the bed and promised to drop by in the morning before he hit the road, then without even thinking about it, he reached out, took her hand and gently squeezed it.

Fred was waiting outside her door. When Scott exited the room he put his hand on Scott's shoulder and they walked out of the hospital together without speaking. The sun had set and the last of the day's glow was fading behind the horizon. The shrubs and trees were still visible in the weak residual sunlight but they had lost all color and looked more like shadows than the vibrant greenery that tomorrow's sunrise would again reveal. The automatic doors slid closed behind them trapping the quiet inside. Scott welcomed the sound of the street.

Even the scream of an incoming ambulance siren was music that would chase the last of the quiet from his head.

Scott stood next to the Charger breathing in the muggy night air. "Feels like we got more rain on the way," he said.

"Yes, it sure does."

"How are you going to get home?" Scott asked. "I don't think that SUV of yours is going to do you much good."

"The wife should be here shortly. I called her while you were in the girl's room." Fred looked at Scott with an inquisitive look in his eye and asked how he ended up traveling with Ashley. Scott told him the story of the Mad Batter.

"Maybe you're that girl's guardian angel, Scott."

"She's in a boatload of trouble if that's the case," Scott said.

Scott got directions to a few hotels from Fred while he waited for his wife to arrive. Fred had seen the golf bag in the trunk and invited Scott to the club for a round. Elks is in great shape this year Fred added. Scott took down Fred's number and said he'd let him know after his visit with Ashley in the morning. Just then a cream colored Chrysler 300 pulled up beside them and Fred announced, "And there's my ride."

Scott countered with, "you got a Hemi in that thing?"

Fred pointed at the C on the fender and waved as he got in the passenger seat and the car disappeared from sight. Standing alone in the ER parking lot Scott Randall felt at peace for the first time in three days and then he looked at the Charger.

Chapter Eighteen

Roger woke to a constant ringing echoing between his ears, bouncing from the left to the right. His stomach retched, but he fought off the urge to vomit. His bladder, which must have tripled in size due to the night's consumption of Corona, had caused a bloated ache in his lower abdomen. A gurgling sound of pouring water somewhere to his right magnified exponentially the urge to relieve himself. So this is a hangover, he thought. Many times he had experienced what he thought were hangovers after college keggers, but they must have been just a warning of what could happen because this was infinitely worse. This is what he got for not heeding those earlier warnings.

With difficulty he sat up on what he now realized was a lounge chair beside the pool. The nude stone woman poured water into the hot tub from her bottomless flask. He rubbed the sleep from his eyes. With some encouragement from deep down, he raised himself to a hunched, but standing position. He tried to straighten up, but the strain on his bladder made that exercise painful. So he began to waddle, bent over like a ninety-year-old, toward the stairs to the apartment over the garage.

"Wow, you really look like shit, Vermont," Beth said. She was standing at the top of the stairs in the same swimsuit she had worn the previous morning. He saw the mockery on her face but it didn't hide the sympathy in her eyes.

Roger wondered briefly through his discomfort, how she could be so stunning and seemingly unaffected by the victory celebration. She had at the very least, matched him beer for beer.

"I feel worse I'm sure," he said in a barely audible whimper.

Beth giggled prancing down the steps. "Nice look, Roger, not everyone could carry it off but it works for you."

Roger looked down to see that he wasn't wearing a shirt. He was barefoot and still had his baseball pants on, which were damp and one pant leg was pulled up past the knee. He looked at Beth inquisitively, she pointed to the pool where his shirt and one of his shoes floated motionless on the sparkling surface.

"You sure got game on the ball field, Vermont, but in a saloon you are one shameful greenhorn."

His stomach retched again, with some panic he squeezed past Beth who was now standing on the bottom step. He climbed the stairs as fast as his triple weight bladder would allow. His gut had settled into a low rumble by the time he got to the guest bathroom. He stood over the toilet expecting the pressure to release in a stream that could rival a fire hose, but what came was barely more than a trickle. His bladder swelled to the point that it restricted flow. So he stood there trickling until the pressure on his plumbing was relieved. A sigh of relief escaped his lips followed by a surge of despair when he felt the inevitable heave.

He heard a light knock followed by Beth's voice, "Roger, are you okay?"

He flushed and said he'd meet her at the pool.

It took him almost an hour to get downstairs. He showered, shaved and brushed his teeth twice. He smelled and looked much better but his head throbbed. His stomach had settled, although his abs burned like he had been doing sit-ups all morning.

"Holy shit, Bethy, look what the cat dragged in," Bobbie said. Bobbie and Beth were sitting at the edge of the pool with their legs dangling in the water. They giggled a bit and Roger flipped them the bird and sat next to Beth.

"How ya feelin', Vermont?" Beth asked in a truly sympathetic tone.

"Give me a few more hours and I'll be good as new," Roger said. He didn't believe that, but he had to cowboy up in front of the girls. "I won't be ready to travel today. You don't mind me staying for another day, do you?"

"Well, if she wants you out of the guest room, Roger, you can sleep with me tonight," Bobbie said, laughing.

Beth punched her in the arm and told Roger he didn't have to leave until he was ready. He thought it unlikely he would be welcome if he were still here in a month, but he wouldn't need the guest room that long.

"I should be fine to hit the road tomorrow."

"God damn, boy, you're as pale as boiled pork."

The three turned to see Jack Walker standing ten feet away wearing a denim shirt, pressed jeans and cowboy boots. "Listen, Roger, you really saved the day yesterday. That was the first time I didn't have to pay for that shindig you attended last night."

Beth was gleaming, as she could see where this was going.

"I understand you have school in the fall but if you want to spend the rest of the summer working here I'm sure I could find a spot for you."

There it was, just what Beth was hoping for. "You seem to be moved in to Billy's old room and you are welcome to it as long as need be."

"I really appreciate the offer, Jack, but I really want to get to the Grand Canyon this summer," Roger said without noticing the smile fading from Beth's face. He stood up, faced Jack and added, "I've been planning this trip since I was a junior in high school and I need to see it through."

"A man who knows what he wants and makes it happen. I like that, son. You go do what you gotta do. If you need to make a few bucks before September rolls around the guest room will be there."

"Thanks, that really means a lot, Jake," Roger said.

"You're still a smartass, son." Jack put out his hand and Roger extended his. With a quick shake, Jack turned and headed back toward the house.

"He really likes you, Roger," Bobbie said. "I can't remember seeing anything like that before. And it's not just the damn ball game. He sees something in you."

Bobbie stood and motioned to Beth as though they had a plan and it was up to her to get it in play. Bobbie walked away, and as she got to the stairs going up to the apartment, she made the same gesture. It was a shoving motion like one you might use to urge a child to join the line to jump off the diving board for the very first time.

"So you're planning to leave tomorrow?" Beth asked in a voice that said, "I don't really want to hear the answer."

"Yeah, I'm already a week behind where I thought I would be."

"I wish you would take Daddy up on his offer to stay the summer."

"Beth, you know I like it here. But it's like I told your dad, I really need to do this." He looked right at her and before he could stop himself he said, "Why don't you come with me?"

"Do you mean it?"

He didn't think he did but he also didn't think he could take it back. Sure it would be nice to have some company and sure Beth was beautiful company, although this isn't what he planned. But he said, "I wouldn't have asked if I didn't mean it."

She kissed his cheek and ran away leaving little wet footprints on the stone. She didn't follow Bobbie up the stairs. She followed Jack back to the main house.

Roger was left sitting on the edge of the pool wondering what had just happened. Two days ago, he hadn't known any of these people and now he was offered a place to stay and a job. He invited a swimsuit model to join him on his trip and she seemed to be willing. The weird thing about that, he wasn't totally convinced he wanted this gorgeous girl to come along. Having all distraction gone, he found the pounding in his head to be unbearable so he went back to the guest room to lie down.

The Nightcrawler

Four hours passed before Roger was brought to consciousness by a honking horn outside his window. Beep, beep, BEEEEEEEEEP. He looked toward the sound and the light streaming through the window caused his eyes to close to slits. He felt much better. The pounding in his head had been reduced to a low grade hum that intensified with each beep. When he got to the window and looked down to the source of the noise, he saw Beth standing beside a shiny lemon yellow Jeep. She waved up at the window with one hand, the other still on the horn of the Jeep.

She stopped beeping and yelled, "Come on down, Vermont."

Roger laughed. Beth had released the horn and was standing with her hands on her hips.

"Well, are you coming down or do I have to come up there and drag your scrawny ass down here?"

He laughed aloud and shaking his head walked to the door leading to the stairs. When he walked out into the sun, which was well past being high in the sky, Roger said, "What the hell is that, Beth?"

"It's a Jeep, Vermont," she said hands still on her hips. "Don't they have Jeeps in the east?"

"Yes we have Jeeps. But what are you doing with it?"

"Well, I told Daddy I was going to the canyon with you and he said, 'Not in that Challenger you're not.' I said 'shit no, we're going to hitchhike.'" Beth broke into a hysterical laughter. "You shoulda seen the look on his face. He said 'Bethy, you go see Billy. He'll have a Jeep ready when you get there.' So here it is."

"So it's Billy's Jeep?"

"No stupid. It's yours. At least for a year. Daddy owns a Chrysler dealership and Billy runs it for him." She threw the keys at him and ran around to the passenger side. "Well, let's go for a ride."

"What do you mean it's mine?"

"For a year, Vermont. Daddy told Billy to set up a one year lease. We have to go see Billy before he closes to finish the paperwork. Come on, let's go."

"Beth, I can't even afford the insurance for a year on that car."

"You don't have to worry about that. It's got Daddy's fleet insurance."

Roger surrendered and quick stepped to the Jeep. The top was off; a tarp was stretched across the cargo area behind the rear bench seat concealing the results of Beth's shopping trip.

"What's all that?" he asked with the look of a nine-year-old who just got the new Schwinn he asked Santa for.

She grabbed the tarp and pulled it back revealing a complete set of camping gear. A tent, sleeping bags, stove, lantern, cooler. It looked like a sample pack for a Coleman salesman. Roger sat stunned and speechless. The gear in the back of the Jeep must have cost more than he made last year.

Beth brought him back asking, "You okay, Vermont?"

"Beth, I can't take the Jeep or any of this."

"Look, the car is just a loan. And the gear, well if you don't want to take it with you after the trip then it will just get stored in the barn until the next ice age. Or maybe me and Bobbie will use it. Now if we don't get moving we're going to miss Billy at the dealership."

Roger started the Jeep and sat for a moment listening to the engine, his hand on the steering wheel thinking. He felt odd, like when he was little and his Granddad used to give him a dollar whenever he came to visit. His mother would always give him a look. Later, she would always caution Roger and his sister that Granddad had better things to do with his money. Surely Jack Walker had better things to do with his money, even if he did own most of Nebraska.

"Vermont, you have to put it in gear or it won't move," Beth said.

Roger followed her instructions without saying anything and the Jeep lurched and stalled. He restarted it a little embarrassed and with a smoother release of the clutch, they sped off toward the long driveway.

They got to Walker's Chrysler about ten minutes before closing. Billy was talking to a pretty young woman at the reception desk. Beth had quipped to Roger that Billy always hired cheerleaders to work the reception desk and then spent a great deal of effort and money trying to get in their pants. She also mentioned that he was fairly successful.

A balding salesman dressed in black pants and a red polo shirt with Walker Chrysler embroidered on the sleeve was sitting at a desk in one of ten cubicles located around the perimeter of the showroom. On the desk a small placard "Bob Johnstone—Sales Associate". Across from him a young couple, both dressed in jeans and western shirts sat nervously as Bob typed in the last of the offer to purchase on a new Caravan. The couple exchanged anxious smiles and then Bob left them while he retrieved the sales contract and presented it to Billy at the reception desk.

Billy and Bob the salesman walked over to the young couple, everyone shook hands, smiled and Billy left Bob to get all the signatures.

Beth and Billy hugged, and then Billy shook Roger's hand.

"How ya doin', slugger," Billy asked.

"Better than I did when I woke up," Roger said.

"No doubt. You were in sad shape when you left the party."

Billy motioned for the pair to follow and they all went in to Billy's office. Billy gave Roger a few pieces of paper to sign and told him to enjoy the Jeep. Beth got up and went to the restroom. Roger expressed his feeling about accepting the Jeep. Billy eased his mind, telling him that Jack was thinking of making it an MVP prize every time Three-B's won the annual ball game. The only thing Roger had to do was bring it back when the lease was up.

When Beth returned, Roger and Billy were sharing a laugh about some of the gaffs from players on both teams during the game. The laughter broke off when she entered and asked what was so funny.

"Billy was just sharing some stories about your childhood," Roger replied and the two men shared another chuckle that broke off when Beth pinched Billy's left arm hard enough to make him squeal. Roger side stepped away from her and Billy told him to be careful around her.

Billy laughed harder; Roger decided it might be best not to respond to this one.

"Okay then, that's all we need to do here. I guess I'll see you both at dinner tonight," Billy said as he ushered them back out to the showroom.

Roger looked at Beth with a confused expression, "Dinner?"

"Oops, sorry, Bethy," Billy said, leaving them, he returned to the receptionist.

"Daddy said that since I was leaving for a few weeks that we should have a family dinner. He said I should bring you along."

Roger had already met the parents, but being invited to "The Family Dinner" was a whole new level. Things were moving way too fast. He wasn't feeling bad about Paige anymore but this felt like a going steady kind of thing and he had only just met Beth. His stomach began to feel queasy but he said, "Sounds like fun."

Things happen for a reason. His mother was fond of that expression. So when he felt his relationship with Beth was based on him saying what he thought she wanted to hear, he thought maybe his responses were just things happening for a reason. Then again, can anything that is based on two days be considered a relationship? He liked Beth and her family. He liked the Jeep and the camping gear. He liked the idea of coming back next summer for a job. However, dinner with the folks, he was not counting on. What he was counting on was being on the road early tomorrow.

"Oh I don't know if fun is a word I would use," Beth replied uneasily.

They had gotten through dinner without incident and Roger was beginning to think he was going to get out without the talk. He had it going through his head since they left Billy's dealership. Jack would take him aside and give him the what for. Shit, the summer had started with him trying to convince his mother that things would be okay. Now he was trying to figure out how he would convince the Walkers the same thing. It was a pleasant dinner. Billy was late and took some of the attention from Beth. He also brought the receptionist and that rubbed Jack the wrong way. Bobbie came in alone, but was dressed in a provocative top that left very little to the imagination. That also pissed Jack off. Beth sat quietly beside Jack like the good child.

Roger began to get nervous early on. Would Billy and Bobbie have Jack so wound up that he would rain down on him and Beth just because he didn't like the way things were going? But that hadn't happened, at least not yet.

Then the axe fell. After dinner, Jack invited Roger to tour the house with him. Beth tried to go to Roger's aid but Jack sent her off to help her mother clean up. How much help she needed with three domestics clearing the table was suspect. Roger followed Jack into his study. That's what he called it, the study. It was a huge room with an equally huge oak desk, a stone fireplace against one wall adorned with brass pokers and a stuffed cougar over the mantle. The cougar was poised to pounce, its ears pinned and fangs exposed, ready for the kill.

Jack caught Roger's fixed gaze at the cougar.

"Beautiful animals aren't they? That one killed three of my cows and my favorite dog before I killed it. If my aim was off an inch either way, I may have been mounted on the wall."

Roger didn't reply, he just made a weak attempt at looking impressed. He was sure that his effort only confirmed to Jack that he was shitting bricks. Make a run for it is what Roger wanted to do.

"I like you, Roger."

Roger cringed at the sound of that. Anything that ever started like that had a colossal BUT, coming right after. His mind raced. Why had Jack dragged him in here? Was he going to buy him off? "Here, Roger, twenty grand and keep the Jeep. Just get out of here before Beth wakes up." Maybe he was going to threaten him. "Roger, if you hurt my little girl I will mount you right up there with that cougar."

Before he could speculate anymore Jack continued, "I don't know if you picked up on it, but Bethy is my favorite. I know parents aren't supposed to have favorites but if you have more than one it's bound to happen."

Isn't this great, Roger thought, the man kills three-hundred pound killer cats for sport and his favorite child is planning to go on a road trip with him. Roger could feel his pores begin to moisten and his scrotum had drawn up so tight his testicles were pushing at his kidneys. He was sure that his face was beaded with sweat and Jack was about to turn up the heat.

"I decided long ago to trust my kids to make good decisions. Bobbie isn't very good at that yet, Billy is beginning to get the hang of it but he still has lapses. Beth on the other hand, I have never had to worry about. So when she came and told me she planned to join you on your quest, I had to support her. However, her little toy car wasn't going to make the cut. Once you get off the highways around the canyon the roads can be primitive at best. And I sure as hell wasn't going to let her hitchhike, it just isn't safe. So I had Billy arrange the Jeep." Roger's mouth began to open and Jack held up his hand to silence him.

"You seem to be as level headed as Beth so I'm not too worried about this," Jack continued then paused again. "Don't disappoint me kid, okay?"

"Yes sir," Roger said. He was desperate to think of something inspired to say to Jack. Something that would ease his mind, or maybe something that would reassure him, but "Yes sir." was all he could muster. Jack slapped Roger on the back and left the room. Roger stood and watched him leave unable to rationalize what was happening to him.

Tomorrow he would be driving southwest toward Arizona in a brand new Jeep. Beth, a beautiful girl he hardly new was going to ride with him. Beth's father who seemed to own most of the state of Nebraska had just given his blessing and there he stood, in the study of a huge mansion unable to make a simple decision like rejoin the group in the dining room.

He stood in the middle of the study when Beth walked in.

The Nightcrawler

"Hey Vermont, you still alive? When you didn't come back I thought maybe Daddy skinned you and mounted you up there with the cougar."

As Roger turned to look back at the cat, Beth charged him, screaming some kind of battle cry and jumped up on him, her arms wrapped around his neck and her legs around his waist. Roger caught her, barely maintaining his balance.

Jack entered the room and raised an eyebrow. Roger realized that he was holding Jackson Walker's favorite child by the cheeks of her ass.

"You two aren't going to make me regret my decision, are you?" Jack asked.

Beth released Roger and ran over to Jack jumped up on him the same way and kissed his cheek. "Calm down, Daddy, I'm just trying to cheer him up after you scared the crap out of him."

"Well, let's get back to the others. Your mom's got a big jug of lemonade or sweet tea waiting," Jack said, leaving them behind.

Chapter Nineteen

At the Prairie Inn, sure, the staff was courteous, and the facility was clean and well- maintained. After the day Scott Randall just had it should have felt like Xanadu. In spite of the hotel's amenities, a state of unease pressed in on him. He hoped work would take the edge off his agitation. He answered all his emails then sat in front of his computer staring at an unchanging screen while the urge to bolt from the room percolated between his ears. There was nothing in particular he disliked about his room or the hotel, but he wasn't comfortable.

His irritation started when the clerk at the front desk said, "Okie-dokie" while handing Scott his keycard. He had come to hate that expression from the first time he heard it come from the mouth of The Nightcrawler in front of Thomas Andrews' office. Now what about that, he had given his hallucination a name. A name that came to him in a dream, well, in a nightmare was more like it. Maybe it was neither. Maybe it was a window to hell. Anyway, when questioned, the clerk claimed that what she said was "you forgot your room key" not okie-dokie, but Scott knew better. She said, "okie-dokie". *What the fuck does okie-dokie mean anyway?*

Then the bellhop in the lobby did that finger gun thing and made the clicking sound with his tongue. *Is there anyone in the heartland who doesn't do that? What is this, cops and robbers? It is not my finger; it's a gun, you dork. For Christ's sake,* he thought. *It's like there's a discussion group going in my head. Hello, my name is Scott and I'm a fucking whack job. Then the group says, "Hi Scott". He goes into a history of Whack Job Scottie, and then there's applause. Shit, that does it, fucking clapping in my head.*

The Nightcrawler

To escape the group session, Scott went for a walk, dressed in the same clothes he had changed into at the hospital. The air was still hot, no hint of a breeze, the rain from the afternoon storm evaporating into a haze that hovered over the area. The moon was full, the sky clear and cloudless, but the lunar glow lacked luster, its reflected rays subdued by the haze. It was quiet, too quiet; eerie was how he would describe it. The only sound was an occasional whoosh of a car speeding by on the interstate a quarter mile away.

He felt like he was twelve. The night he had run away from home was just like this. His dad had scolded him for not trying to stretch a double out of a line drive to left center. When he got home, he ran to his room. He sat there for what seemed like hours, just sitting on the bed stewing over his dad's tirade. Why couldn't his dad be happy that he got a base hit? He moved the runner over to third and was safe at first. Then Robbie hits one right at the shortstop and poof, double-play. Scottie improved his batting average but his team lost the game. Sure, if he stretched his hit into a double, there would have been no double play, but that didn't make the loss his fault. So, he ran away. When it got dark, he opened the window, threw his glove out on the back lawn, and climbed down using the TV antenna tower. He went to the ballpark and sat on first base. He screamed into the darkness, "I'm still safe." Then he got scared. He lasted about an hour out there, in the night. Crickets chirped, an owl hooted and the wind was moving the trees, but Scottie didn't feel any breeze. He just saw the trees move and heard the leaves rustle. He had to fight back the tears that welled in his eyes. He ran home, picked up his glove from where it fell on the back lawn and climbed back through his bedroom window.

Twenty years later as he walked beneath the streetlights he again felt frightened. He looked up at the trees and watched them move in the wind. Scott did the Boy Scout test, finger in mouth, hold to the air, feel the breeze. Nothing there and yet the trees swayed to a rhythm of some unheard music.

Crickets chirped all around, louder and louder, as if amplified. At first, it was just chirping, and then it became a raucous chorus of catcalls. It seemed like the whirr of noise that comes from a crowd of people all speaking at once. Then the whirr seemed to slow into a rhythm. The kind the sports fans get when they chant a player's name in unison. But it wasn't a name he heard, it was, "okie-dokie." Scott clamped his hands over his ears. The chant was muffled, but still audible. He squeezed harder, his hands like a vice now, pressing against the side of his head. His ears started to ring, he sat on the grass eyes closed, hands over his ears, rocking to the chant, "okie-dokie, okie-dokie."

Then a voice broke the chant, "Are you okay, sir?"

It was quiet again, even the chirping was gone. A cool breeze brushed Scott's cheek as he opened his eyes to see who stopped the noise. A woman dressed in green scrubs was standing on the sidewalk looking down with a concerned expression. She was an average looking woman, not pretty, not ugly. One of the many someone's, who could walk into a room and not be noticed. Her hair was cut in a bob, she wore no makeup, and her purse had straps like a child's backpack and was strung over her left shoulder.

"What, I'm sorry, were you talking to me?"

"I asked if you're okay." She still had a worried look on her face and added, "Do you need any help?"

"No, I'm fine thanks."

"All right, but you really should get up off the ground, I work in this building and the sprinklers will be coming on in a…" Sure enough, they did. Scott managed to jump to the safety of the sidewalk with just a few water spots dotting his shirt and shorts.

"Well, it looks like you saved me from a cold shower." By now they were both laughing, the controlled laugh you enjoy when you're with someone you don't know.

"Hi, my name is Scott. Let me reward you by buying you a drink."

"That won't be necessary, Scott."

"Look, I've been on the road for what seems like forever, I'm just looking for some friendly conversation. How about it? Just drinks and conversation."

"I tell you what, Scott, I just got off work. My house is a couple of blocks from here." She paused, almost as though she was debating in her head whether to continue with her current response. "If you like I could run in and change and then I might be open to grabbing a quick bite if you're interested."

"Sounds good to me," Scott answered with an enthusiastic resonance. It was a tone reminiscent of his response to an invitation from his dad to Dairy Queen after a ball game.

His childlike demeanor had brought on another giggle that she tried to muffle by putting a hand over her mouth. Before he could say anything more she said, "My name is Gwen, it's a pleasure to meet you, Scott."

Gwen started along the sidewalk without saying anything and Scott followed suit, walking slightly behind and to her left. A luminescent glow gave the trees along the road ahead of them a surreal spookiness. They walked along without speaking. Scott stared at the freakish skeletal shapes of the tree limbs, like he was waiting for someone, or something to jump out at them. Or maybe he thought the trees themselves might just come after him. After all, if worms could mold themselves into people, and crickets could chant, "Okie-Dokie," then why couldn't trees chase him through the streets of Salina, Nebraska.

"Yer kinda quiet there, Scott, you sure you're alright?"

"Sorry, what was that?"

"I said, you sure yer okay?"

"I'm good," he said. "Gwen, what's that light up ahead?"

"Oh, that's Heritage Park. Most likely a little league game's goin' on. Usually three or four at a time every night. They also got some old farts playin' slow pitch. I stop and watch sometimes. The kids are fun, I call slow pitch 'toss and giggle'. It's a pale comparison to baseball."

This brought a chuckle to Scott's lips that he didn't bother to hide. He had played on the company slow pitch team in the past. It was just an excuse to go out on a weeknight and swill beers with the boys. With the exception of a few guys, the talent pool on the team was weak, but the after-game libation made the embarrassing losses on the field tolerable. He quit playing the year Tad McKinney took a bad hop off the side of the head that turned him into an idiot for the rest of his life. Tad was his best friend and an up and coming star player in the company, but now he needed help tying his shoes.

"Hey Scott, there's always a weenie wagon at the park when there's a ball game. You up for ballparks and a Coke?"

"Now that, my friend, sounds like a winning plan."

"Great, then I won't need to go home and change."

They walked the rest of the way without talking. The sounds of the ballgames at the park ahead gradually broke the silence. A car full of teenage boys sped by, first honking then one of them yelled, "Fuck her, I did." Gwen flipped him the bird but didn't say anything. Scott just shook his head; he figured he was probably just as obnoxious when he was as young as those kids are now. They watched the car's taillights disappear around the next corner, and their attention focused on the sound of the kids' voices at the park. A light breeze carried the mouth-watering smell of hotdogs and sausages.

When they got to the corner of Partington and Ashland, there were no more trees to obscure their view of the park. It was clear that all the games were little leaguers'. The hotdog vendor set up between the backstops of diamond's two and three. The park, illuminated by large lights mounted on fifty-foot high poles, gave the whole place the glow of midday. It was like sitting at Dodger Stadium for a night game. Swarms of flying insects hovered around the lights giving the effect of living halos. The air was filled with the drone of young boys, chatting it up in the field, "um batter, batter", "give him the heat", "he ain't got nothing", the sounds of kids who play a game because they love it.

Scott began to think about some of the spoiled millionaire athletes he's dealt with at Cobra, and then looked back to the kids. There were four games going on, fifteen, maybe twenty kids per team. Eight teams in all, which meant there were as many as one hundred-fifty kids out on those fields. Maybe, not very likely, but just maybe one of those kids was going to be a star on a pro team. When that happened, the fun will have left the game for that kid. Some of these kids will play ball and enjoy it until they can't find the time, or they can't swing a bat because age has taken away their ability, but the kid who makes the pro's will lose the fun when the game becomes a business and not a game. What a shame that will be; taking the fun out of a child's game should be against the law.

Scott and Gwen crossed Ashland and went directly toward the gap between field two and field three. When they arrived at the hotdog wagon a boy about ten, wearing a Kansas City Royals jersey and hat was just walking away with a Cherry Coke in hand. A young woman, wearing a Cardinals shirt and a Royals hat was tending the weenie wagon. She was a pretty girl with a smile that glowed as bright as the lights surrounding the park.

"What can I getcha?" She asked, her smile not waning as she patiently waited for an answer.

"What'll it be, Gwen, dogs or sausages?" Scott asked.

"Sausages, absolutely sausages, and Dr. Pepper, if you have it."

"Same thing for you, sir?" the girl asked Scott.

"That sounds about perfect," Scott replied smiling back at her. He wondered if she ever worked at McDonalds, where they used to have "Smiles are free," up on the menu. "You are quite a fence sitter aren't you?" Scott said as she handed him two sausages.

"I'm sorry," she said her smile fading a bit, not understanding what he meant.

"Royals hat and Cardinals shirt. You couldn't make up your mind?"

She handed him two cans of Dr. Pepper and said, "That's eight dollars." Scott handed her a ten and told her to keep the change. She thanked him then said, "It's the people around here, some like the Cards, and some the Royals. Me, I like the Yankees but if I wore a Yankees cap or shirt I would never get any tips. Her smile returned bigger than ever as she stuffed Scott's change into the back pocket of her jeans in a deliberate motion as if to accentuate her point.

When Scott returned his attention to Gwen she was handing him one of the sausages. "I hope you like mustard and onions."

"A woman who knows what I like." He took a sausage and handed her a soda. "Shall we take a seat in the nose bleeds?" he joked as he motioned to the bleacher seats behind field three.

"Lead the way, sir," she answered.

Scott made his way to the top row of bleacher seats. They sat in the middle of the last row, having the whole thing to themselves.

After settling into their seats, Scott took a bite from his sausage, and with cheeks bulging like a chipmunk announced, "Now thas a goo thauthage." Gwen was chewing her food and just made an appreciative, "Hmmm."

Scott hadn't realized how hungry he was and finished eating without another word. He opened his Dr. Pepper with a snap and drank it down without taking a breath. Gwen was not quite half done her sausage, so while she was finishing, he looked around the park. There was a well-lit parking lot behind field four filled with minivans and SUV's. Opposite the parking lot was a municipal swimming pool. The only sign of life near the pool was a young man dressed in a T-shirt and swim trunks vacuuming it. Behind the pool was a playground, swings, slides, climbers, all the usual public park fodder.

He brought his focus to the people in the seats, men and women, mostly in their thirties. Moms and dads watching their kids play ball. Some had other kids in tow, some quietly sitting with their parents, others not so quiet, and still others annoyingly running up and down the aluminum benches. It was amazing how such small people could make such loud footfalls.

They all seemed too polite. There were no raucous catcalls aimed at the umpire, no dads chewing out the boys for not stretching singles into doubles. This was not the kind of little league crowd he knew as a boy. If the bleacher throng were better dressed Scott would have thought he was in Stepford.

Out on field three a chubby boy hit a sharp ground ball to a scrawny kid at second who scooped it up with the grace of a cheetah and fired it over to first beating the chubby kid easily. The game ended and the polite parents gathered their kids and headed out to the diamond to collect their budding stars.

Scott checked his watch it was nine o'clock. He hadn't noticed the other games had already ended and out on field two the beer bellied slow pitch players were already doing their warm ups. They were a sad looking bunch, soft middles, knees braced and elbows wrapped. A few were out in the field with cigarettes hanging loosely from the corners of their mouths. A short, round man with a salt and pepper beard was fielding balls at first, an open can of Bud on the ground next to the bag.

"This is where the real comedy starts," Gwen said, nudging Scott with her elbow.

"I have no doubt," he said as he motioned to the hotdog girl. "I'm going to get another Dr. Pepper. Would you like one?" She shook her head and he was down and back before she had time to think of a reason to take her leave.

"Scott, what were you doing on the lawn in front of the nursing home?"

"Nursing home? Oh is that what that was? I've been under a lot of stress lately and I had a pounding headache." He didn't think it wise to tell her he was trying to block out a chorus of crickets chirping, "Okie-dokie."

"It was a little creepy. I was going to walk by. To see a grown man sitting on the ground chanting "Okie-dokie" and rocking back and forth was a bit unsettling."

A chill went through Scott when he heard that. It wasn't the crickets. It was him. Shit he was cracking up, he'd be in a rubber room before the end of the week if this kept up. In an attempt to divert some of the attention from his nutty behavior he said, "So you work in a nursing home?"

"Well, I used to work in a burn unit but that was just too heartbreaking. People in so much pain and not too much you could do. They just had to endure while the healing came slowly." She shuddered a bit and took a sip of her Dr. Pepper. "What do you do, Scott?"

"I sell exotic cars."

"What's an exotic car? Some kind of limo with Hula Dancers in the back?"

They both had a hearty laugh at that then he explained why he was driving through Kansas and about Cobra Exotics, about the customer waiting for the Aston Martin. She had some trouble believing that people needed help finding a car. Even if it was a quarter of a million dollar English sports car.

Just then she grabbed his knee firmly to get his attention and said, "Oh watch this guy, I've seen these ol' boys before." Scott looked out at field two, where a guy who looked to be about fifty and carrying triplets, stood at the plate. He had a very muscular upper body that seemed to disappear into the bulbous growth hanging way over his belt.

"He hits the ball farther than any of them but if it don't clear the fence he only gets to first and then they get him out at second when the next guy hits into a fielder's choice." True to what she said the guy hit a line shot that one hopped off the center field fence for a single. Gwen laughed as the guy stood at first, hands on his knees trying to catch his breath.

She looked over at Scott who was staring at the spot where the ball had bounced off the fence. "I told you he hits it far, didn't I?" Scott didn't answer; he just continued to stare at that spot in the outfield. "Hey Scott, are you okay?"

"What? Ya I guess, I mean did you see that guy in the outfield?"

"The one who threw the ball in, sure I saw him. Not much of a throw but you don't need a great arm to send that mook back to first."

"No not him, the guy behind the fence. He had long greasy hair, dirty clothes. Did you see him?"

"Didn't see anyone like that, Scott. It's kind of dark out there past the fence. Are you sure it wasn't a shadow? Or maybe it was that crow on the outfield fence."

"Maybe, I guess it could have been a shadow." He hesitantly looked back, sure enough a huge crow sat perched on the center field fence. It seemed to be looking directly at Scott. When he was convinced that the bird was staring him down he looked away. When he looked back it was gone. Then that awful clicking sound was coming from overhead. Scott and Gwen both shifted their gaze to the noise and there it was, atop the chain-link backstop not twenty feet away. A crow, big and black, with a few feathers jutting out at differing angles that gave it a scruffy appearance looked down on them. It looked diseased. In the crow's beak dangled a huge worm that moved only slightly with the night breeze. With a sudden quick motion the bird's head tipped back and the worm disappeared. Scott was sure it was the same crow. The one he had seen back at the Best Western. Shit, if The Nightcrawler could be in the outfield then why couldn't this same crow be here also? The clincher came when the bird flew off, making that same caw-caw-caw, that sounded more like mocking laughter than the meaningless nattering of a dumb bird.

Scott's mood turned sullen, and his face lost all expression.

"Well that was a bit gross, eh Scott?" Gwen said not noticing that he had gone off to another place. "Scott, are you still with me?" She put her hand on his shoulder and tried again, "Earth to Scott, come in please."

"What," he answered, with a groggy, just got out of bed slur.

"You're a bit of a flake sometimes, aren't you? Where the hell were you just now?"

"I'm not sure, Gwen. It may have been hell. I've been in a real bad place the last few days, and it doesn't look like I've gotten out yet." He stood and gave another look out to center, no crow or vagrants to be seen. "I should get back to the hotel, thanks for the company, I wish I could say we'll do it again sometime but I really don't see myself dropping in on Salina, Kansas, again in this lifetime."

"I'm not surprised, it's not much of a tourist Mecca, is it?"

He didn't reply, he just made a diagonal descent across the bleachers to ground level. Scott paused for a moment, turned to look up at Gwen. He forced a wave and what he hoped was a warm smile. She returned the wave but her face showed only concern. Gwen began to make her way to where Scott stood but he didn't wait. He turned and faded into the shadows beyond the trees near the park's edge. In the darkness he looked back one more time to see Gwen watching him go, concern never leaving her face. Scott plodded back along the same route he and Gwen had used to get to the park. As if on autopilot, he continued, barely aware of where he was or where he was going. His mind began to rewind to the bum, the crow and the worms. Then chirp, just a single chirp from a solitary cricket. He looked up to find himself in front of the same building, the nursing home that Gwen had emerged from. The grass in front of the stately two and a half story manor glistened, millions of little droplets from the sprinklers reflecting the lights from the street lamps giving the lawn an almost celestial brilliance.

The solitary cricket made a friend across the lawn and they began to banter back and forth, then three, four, ten, and then the whir became the same chant, "Okie-dokie, okie-dokie, okie-dokie." He hurried toward the hotel, walking at first then a jog and finally a flat out run. The chant faded with distance until three blocks away it was gone all together. Stopped, exhausted, hands on his hips, his breath coming in deep gasps, he listened. Scott turned in all directions and listened, nothing but the sound of the occasional passing car, a dog barking in a far off yard and the leaves slightly rustling in the breeze.

He inhaled deep into his lungs and let it out, his breath still hurried, but close to normal, he continued, his stride more deliberate now. A tune popped into his head, he didn't know what it was called, nor did he remember the words but it was very familiar. It was a child's song and he began to whistle it. The song calmed him, and the good

The Nightcrawler

mood he had before he saw the shadow man behind the fence in centerfield returned. He could see the glow of the hotel sign two blocks up. There was no joy in returning there so he slowed his pace and began to look around at the old buildings. They were all two to three story houses, converted into restaurants, convenience stores, women's boutiques and doctor's offices. This was assuredly the place where the well-heeled of Salina lived during the twenties and thirties. The structures were well-built and still had their original charm.

In front of one of the old houses, which was now the Just Like Mom daycare center, was a silhouette cutout of a man leaning on a tree. It was mounted against a huge Sycamore and with the floodlights illuminating the front of the building; it could have been a real man. Scott stood watching the plywood man, standing on one leg the other bent at the knee, foot resting against the trunk of the tree. He began to feel better about what he may or may not have seen in the outfield. If light and shadows could make this thing look like a real person then maybe Gwen was right, maybe it was just shadows playing tricks on him.

Scott waved at the wooden lawn ornament and said good night. As he turned to head back to his room something moved in his peripheral vision and on instinct he looked back to see the plywood man tip his hat and say, "Goodnight Scott." Scott held his ground, looking directly at the plywood man. It stood motionless against the tree. Okay, he thought, lights and shadows can't say goodnight. He needed a closer look so he crept up the sidewalk that split the front lawn in half. The man was still two dimensional and still not moving. When he got to within six feet of the old sycamore something crunched beneath his foot stopping him in his tracks. Scott looked down. He was surrounded by crickets; the biggest blackest crickets he had ever seen. They began to fall from the branches of the big tree like black rain. The chirping started up louder than ever, "Okie-dokie, Okie-dokie…"

He ran, he ran like he had never run before. He ran as if his life, or at the very least, his sanity depended on it. He didn't stop running until he was pushing the elevator button in the hotel lobby.

155

Inside his room it was safe. He leaned his back against the door, his chest heaving, his lungs burning. He stood there for what seemed like hours. His breath coming in slower waves, his lungs were no longer on fire. He could feel the tightness in his legs as he slowly made his way to the bathroom. He stood under the harsh light reflecting off the mirror. His own reflection sickened him right now. He had acted like a frightened child and he was no child. As he looked himself in the eye, his attention was drawn to a small dark spot on his shirt sleeve. A big, black cricket was clinging to the fabric, his little antennae twitching in all directions. "Uh," he moaned, as he brushed the insect off and stomped on it with his full force. When he raised his shoe there was nothing left of the bug but a dark spot on the tile floor of the bathroom. Scott stared at the cricket's remains and was startled to see the stain on the floor had the same shape as the plywood man from the daycare center. He pulled a handful of tissues from the box on the counter, picked the cricket up from the floor with them and tossed the whole mess in the toilet and quickly flushed before it could leap out. He then stepped carefully around the spot where the cricket had been, clicked off the bathroom light and went over to the bed, sat down then let his body go limp and he fell back. Scott just lay there in his clothes, staring at the shadows on the ceiling until exhaustion and sleep took him away.

Chapter Twenty

Roger woke with a convulsive jerk through his whole body. His skin clammy, his heart beating faster than it had been when he finished his round tripper in the slow pitch game. He had never been this awake this fast in his life. He had another bad dream, but this one didn't linger in his conscious mind. He had a vague feeling that there was a big dog with glowing red eyes. Someone else was there, maybe it was Beth, he didn't know for sure. As the seconds turned to minutes, his whole recollection of the events in the dream melted away.

His attention drifted to the orange glow of dawn creeping through the window of Beth's bedroom. The pale light gave the whole room the appearance of a photonegative. The mirror over the chest of drawers had an odd reflection of the luminous window. The floral print wallpaper, barely discernable in this light looked more like poorly done graffiti. An ominous gleam off the eyes of a wooden rocking horse gave Roger an anxious feeling. Partially covered with clothing, the horse looked like a blob with eyes. Roger stared at the eyes thinking they could have been the eyes in his dream. With each passing second, as the sun climbed higher in the sky, the eyes glared ever brighter.

He diverted his gaze from the horse to the window. Recollection of the events from the previous night replaced the faded images of the nightmare. The Jeep, the stop at Billy's dealership and Jack's heart-to-heart. Mostly Jack's heart-to-heart. His chest began to pound as it had when Jack described the cougar hunt. The biggest thing, the event that weighed heaviest on him was Jack's admission that Beth is his favorite. Roger began to feel as uncomfortable now as he did standing in Jack's study getting the *don't make me regret my decision,* speech.

He looked over at Beth lying next to him. The dim light brought in by the sun as it only now breached the horizon cast an angelic glow on her. Her hair spread across the pillow framing her face. The top edge of her floral duvet left only her face, left shoulder and neck exposed. As he looked down at her, her right leg moved out from under the covers and took on a radiance in the subdued light from the window.

Shit, now he had done it. He didn't want this to happen. He liked Beth, hell he liked the whole Walker family, but he wasn't ready to start another relationship. He wasn't over Paige when he left Vermont and now he was lying naked next to Beth, who as far as he knew was also naked. Last night had been great. Beth had hugged him when they got back upstairs, the hug turned into a kiss and the kiss into, well into this. What, after all, was this? What ever it was, it made him feel just a little ashamed. He wanted to be here with Beth, but he also wanted to run like hell.

Roger left Beth's room as quietly as he could, gathering his clothes on the way out. He returned to the guest room, used the bathroom, then went over to the window where he leaned on the sill and watched the sun rising, casting long shadows over the pool. The statue of the naked lady continued pouring water into the hot tub. The Jeep was directly below the window, its yellow finish gleaming in the early morning light. The cattle in the far off fields were beginning to vocalize their hunger. A rooster crowing brought a smirk to Roger's lips. How cliché was that, the rooster crows at sunrise.

He was second guessing his invitation for Beth to join him on his trip, he began to wonder whether it might be best to pack his stuff and hit the road before anyone had a chance to wake up. He went into the bathroom, thinking it might be a while before he had a hot shower again. He shaved as quickly as he could and took a shower in record time. He brushed his teeth then packed all his bathroom stuff into the small plaid pouch he got from his dad. It was a little tattered; having seen several of his dad's business trips but it served Roger well now. He straightened up the bathroom, hanging the towels and wiping the water off the counter. In the bedroom, he pulled some clothes from the bureau drawers. He tossed them all on the bed, if only he hadn't unpacked. He could be gone already. He dressed in the same clothes he wore the day he met Beth at the rodeo. He picked up the rest of his things and began to stuff them into his backpack, stopping briefly, when the sweet smell of the freshly laundered clothes gave him another twang of confusion, or was it guilt. The clothes even made his old pack smell nice. Who washed the clothes, he wondered. It couldn't have been Beth, they were never apart long enough. He didn't think Bobbie would even know how to wash clothes.

Roger sat on the bed, the sun well up in the sky now, and the light of a new day filled the room. He picked up his pack and returned to the window. Roger looked down on the pool, and his mind drifted back over his time here with Beth. He stood statue-like, wrestling with his emotions.

Suddenly the sound of the pouring water stopped. The stream from the flask looked frozen. The surface of the water no longer sparkled. It was as still as the surface of a mirror, or a frozen pond. He caught a slight movement in the corner of his eye. The naked lady was gone, replaced by a young girl dressed in a snowsuit dragging a toboggan. She stepped down from the edge of the hot tub, steam billowing up from the surface. Roger then noticed the pool; it was now surrounded by snow. How is that possible? He swam in it yesterday. He was standing next to an open window and the warm breeze was bringing perspiration to his face. The girl now stood on the frozen pond, not pond, pool, her face no longer obscured by the steam from the hot tub. It was Lisa, his sister. His dead sister standing on a frozen pool in the middle of a heat wave, dressed in winter clothes, over two thousand miles from the only place she had ever lived. Roger absently raised his trembling hand and waved. She just stood there looking up at him. He pulled the second strap of his backpack over his left shoulder. At that moment, Lisa shook her head. He stared down at her, clipping the chest strap on his pack but not taking his eyes off her and again she shook her head.

She didn't speak, not a sound came from the pool, but Roger knew what she wanted. When they were little Lisa was always able to get Roger to do what she wanted without even asking him. He dropped his pack and she smiled up at him. Her smile seemed so familiar, like he had just seen her yesterday. She waved and turned, walking back toward the hot tub. She had taken three steps and a long sound sent shivers all through Roger's body. It sounded like a tree breaking under the heavy strain of an early spring ice storm. But, it wasn't a tree, it wasn't spring and there wasn't any ice storm. The girl looked down at the ice she stood on. A large fissure was working its way across the pool. She looked up at Roger, a frightened little girl, rooted to the spot.

He wanted to yell something encouraging. Don't move, I'm coming, I'll be right there, it'll be okay. Before he could say any of those things, she disappeared through the surface. His knees buckled and he fell to the floor. For the second time he had watched her fall through the ice and for the second time he was helpless to prevent it. With resolve he sprung to his feet, he wasn't a little boy anymore; he could get her out before it was too late.

"Hey, Vermont, what's shakin'?" Beth was now standing in the doorway.

Roger looked out the window at the pool. The water flowed into the hot tub from the naked lady's flask, the snow was gone, the ice was gone. Lisa was gone. Lisa had come to tell him not to leave and then she left. She left him the same way she left him when he was nine. He was shaking, his mouth was open just slightly and his eyes stared unblinking at the pool.

"Roger, are you okay?"

He still didn't answer. He staggered back to the bed and sat down. He looked at Beth, then back to the window. Bewildered, he didn't know what to say and even if he did he wouldn't know how to say it.

Beth sat beside him and put her arm around his waist. "Did you have another bad dream?"

"You have to be sleeping to have a dream, right?"

"So, what then?"

"I wish I knew." He got up and shuffled over to the window. Peering out, he saw a gorgeous summer morning. The sun was completely above the horizon now; the view could have been a picture from Better Homes and Gardens. The sky was metallic blue, only a jet stream, streaking from the east broke the monotonous hue. The lady statue continued to pour the crystal clear liquid into the hot tub, the gurgling sound gave the whole scene a serene feel. No sign remained of Roger's dream, hallucination, or apparition. All seemed to be well in Nebraska this fine summer day.

He did his best to explain what he had just seen, or what he thought he had just seen. Beth felt a twinge of sadness at not having anything to say that might help. She had thus far lived a charmed life. She hadn't lost anyone close to her. She was not equipped to deal with this kind of thing, so she tried to cheer him up by joking that he wasn't allowed any more late night snacks. Then she opened her robe, flashed her naked body, and giggling like a schoolgirl, she ran back to her room.

When she emerged, she was dressed in denim shorts, a tight white T-shirt and bright white Reeboks. Roger had gone out to the playroom. That was Beth's term for the main room of the apartment. The room with the huge TV that came on when you entered. She sat beside him on the couch, kissed his cheek and said, "Well, are we going to the Grand Canyon or are you going to watch TV all day?" Roger had settled into a gloomy reprise of the scene at the pool and jumped a bit at the sound of Beth's voice. He was sitting, staring at the TV, but not seeing it. He was unaware of the veejay, introducing a video by Alanis Morissette. The skin on his arms and neck had crawled to life, covered in gooseflesh, as though he were actually standing beside that frozen pond.

"Well, the Jeep is gassed up, packed and ready to hit the open road," she added, hands on her hips.

Roger finally turned his attention to Beth and smiled.

"Race ya," he said, grabbing his pack. He sprang from the couch and bolted for the door. He opened it and, like the perfect eastern gentleman, held it open for his lady. He stepped out behind her and as he pulled the door closed Alanis sang that everything was going to be fine, fine, fine. Roger pushed the door open, looked at the TV, he swore Alanis winked down at him from the big screen TV. He shook his head, closed the door and took the stairs three at a time, his pack bouncing around on his right shoulder, his left hand gliding down the rail, guiding his decent.

Beth had already settled into the passenger seat, the engine running and the radio was crackling some hideous rap thing. Roger tossed his pack behind the driver's seat and immediately killed the radio, then said, "I don't think so."

"Is that so, and what would you prefer, Mister Sophisticated Easterner?"

He reached behind his seat and fished a CD out of his pack. Beth took it from his hand, without looking at the disc, she turned the radio on, inserted the disc and Warren Zevon began to sing the story of Werewolves of London.

"Songs about werewolves eating Chinese food. Christ, Vermont, no wonder you have nightmares," Beth said giggling while Roger guided the Jeep along the long driveway flanked by cattle pastures.

The Jeep was topless and Beth stood up howling with Warren, her arms held out to her sides like the wings of an eagle, her hair blowing wildly in the wind. Roger laughed aloud and joined in. AHOOO, Roger, Beth, and Warren Zevon howled all the way to the road.

In the main house, Jack Walker stood in his second floor bedroom window watching the Jeep carry his favorite child away. Away from the safety net he had provided for her, her whole life. He still trusted Beth to do the right thing, and he felt comfortable with Roger, but Jack knew how much bad there was in the world. It was that *bad* that made him wish he hadn't let her go. He watched as the brake lights glowed brightly at the gate, he watched as the Jeep turned left on Route 6, he watched that Jeep until he couldn't see it anymore.

Aside from the annual slow pitch games, Jack Walker didn't lose, but he had a strong sense of losing something as the Jeep disappeared from view. This wasn't the loss of a ball game, or even a business deal, which Jack Walker had never experienced. This was true, gut-wrenching loss. He wasn't concerned for her safety really. What he was feeling was his little girl no longer needing him. It was different with Billy, he was a man, and Jack expected him to go out and do his thing. It just turned out that Billy's thing was the dealership, which kept him under Jack's thumb.

Bobbie had always been a wild child but she also seemed to love the ranch so he didn't anticipate losing her any time soon.

Beth was another story, he knew it would come, but knowing the potential and living the reality were completely different. So there he stood, forlornly gazing out at the empty road, the Jeep long gone, a huge gap left empty somewhere deep beneath his rugged exterior. He wiped a tear from the corner of his eye and turned back toward his bed. He hadn't realized that Nora was standing right behind him.

"Jeez," he said. "You scared that shit out of me. One of these days I'm going to tie a bell around your neck so I can hear you coming."

"So, they're gone, are they?" She put her arms around him and he held her tight. Nora let Jack believe that he was comforting her, but really, he was the one who needed someone to lean on.

"She'll be back in a few weeks, Jack."

Nora had known for years that Beth was the brightest star in Jack's sky. She also knew that he wasn't as tough as he wanted everyone to believe and his secret was safe with her. He was that tough until Beth came along. That little girl melted Jack Walker's icy interior just as sure as the spring melts the snow covering the pastures.

Roger and Beth stopped for lunch in Loweville, Colorado, population seven hundred and thirty-two. Main Street had a bar, a church, a general store and Lainie's Café. Lainie's had an extensive menu that included anything your heart desired, so long as your heart desired burgers and fries, or steak and fries, or meat pie and fries. Roger and Beth both went with the burger deluxe, which included a burger, fries, and a can of soda. They ordered it to go and ate in the Jeep, parked under a huge oak in the only park in Loweville.

The morning had flown by as fast as the scenery on the side of the highway. The monotony of the Nebraska landscape changed to the less daunting Colorado countryside. The foothills of the Rockies became discernable on the far off horizon. The driving turned more enjoyable with the first sight of those hills.

The scene over Beth's pool in the early morning had weighed heavily on Roger's mind as they left the Walker ranch. Beth had an instinct for reading his moods and an even greater knack for improving them. She was forever talking, but she never got boring. Beth had a way of telling a story, her enthusiasm was intoxicating. She had an endless catalogue of one-liners, which she delivered with the skill of the best stand up comics. She would make up limericks on the fly that could make a saloon full of cattle ranchers blush. Most of all she could bat her eyes, tilt her head and smile at him in a way that infected him. Roger could feel himself flush as her zest spilled out and he absorbed it like a sponge. Beth had more life than any person should and Roger felt better for sharing in just a small piece of that life.

By the time they stopped for lunch, Roger had heard every indiscretion of Bobbie's life. The time Jack caught her boffing a cowboy in the hot tub. How she took Jack's RV to last year's rodeo and had her own little party. The swimming coach, her history professor. What really shocked the family on that one was that Professor Kindel was a forty-five-year-old woman. Oh, nobody really thought Bobbie was a lesbian or a tramp for that matter. They all believed she did these things to get attention from Jack.

Billy's history was less colorful, most of it concerned his Receptionist of the Month club and how long it was going to take before the dealership got sued for sexual harassment.

This made clearer the points Jack brought up in his study the night before. Why he felt he could trust Beth and why Bobbie and Billy were struggling with the concept.

There they sat in the Jeep; the sun was bright, but not as hot as the past week had been. The sky a glorious shade of blue, sparsely populated with small clouds that appeared motionless as if in a snapshot. The breeze that occasionally passed through was barely strong enough to move the leaves on the only oak large enough to provide shade in the park.

The burger and fries had a soporific effect on Beth, the jokes and stories ceased. She sat quietly, looking at the small clouds with a serene look of contentment. Roger was happy to just sit and watch her. He didn't think it possible to fall in love with someone after just a few days but he felt it happening to him. The tears he wiped from his cheek in the cab of old Pete's truck after sharing his story of Paige were as distant a memory as could be and would not be completely forgotten.

"Well, you about ready to hit the road, Beth?"

"Ready as ever, Vermont," she said in her typical upbeat way. "Check this out, I picked it up in the café."

She handed him a small pamphlet and before he had a chance to read it she continued, "It's the world's only lint museum." Beth began to laugh as Roger looked at her trying to find something funny. "Oh come on, Vermont, where's your sense of adventure? When are you ever going to get a chance to see a museum that showcases some old lady's artwork that she has sculpted from the lint she took out of her dryer? Shit, that has got to be worth a slight detour doesn't it?"

Roger just laughed. It was as if Beth had suddenly turned into the Loweville, Colorado tourist board. "Well, ma'am, where do we find this riveting piece of Americana?" he asked.

Beth's laughter became loud and raucous. Roger was laughing at her, laughing at him, and he knew full well, that she was indeed, laughing at him. She pointed over his left shoulder and there it was, just across the street.

They visited the world's only lint museum. It would be the first of many curiosities and actual points of interest they would visit on their journey, Beth snapping pictures of them all. She would even recruit passersby to take pictures of her and Roger arm in arm, in front of each attraction. Things like a giant ball of string, a tree growing out of a rock, the Guinness Book's record-breaking ear of corn. Beth and Roger were digitally immortalized with all of these quirky things on her camera's memory chip. She would also get photos of scenic landscapes, the capital buildings in Denver, several mountain peaks, countless valleys and canyons. She was especially anxious to see a shot she took just before sunset, of the moon sitting directly between twin summits near Aspen. The moon was a bright yellow and the eastern sky was purple. They both felt a bit odd looking at the dark sky in the east and the orange sunset to the west. The lint museum was just the beginning of these Kodak moments.

When they left the lint museum it was close to two-thirty. Roger had resigned himself to the fact that the journey, not the destination, would be the highlight of this vacation. Beth, he was beginning to realize would definitely be the main highlight of the journey.

It wasn't long after they got back in the Jeep that Beth fell asleep. She was telling another story, this one about how she managed to pull one over on Jack and Nora in order to go to a Bon Jovi concert, which she was denied permission to attend. She just stopped talking and Roger looked over to find out how the story ended but Beth sat still, her head back against the headrest, her eyes closed and her mouth slightly open. Roger smiled, and inserted a CD into the Jeep's stereo.

The disc was one that he and Paige had burned together. He listened with a nostalgic sadness. It was sadness for something lost, but not an overwhelming loss. That was when he knew that it really was over with Paige. If it had been true love, whatever that was, then he would feel worse, much worse. Maybe they both knew it. Surely, Paige knew it first and that must have been why she had made such a clean break. Why she didn't return his calls, or even see him to talk it out. That realization brought a smile to his face and he listened to the music he and Paige collected together. When the last song played, Roger ejected the disc, put it in the case, thought of tossing it out of the car, but instead, he reached back behind the seat and stuffed it into his pack.

The Nightcrawler

With his past tucked safely away, it was time to return to the present. Roger tapped the brakes and the Jeep made a sudden lurch. Beth's arms flung out to grab hold of anything they could find. Her right hand found the window crank and the left got the edge of Roger's seat. Her fingers were white knuckled as her brain tried to catch up with where she was.

"Welcome back," Roger said through a suppressed chuckle.

"I'll kick your ass, Vermont. That shit's not funny."

Roger saw that Beth was not kidding around, she was genuinely angry at his little stunt. This made the moment that much more enjoyable for him. His chuckle turned to an all out laugh as he reached over and tried to console her with a hand on her shoulder. He made a mock pout, his bottom lip quivered; his eyes drooped as best as he could. Beth pushed his hand off her shoulder, punched him hard in the arm and as he grimaced she smiled and said, "Pull over Vermont, I want to drive for a while."

"There's a rest area just ahead. We can stretch our legs and then you can drive, okay?"

True to his word, just past the next rise an exit lane lead the way into a highway rest stop. It looked like every other rest stop on every interstate in the country. Picnic tables scattered around beneath mature trees. Barbecues cemented into the ground with iron grills covered in the crud of a thousand burgers. The grass was six inches long and swayed in the wind giving the illusion of waves over a small lake. There was one building that was maintained by the tourist bureau, men's room on the right, ladies to the left. It was a rustic log cabin-like structure that seemed quaint from the car, but in need of a paint job and a good cleaning when you got up close. The front wall between the two restrooms was lined with slots, containing pamphlets for the many attractions in Colorado. After Beth used the bathroom, she took one of each of the pamphlets.

When she found Roger, he was sitting at the picnic table closest to the building drinking a Coke he got out of the vending machine behind the restrooms. Beside him sat a large crow staring at him. It had landed there immediately after he sat down. It tilted its head first to the left, then right, as if trying to figure him out, its gaze never breaking Roger's. In the bird's beak was a large nightcrawler, still wriggling for life.

Roger looked at the bird, and asked, "Are you Heckle or Jeckle?"

"Hey, Vermont, who's your friend?"

He hadn't noticed Beth walking up behind him and he flushed a little, embarrassed that she caught him talking to a crow. He took a sip from his Coke and tossed one over to Beth. The crow cawed at the sudden movement, flared its wings but held its gaze on Roger.

Beth walked over to the table and sat across from him. The bird held its ground, looking away from Roger only long enough to make sure Beth posed no threat. After she was seated the crow looked back at Roger.

"I think your feathered friend really likes you," Beth said.

They both had a confused look of curiosity as they watched the bird. The fact that it appeared so fearless of two people in such close proximity was odd, but what held their interest more was how it concentrated on Roger's every move.

"So, do you think she's saving the worm for later?" Beth was getting a little creeped out and was trying to make light of the scene.

"Maybe he was saving the seats for his friends and we're getting in the way," Roger said as he finished his soda and stood up. "Are you ready to go?"

"Later, bird," Beth said. Following Roger's lead, she got up, and skipping back to the car, Coke in hand, called, "Race ya."

She sprinted for the parking lot. Roger ran after her, slowing a little near the trash barrel to toss his empty can. Beth was sitting behind the steering wheel when he trotted up. Roger tossed her the keys and climbed in.

A momentary darkness spooked them, and then an odd noise followed as the crow landed on the hood of the car. The worm still wiggled in its black beak.

The Nightcrawler

"How weird is that?" Roger said.

"Pretty weird," Beth answered, then started the car and backed away from the curb. The crow dropped the worm on the hood and flew away, caw-caw-cawing as it disappeared behind the restrooms and trees of the picnic area. Roger got out, picked the worm off the hood and threw it on the ground near the edge of the pavement. "Pretty fucking weird," Beth said driving off toward the highway.

They said nothing else as Beth guided the Jeep along the ramp leading back to the highway. Roger sat quietly, enjoying the rest from driving. The pavement on the ramp angling toward the edge of Highway 6 was blacker than any pavement he could ever remember seeing. The faded grass on the sides looked sickly pale next to the ultra dark blacktop. The bright sun, risen high to its midday point, made the sky look almost metallic. The surrounding trees, although not plentiful, looked much greener and more vibrant than the scrub they had left behind in Nebraska. Roger looked to the horizon but it was not visible through the heat waves shimmering up through the hot air. The surface of the highway was pale looking, almost white where it met with the lane exiting the rest area. A destination sign ahead read, "Sterling 80 miles". As the Jeep approached the sign, a large crow, in Roger's mind the same crow, landed atop the sign. Perched on the sign, its eyes as they had on the picnic table, appeared to lock on Roger. Its head cocked to one side, as if still trying to communicate with him. At least that was what he thought. Roger looked over to Beth, but she was shifting gears accelerating to merge onto the highway and checking for traffic, so didn't appear to notice the bird, or she didn't think a bird perched on a sign was anything unusual. Of course, a bird on a sign was perfectly normal, but it looked like the same bird, and Roger felt like he was being stalked, stalked by a crow.

The crow seemed to watch them as they passed. Roger turned to see if it would follow, but it didn't, and as they zipped along the highway, the sign and the bird disappeared in the same heat shimmer that obscured the western horizon.

Having dismissed the idea that a crow could stalk him, or try to communicate with him, he reclined his seat a notch, put on the cap he got with the baseball uniform, and added his wraparound sunglasses. He pulled the bill of his cap down low. He propped his head against the headrest, his left hand on his lap, his right arm resting on the top of the door. He cupped his hand and angled it into the wind, raising and lowering the angle, his arm lifting then dropping with the changes in lift of the oncoming air. Roger didn't notice Beth look over at him. She smiled when she saw him, the way a mother might smile at a little boy playing with the rushing wind from the car window.

Beth returned her attention to the road; Roger stared at his hand, up and down, up and down. He changed the position of his hand and it began a left, right motion in concert with the up and down. Like a boy playing with his toy plane, he continued for miles. It brought back memories of childhood road trips, him and Lisa in the backseat of the Taurus wagon, him on the right, her on the left. It was always the same, him on the right, her on the left. It was like assigned seats in school.

He adored Lisa when he was little. At least that's what his parents told him, over and over again. He found it harder with each passing day to remember anything about her. Now as he sat watching his hand cut through the air he felt close to her. Memories of Lisa that he had long forgotten came flooding back.

As if it had happened yesterday, he was reliving his first day of kindergarten. It had been unusually hot for early September in Vermont. The morning air was warm and humid. Summer flowers in his mother's garden were bright and vibrant. Lisa wore a blue dress with white trim around the neck, and knee socks, as white as any fabric could be. Roger felt calm, as though he was there with her, still wearing the same shorts, Sea World T-shirt and white sneakers. He could almost feel the weight of his backpack straps pulling on his shoulders. There was a slight breeze that day and it carried the scent of his mother's marigolds and snapdragons across the yard. He remembered telling his mom the previous night that he was scared of the school bus. When she reminded him that Lisa would be on the bus his fear faded.

When he got to the bus he stopped. The big yellow doors folded open like a gaping mouth ready to swallow him whole. His fear had taken over. Lisa took his hand and he followed her without hesitation, because he knew she would never lead him into harm. He hadn't let go of her hand until she led him right to his room. Lisa told him that Mrs. Miller was his teacher and she was going to take care of him. He always believed Lisa, always.

Still feeling the warmth of Lisa's hand he looked at his left hand, resting atop of it was Beth's. His right hand was still flying outside the Jeep's window. He let it drop to the door and closed his eyes. The radio was playing something of Beth's that he didn't like or recognize. The music faded and he was with Lisa again. He was in grade two, and Billy Clarou had just pushed him to the ground. From out of nowhere, Lisa had come and pushed Billy down so hard he bit his tongue and ran away crying, blood clearly visible in his mouth as he retreated.

It was odd, unexplainable even, that he so vividly remembered her now. After all this time with barely any recollection, her memory had returned to him with such clarity. Sure, he remembered what she looked like from the pictures at home, but the sound of her voice, expressions she used, those kinds of things had been long gone for him. So now, all of a sudden, he wasn't just having flashbacks, he was feeling that adoring love for her that he had forgotten how to feel. Why now? Was it Beth? Could she be bringing on these feelings? Maybe it was being out here so far from home.

He fell asleep before he got an answer. Beth had just started to tell another tale and noticed he was in slumber land. She smiled as she looked back to the road. She had been working her own inner thoughts, which brought up the story she was about to share. It was about Dan Mandville, the Double-D's captain, her boyfriend of a year ago. She hadn't dated Dan long, had only really dated him because she was pissed at Jack, and she knew he wouldn't approve of Dan. To this day, she couldn't remember why she was pissed at Jack; she didn't really care anymore and Dan was long since history. While Roger snored next to her, she filed that story away for later. The music on the radio had given way to a commercial break and Beth began to scan for something better. She stopped at a syndicated talk radio program, the current topic, Racism in America. The host had just welcomed a man who introduced himself as Bob from Alabama. Bob had started, very polite and cordial, but then became quite the opposite. The "N word" had become his word of choice. The producer was working double time bleeping out all the profanity. Most of Bob's tirade was bleeped, but his message of hate still came through.

The next six callers were all calling in response to Bob. Four of them were appalled that the network would even allow him to finish, or that anyone in their fair land could spew out such trash. Two hailed Bob as a hero and nominated him for president. Beth agreed most with Judy from Ohio. Judy called in to say, that we all need to look at each other as people. She is a woman, not a black woman, and him, he is a young man, not a young white man. Why not congratulate Denzel Washington and Halle Berry for winning the Oscar, not for being black and winning the Oscar. Forget minority rights, concentrate on the rights of all the innocent, good people in the country, in the world even. This, in Judy's mind, was the kind of thinking that was going to get the world where it needed to be.

Judy's speech of hope for humanity kindled a long discussion from the host, as well as several callers. Some dismissed her words as rhetoric, or liberal, or even communist, while many called to bless her heart.

While Beth was focused on Judy, her supporters and her rebutters, Roger was sleeping restlessly. His head moved slowly from side to side. Sweat gleamed on his face. His eyes squeezed tighter, and tighter, causing his face to look almost wrinkled and old. He was having another bad dream. Beth seemed to sense his agitation and her attention drifted from the road to Roger and back.

He sprung to attention with a spasm that caused Beth to utter a startled squeak.

"Another bad dream," she said.

"It was all there, not exactly the same but close."

"What?"

"The dream I had that night. You know, when you came into my room. The dark highway, the far off rumbling of impending doom." Impending doom, that was how he felt when he recalled the dream. He saw the same glow of headlights, the light standards on each side of the road appearing to bend inward to the road as if being sucked down by the speed of a devilish red machine. He stood rooted to the spot, unsure why it was all so familiar. He was also dumbstruck by the oncoming demon. He stood anchored, breathlessly waiting to be mowed down.

"Just when I was going to be killed by the car I heard her voice."

"Lisa's voice?" Beth asked.

He just shook his head. "Roger," she called. I didn't answer her. I was sure it was the wind through the desert brush. "Roger," she called out louder. I still didn't respond. "ROGER," she screamed, then I couldn't ignore what my head told me couldn't be there. I turned to see Lisa, my own guardian angel, standing beside me. She was still twelve, wearing a nice floral print dress.

"She told me to get off the road, in a calm almost nonchalant tone. I was looking at her, the street lights were sparkling halos in my eyes, while I tried to focus through tears that had come when I saw her. "Lisa, I c-c-can't move my l-l-l-legs," I stammered through the tears.

"Roger, you have to get off the road," she repeated.

"I just stood there, like a little boy, like the ten-year-old little boy I was the last time I had seen her alive. I just stared at her, waiting for her to fix everything."

He took a moment, looking away from Beth while he wiped the tears from his eyes. Not wanting to rush him, or intrude on what was obviously a very personal moment, Beth sat in silence.

"Now!" Lisa screeched, and with a mighty shove using both her hands in the middle of my chest, I fell backwards off the embankment that was the edge of the road. I looked up in time to see her, but it wasn't her, it wasn't Lisa at all. You were standing on the road. You looked down at me, lying in the gravel and dirt and smiled. As the savage machine raced ever nearer you smiled down at me, lying in the gravel and out of harm's way. I reached out trying to snatch you out of the path of the demon, but I was too far away and it was too late, it sped right through you. There was no sound but the howl of the engine.

"NOOOOOOOOOOOO," I cried, but you were gone. You were gone and Lisa was gone. "

Chapter Twenty-One

With a crick in his neck and a pain in his side, Scott woke to the sound of a nurse entering Ashley's room. After a fitful two hours in bed at the hotel he went back to the hospital for a visit and fell asleep in the chair beside her bed. He pushed himself upright from his slouch over the arm of the green faux-leather chair and massaged the spot on his side where the wooden arm had been digging into his ribs. He watched the nurse while she performed her ritual.

"She'll be fine," she said to Scott.

He gave her a nod then looked over at the sleeping girl. Her head was still bandaged and a purple bruise above her right eye had started to spread out from under the bandage.

"Is she your sister?" the nurse said.

He shook his head and asked where he might find a phonebook. Scott returned to Ashley's room about an hour later. She was sitting up channel surfing on the tiny TV.

"Man, TV is lame in this place," she said. "They said I have to stay a day or two. I don't know if I can stand it," she added, rolling her eyes at the tiny screen.

Scott approached her bed and handed her an envelope. "I'm going to miss having you around," he said. "But I have to get back on the road."

"I know," she said. She smiled in an attempt to ease Scott's mind but the tears in her eyes showed her true feeling.

"Listen," Scott said. "Hitching is not safe for anyone but especially a pretty young girl like you. In that envelope is an open-ended train ticket to LA. My card is in there, too. Call me at the office and let me know when you're getting in and I'll make sure you have a ride. If you don't have a place to stay you can stay in my guest room until you get on your feet."

Ashley was overcome by his gesture and began to cry in big sobs.

"Hey, don't go thinking I'm doing you some big favor. If you stay in my guest room, you will be working it off. I hope you can cook, and you better not be afraid of dogs because Max needs to be walked twice a day."

She laughed through the sobs and he gave her a hug then left the room without another word.

Scott returned to the hotel, had a quick bite, and then went to his room for a shower. With a fresh change of clothes he was ready to get back on the road. He took little notice of the clerk while checking out. He took care of business, carried his bags to the car and drove off. The hotel was close to the highway and he was speeding west, on I-80 less than ten minutes later, the morning sun above the horizon, burned bright in his rearview mirror. The trees, pathetic as they were, cast long ghostly shadows on the ground along the highway's edge. He turned the radio on but wasn't listening; if he had been he would surely have changed the channel. Ashley had been listening to top-forty, Scott's least favorite form of dribble. Well, next to rap that is. The perky drive time hostess played a song, took calls from the listeners, and did the news, the weather, and traffic. Hearing the traffic report put Scott in a cheerful mood. He actually chuckled. Traffic in Salina, Kansas at this time of morning was Old MacDonald's tractor, Farmer Brown's combine and a scattering of eighteen-wheelers out on the highway.

It was eight-thirty when the next traffic report came on, then a Britney Spears song began and that was all he could take. He shut it off and relaxed, listening to the wind rushing in the open window. The air was dry and considerably cooler than it had been. It felt fresh, and his left arm was chilled to gooseflesh resting out of the open window, but he didn't bring it in. After the oppressive heat of the last few days, this was invigorating.

The Nightcrawler

"She'll be just fine," he told himself, thinking of Ashley.

"I have absolutely no doubt of that," said a voice from the backseat.

"Huh," Scott uttered at the suddenness of the words coming from behind him. He looked in his mirror and there it was, the Nightcrawler, seated on the passenger side of the rear seat, smiling his yellow smile.

"Jesus," Scott cried.

He spun around as if maybe it was a trick mirror, the seat was empty, had to be empty.

"Mornin', Scott," the bum said. He pointed to the front. "You'd better watch where you're going, you'll kill yourself."

Scott turned his eyes back to the road, just in time to prevent the car from entering the median, and possibly the eastbound lanes. He jerked the wheel to the right correcting his position then looked back at the figure behind him.

"You really need to watch the road, Scott, or you will seriously end up dead."

"If I die in here so do you, asshole," Scott said with contempt. "How the fuck did you get in my car?" Scott was shaken, but was doing a good job of keeping his voice steady. "Never let them see fear, Scottie", his dad would always say.

A slight laugh came from the backseat, "Scott, think about that for a minute. I am a homeless man from Detroit. How can I be in the backseat of this car? Now, if I can't be here, then I can't die here." He was very calm, soft spoken and articulate.

"Of course you can be here. I can see you, and I can hear you. In fact, I've seen you all over the country. In Michigan, Indiana, Kansas. Hell, you might just as well stay in the backseat, at least there won't be any surprises that way," Scott retorted, trying desperately now to sound like he was in control.

"I can see that you're getting upset. You have no reason to fear me, Scott."

177

"How the fuck do you know my name?" Scott was getting more agitated by the minute, his efforts to stay calm failing, his voice getting noticeably higher in tone and volume. "And since you seem to know who I am, who the hell are you?"

"Who I am isn't important, is it, Scott?" He paused briefly then continued. "If it were up to you, me and everyone like me would be exterminated, isn't that right?" He was still calm but his dark eyes had become cold. "But if you must have a name to call me, why not Matt? Yes, I think Matt will do fine. After all I'm no more than a doormat for you to wipe your shoes on, isn't that right?"

"I don't know what the hell you're talking about. I sure as hell don't know why you're in this car, but I'm going to pull over to the side of the road and when the car stops you'd better get the fuck out." There was an air of confidence in his tone, and he guided the Charger to the shoulder. "Now get the f..." The backseat was empty when Scott turned to banish his unwanted guest. He sat for a moment, took three deep breaths like he was practicing yoga relaxation. He began to guide the car back onto the highway when the thunderous roar of a truck horn brought him back to reality. Had he been a little quicker he would have become one with the bugs on the grill of that truck. His heart beat quickened and he checked for traffic, and then returned to the road. His breathing was hurried and shallow. The air was still cool and the nervous sweat on his skin made him cold.

Safely back on the road, Scott quickly accelerated. When he noticed Matt, the bum, the Nightcrawler, not in the backseat this time, but in the front next to him, dressed in the same filth he wore in Detroit, Scott flinched as though some unseen object struck him in the face. Of course, he would be dressed the same, Scott thought. It isn't like he could just go to his closet and pull out a change of clothes for his field trip through Scott's sanity.

Matt sat quietly looking through the windshield, his hands crossed in his lap, his dirt encrusted lap. He turned to Scott, smiling his yellow smile. At least the teeth remaining were yellow. There was something different about him though, it had taken Scott a while to realize it, but

The Nightcrawler

it was quite obvious now. The rancid smell that repulsed him in Detroit was not in the car.

"You don't like me much do you, Scott?"

Scott's jaw dropped, but no words came out. He had always been confident in his verbal skills, always able to meld into any type of conversation. Without a doubt, he could for sure handle an unfriendly attack, with jibes that would usually send his adversaries away with their tails between their legs. So why was it, that in the presence of this low life, he found himself at a loss for words.

"Well, no matter," Matt continued. "I'm sure there are dozens of people, in every city across this great land that you find as revolting as me." He paused to survey the scenery, and resumed not waiting for Scott to respond. "Yes, it is a beautiful country, isn't it? I bet there are millions in this country who don't deserve to ride in the same car as you. Don't you agree, Scott?"

"What the fuck are you talking about? And why are you here?"

"Come now, Scott, it's not just vagrants who don't measure up next to you, is it? What about the welfare recipients, now there's a group of people the world can do without, wouldn't you say? They'll for sure drag this nation down to a level it can't afford to be at, am I right?" Matt spoke with clarity and intelligence. His tone and demeanor were more apt to be in any boardroom of any big company. Yet he was far from the CEO type. As far from it as anyone could be. "What about the mailman, the garbage man, store clerks, all useful people, but still not worthy to sit beside you, are they, Scott?"

"Would you just shut up?" Scott yelled. "Just shut the fuck up."

"Such language and you being so upper crust, I would have thought more from you. Of course you didn't mind spending a little, shall we say, quality time with that nice young lady in the parking garage, did you?"

"Listen, you prick, you leave Sarah out of this, and get the fuck out of this car."

"A bit of a sore spot there, I see. Oh, by the way, Scott, you really should slow down There's a state trooper just over this rise."

Scott looked at the speedometer. It was at eighty-nine and climbing. He slowed to sixty-five, and just as the Charger crested the hill he saw a radar gun pointing out of the window of white four-door sedan. On the side of the car in black, KANSAS STATE TROOPERS.

"Well, it looks like you owe me the price of a ticket, don't you, Scott?" Matt said, in a pleased with himself tone. "I was sure you were going to stop and ask the nice officer to take me away. Have you figured it out already, Scott?"

"Figured what out?"

"If you're asking then the answer is no. So we continue. Where is it we're going, anyway?"

"Where are we going?" Scott looked at him and laughed. "Where are we going? That's rich. You invite yourself into my life, stow away in my mind and you don't know where we're going."

"Oh, you can be so sensitive," the bum interjected. "Why didn't you wait for the pretty girl at the hospital before you left town? I'm guessing she's sitting in that room crying her poor self to sleep. Of course, you don't have time for her. She's just a wanna-be-actress. Sure, she was handy to have driving the car so you could work, all the while ignoring her stories. She poured her heart out to you. What did you do? You tuned her out so you could take care of important business. You were dealing with serious issues like your dog, or this car, emails, and quarter-million dollar cars for the rich and famous. No time for Ashley's life, is there? She would just be an unnecessary delay now, wouldn't she?"

"What do you know about it?" Scott yelled. "What do you know about anything?" Calming his voice down a bit, trying to regain some control of himself, he continued, "You don't know shit, you don't appear to know how to use soap and water, and you sure as hell don't know how to get a job." A slight grin crept to the edges of Scott's lips, feeling he had just scored a blow for the taxpayers of the world.

"And there you have it in a nutshell, I don't have a job," Matt said,

The Nightcrawler

his voice never wavering. He continued to speak like he was giving directions to a passing motorist. "Anyone in this world who does not get up and go to work every morning must be worthless."

Scott sat quietly, his grin still in place, his demeanor now smug. The anxiety that had been building from the time Matt (or the Nightcrawler, or Stink Man, or whatever his name really was) had entered the car waned. Scott stared through the windshield, his head angled toward the left. He was determined not to look to his right. If he couldn't see him, and he couldn't hear him, then maybe, there was no him at all. He glanced at his watch; it was almost eleven. He checked the speedometer, just shy of eighty. He had no idea where he was, he had been preoccupied with the bum, but if he had been maintaining this speed all morning, he must be nearing Colorado.

A long silence had given him a sense that his encounter with Matt had ended. He started to take in the surroundings that he had missed from the time his company arrived. The landscape had become greener and the sky bluer. He wondered with skepticism, whether the air felt thinner. The oppressive heat of the prairies replaced by a comfortable, dry, seventy-something. He felt a relaxed calm settle in, making everything seem more beautiful, even poetic. The way the trees along the border of the fields swayed in the breeze, each leaf like a little hand waving at him, as if he were the Grand Marshal in the Independence Day parade. The long blades of grass swaying along the edge of the road reminded him of a wave making its way around a football stadium. The air even smelled cleaner than it did back in Salina.

Scott felt like himself again. He was young and strong and arrogant, yes even he considered himself arrogant. He attributed part of his success to that arrogance. It came in handy when dealing with the rich and famous who about cornered the market on arrogance. Scott inhaled deeply and with all the confidence he could muster, glanced at the passenger seat.

It was empty.

He chuckled aloud, of course it was empty, that bum was back in Detroit, probably standing on a sidewalk panhandling the whole time

Scott imagined him sitting in the car with him.

The sight of the empty seat gave Scott the feeling of refreshing coziness that filled him with glee. It was a feeling that to Scott Randall compared only to a Labor Day weekend long gone. It was the last Labor Day before Gramps had the stroke. They had gotten up early that Saturday to go fishing. Gramps had an old rowboat behind the cottage. They paddled out to the middle of the lake. Scott had asked Gramps at least a hundred times why he didn't get a motor boat. Gramps would just scoff, "Noisy contraptions scare all the fish away."

They had been out on the lake before dawn. Scott sipped coco from his thermos while Gramps slowly rowed that old boat out across the golden water. The only motion on the surface came from the boat and the oars. The chill air hovering over the water, still tepid from the hot summer, brought a layer of mist that reluctantly parted, then closed up behind them as the boat glided serenely toward the sunrise.

The cool damp air sent shivers down the back of his neck. He remembered Gramps smiling at him after a shiver ran down his spine and with that smile a warm breeze blew across the lake, taking with it the goosebumps and the shivers. He smiled back at his Gramps, feeling safe and protected.

Now Scott was feeling a disturbingly similar feeling in the Charger, looking over at the empty seat. He was barely aware of himself guiding the car west on I-70. The loud sound of a horn startled him back to the present. A green Mustang convertible passed. There were four teenage boys in the car, the two in the backseat stood and mooned Scott, howling and laughing all the while, their white asses seeming brilliant in the late morning sun. Scott laughed aloud, honked his horn and waved as they sped off.

Just then, he had noticed the gas gauge was nearly bottomed out. If he didn't stop soon he was going to do some walking. He drove in silence for another ten minutes, and then the boys in the Mustang offered him another chuckle. They were parked on the side of the road, a white state trooper sedan, lights flashing parked directly behind them. Scott gave the horn another toot and waved as he passed, but this time the boys were not laughing.

A short while later he took the exit leading into Staples, Kansas, population 753. He pulled into a Texaco station at the edge of town. It was like he had driven back in time. The pumps had the old spinning cylinders numbered zero to nine. The big red Texaco star was mounted high on a post out near the road. It even had an air hose across the ground that rang a bell inside the one bay garage when a car ran over it. A man in a grey Texaco uniform came meandering out wiping grease from his hands with a rag that was so dirty he may well have been wiping the grease on his hands as much as off. He looked to be in his forties, but too much hard work and way too much time in the sun gave his features a creased, older look.

His shirt had the Texaco star on one pocket and his name, Stew, embroidered on the other. Scott was always reminded of his dad's advice when he saw this type of uniform. "Scottie," he'd say, "Get a good education; you don't want to find yourself sluggin' it out in some grunt job, sportin' your name on your shirt." Of course his dad would always qualify his statement with, "Nothing wrong with hard work, but it pays better to work smart, not hard."

"Well, Dad," he thought as he watched Stew approach, "I'm working smart not hard."

"Fill it," Scott instructed as Stew stepped to the pump. Stew just nodded and began to squeeze the nozzle, the wheels in the pump display started spinning and clicking, one set counting off the gallons the other tallied the dollars and cents.

Scott surveyed his surroundings and turned to Stew, poised to speak; Stew just pointed at the garage and said, "Restroom's around the corner. Light's broke in there so just leave the door open a crack."

Scott walked around to the side of the building, a narrow gravel drive lead to an auto graveyard out back. Looks like Stew had his own supply of spare parts for dozens of cars. The trouble was, these cars most likely had very few brothers still on the road. The weeds grew tall between the old wrecks. A thick layer of dust blanketed the steel carcasses giving them a ghostly dull look.

Scott opened the only door in sight and a smell so foul he nearly gagged, bombarded his senses. He thought better of going in and walked over to a rusted K-car. He urinated on the front wheel of the old Reliant, resisting the temptation to write his name in piss on the car door.

"That's quite a collection you've got out back," Scott said, approaching Stew, who was returning the nozzle to the pump.

"Well, folks who got no money try drivin' cars that got no business bein' on the road, from who knows where to Californ-I-A. Everybody thinking they could be a movie star." Stew chuckled, more like a grunt than a laugh, but Scott thought it was as much of a laugh as Stew had in him. "Them shitty cars break down and I tow 'em here. When they find out how much it costs to fix, they go out to the highway and stick out their thumb." With the same grunt-laugh he said, "That'll be thirty-two even."

"Would you check all the fluids, Stew?" Scott asked.

"Did I scare ya, mister?"

"Scare me?" Scott asked, confused.

"About the cars breaking down, 'cuz I don't think you need worry about this car."

"No, you didn't," Scott answered. "I drove this car from Michigan. Better safe than sorry, you know what I mean?"

"Sure thing," Stew said. "I could change yer oil for ya, if ya like. Be done in a half hour, maybe twenty minutes."

"That might be a good idea if there's any place nearby to get a bite."

"Mollie's, 'bout a mile up the road. You can take my old truck over there. Key's in it."

"Sounds like a good deal," Scott said. He didn't realize how big a grin he was sporting until he saw himself in the mirror in the truck. Did people actually live like this? Here take my truck, and go get yourself something to eat. Scott was sure Sheriff Taylor and Deputy Fife would be at Mollie's having a cup of coffee when he got there.

The Nightcrawler

He drove alongside the Charger and told Stew to top up the tranny and rad if they needed it, then drove away from the Texaco station, a cloud of gravel dust following him half way into town.

From the outside, Mollie's was reminiscent of Charlie's, where Grace had shown him more than ordinary hospitality. The whole room inside was done in knotty pine. The walls were tongue and groove pine straps. The floor was covered with long slabs of ten inch pine. The window and door frames were made of split pine logs. The wood glistened in the sunlight streaming in the windows. All the windows and doors were flanked by carriage lights that gave off a yellow glow.

The circular tables, and matching chairs, were a perfect match to the window and doorframes. The inside could not have been more different from Charlie's and Mollie could not have been more different from Grace. Mollie was a heavy woman, with silver hair and rosy cheeks. She wore a loose fitting tank top and a knee-length skirt. Covering the top and skirt was a white apron with Mollie's embroidered over her left breast.

"Sit where ever you like sonny," she called from across the room.

Scott sat at the table nearest the kitchen, and Mollie walked over with a pitcher of water and a large glass. After filling the glass, setting it in front of him, she said, "Car trouble, sonny?"

"I'm sorry, what?"

"I see you drove up in Stew's truck. So, either you have car trouble, or you stole that truck. And you don't look like a car thief."

"I stopped for gas and lunch. Stew mentioned an oil change and I thought it might be a good idea."

"I bet Stew put that good idea in your head."

"As a matter of fact he did, but it was a good idea. I drove the car from Michigan."

"That Stew," Mollie, said shaking her head. "You need a menu, sonny?"

"What's good here, Mollie?"

"Everything's good, sonny, but I make the best burger in the country and the fries are fresh cut, none of that frozen stuff."

"Then a burger and fries it is, Mollie. I'd also love some lemonade if you've got some, a Coke if you don't."

"Burger, fries and some of my fresh squeezed lemonade comin' up."

Scott was back on the road, feeling better than he had in days. The warm feeling that flooded over him earlier had remained through lunch. Mollie was true to her word, the burger was great, the fries fresh. When he got back to Stew's Texaco the Charger was gassed up, the oil had been changed and Stew was toweling off the water drops left by the wash he had just finished. Scott left Staples with the feeling that if he were ever to settle in a small town, he would want it to be like Staples, Kansas.

By two that afternoon, he had crossed into Colorado with no more visits from Matt the bum, and all was right in Scott's world.

Chapter Twenty-Two

The air in the tent was cold and damp. Rain that started to fall during the night had slowed to a drizzle. Roger woke with Beth wrapped around him inside the doublewide sleeping bag like a hungry boa constrictor. The mountain air must have agreed with them both he thought, having slept more soundly than he had since leaving Vermont and Beth was still sleeping soundly. He moved her arm off his chest and she rolled away from him. Squirming like a snake, he managed to get out of the sleeping bag without waking her. He wrapped his arms tightly around his chest to battle the cool air. His T-shirt and briefs along with his skin were damp with sweat from the warmth he had just left, adding to his chilled condition. The sun already risen, its light weakened from the overcast sky gave everything inside the tent a greenish hue. He crawled to the tent door opened the zipper and stuck his head out into the drizzle.

"Great," he said to himself as he made a dash to the nearest tree to relieve himself.

"Mornin', son."

Roger spun around with a start to see a woman, dressed in jeans and a denim jacket, holding a large red and white umbrella over her head. Her straw cowboy hat covered her dark hair that flowed down over her shoulders. She grinned at Roger with a bit of flush in her cheeks.

"Gotta tell ya son, that's the first time in a while I've been greeted like that."

Roger then realized he was still holding his penis and spun back around to put himself together. He no longer felt the chill in the air, in fact he felt flushed and hot. Fear and embarrassment engulfed his emotions. He turned back to face the woman, his T-shirt stretched down as far as he could, trying to hide his Fruit of the Looms.

"Sorry about that, Mrs. Miller."

Beth had left the highway while Roger was sleeping, she said she wanted to see the country, not speed through it seeing nothing but a four-lane highway. Tiring and sure they weren't going to find a campsite, Beth pulled into Mrs. Miller's driveway. She stopped the Jeep right in front of the house, boldly walked up the front steps, and knocked on the door.

"Hello, my name is Beth and that's Roger." By this time, Roger was out of the Jeep and standing behind her. "We're on our way to the Grand Canyon and we need a place to camp for the night."

"There's no campgrounds anywhere near here," Mrs. Miller said.

"Yes, ma'am," Beth continued with the confidence of a career politician. "What I was hoping was maybe you wouldn't mind if we pitched our tent on your ranch here, just for the night."

"Where are you kids from?" Mrs. Miller asked.

Beth went into a long explanation of where they were from and how they came to be on her doorstep. She stressed the part about Roger's lifelong dream of getting to the Grand Canyon. Roger was waiting for her to add a terminal illness to her story but it wasn't necessary.

Mrs. Miller didn't just give them permission to camp on her property; she invited them to sleep in the house. Beth declined that without consulting Roger, but thanked her for the offer. They did however accept Mrs. Miller's invitation of food and drinks.

They sat up well past midnight, listening to Mrs. Miller regale them with stories of her past, which included three husbands. The first had died in an avalanche. She chuckled with the telling of this, she seemed to find humor in the fact that a mountain guide got himself killed like some stupid tourist. The second had passed while making love to her on their seventh wedding anniversary. She laughed even harder at this one, "It was the only orgasm he ever gave me," she stuttered through her snickering. The last one she divorced after only a year,

"He couldn't get it up," she told them.

Now Mrs. Miller lived alone on five hundred acres, in the shadow of Scruff Peak. Twenty of those acres were cleared, and she kept a menagerie of odd bedfellows, which included a five hundred pound Siberian Tiger named Zeus, seven pygmy goats and an ostrich. She told them all about her collection of critters, how they had found their way to her, and how the money from her husbands paid for the whole thing, food and all.

"Don't sweat it, son," Mrs. Miller said now referring to Roger's obvious embarrassment. "When Bethie wakes up I want you two to come up to the house to have some breakfast."

She gave Roger another once over then went back to the house giggling to herself.

Roger trotted back to the tent, wet and cold. He hadn't really been aware of how wet he was getting until Mrs. Miller had turned to walk away from him. He pulled the wet fabric from his skin and realized that everything he was wearing was pretty much transparent. He may as well have been standing in front of Mrs. Miller naked. He felt his ears start to get warm again and hurried to the tent. He abandoned his concern for waking Beth in his rush to get out of the rain-chilled air. Once inside the tent it occurred to him that their packs were in the Jeep and his dry clothes were in his pack. He scurried outside again and sprinted to the Jeep not bothering to zip the tent behind him. The rain stopped just as he arrived behind the car; opening the back he got the towel from his pack, looked around for Mrs. Miller, stripped down and quickly dried himself.

"That's what I like to see first thing in the morning," Beth hollered, her head sticking out of the open tent, now laughing aloud at Roger as he fumbled to cover himself with the towel.

"Shit," he said, just loud enough for Beth to hear. "I thought maybe it was Mrs. Miller again."

"Again?" Beth laughed even louder as she raised an eyebrow trying to look shocked but failing miserably through her laughter. "What is that supposed to mean?"

Roger put on dry underwear and jeans then pulled over his head a white T-shirt with Green Day in big blue letters on the front. He took Beth's pack from the Jeep and walked as casually as he could to the tent.

"Mrs. Miller has invited us to breakfast, if you're interested."

"Sounds better than granola and bottled water. I'm in."

Roger put her pack in front of her and she retreated inside. "Are you coming in, Roger?"

Her tone and the fact that she called him Roger and not Vermont had him dashing inside. Beth wrapped her arms around him, kissed him like a newlywed on her wedding night, then pushed him away scolding, "Mrs. Miller's waiting, Vermont!" Roger chuckled playfully then tackled her.

They left the tent twenty minutes later. Roger got out first and barely before he had stood upright, Beth was out of the tent, and had jumped on his back. They both laughed all the way up to the house, Beth still riding piggyback.

Mrs. Miller hadn't answered the door right away and while they waited Roger took in the breathtaking beauty that was the ranch. From the front porch, deep forests of pine climbed the steep face of Scruff Peak. About two thirds of the way up, gray rock replaced the trees. The rock disappeared into the low hanging clouds. Even on a dreary day like this, it was still stunning. The house was a small story and a half bungalow, painted white, with black shutters flanking every window. Flower boxes below the windows, each side of the porch bloomed red with geraniums that looked like a picture from a Miracle-Gro ad. A horse whinnied to their left attracting their attention. Three horses galloped freely around a paddock, chunks of mud flew off their hooves clearing the white rail fence. The steel sided barn just beyond the paddock was also white with a green hip roof.

When the loft door flung open and loose hay began to cascade down into the paddock, all three horses stopped their morning mud dash and settled into breakfast. Mrs. Miller appeared at the edge of the opening the hay fell from. She gave a wave to Roger and Beth who returned her greeting.

Beth, raised with horses and cattle yelled, "I'm comin' up," and sprinted to the barn. Roger watched her as she disappeared inside the cavernous opening at the end of the stables. He began to think back, back to his misgivings about Beth joining him on his trip. He had his reasons. It was his trip, and he didn't want to be on anyone else's schedule. He did not want to miss anything because his travel companion didn't want to, or was afraid to do, what ever. Neither did he want to be dragged into one boring excursion after another delaying his arrival at the east rim. So on the morning they left Beth's place he was torn between his desire to continue getting to know Beth, and his need to finish what he started; he had to see the canyon.

Now, with a full day behind them he could not imagine this trip without her. If Beth hadn't come along, he would never have gone out of the way to see the Steve Canyon statue in Idaho Springs. He sure as hell would not have stopped to see the Swetsville Zoo, near Fort Collins. A zoo occupied with not a single live animal would surely not have drawn Roger's interest, but it was very cool, he had to admit. Who would have thought a zoo full of animals sculpted from car parts could be cool. Then there was Mrs. Miller's ranch. There is no way he would have knocked on a stranger's front door and asked permission to camp on their property. A distant roar scared the shit out of him. Roger assumed that Zeus was now getting his breakfast. How many cans of 9 Lives tuna could a full grown tiger eat, he wondered.

His wondering took him back to his recollections of the trip with Beth. The twenty-dollar tip she gave the teenage waitress who was pregnant. Beth made comment of the sad look on her face. "Nobody who is getting ready to be a mother should be sad," Beth said. Then she added that a girl her age should not be having sex let alone giving birth. At that point she went on a passionate speech about the government's lack of action when it came to help for underage mothers. She almost appeared angry and five minutes later, she was laughing about Billie getting caught by Jack, banging one of his girls in the backseat of a brand new 300C.

The next time they ate was in a McDonald's. The guy at the counter got a bit flirty with her and almost as if it was he who had abandoned that poor pregnant girl, she automatically disliked him. He took a little long getting the order and then he got it wrong. Well Beth tore a strip off that guy and two minutes later Roger and Beth were sitting down eating a free meal, compliments of the shift manager. He also gave them a coupon for two Quarter Pounder's for the next time they came in.

When Beth and Mrs. Miller arrived on the porch, Roger had a look of mischief on his face. Unknown to them, his trip down memory lane had just taken him back to the tent. After changing into dry clothes, he and Beth had begun with a playful tussle in the tent that lead to an intimate encounter. Those were the images he had in his head when Beth and Mrs. Miller arrived on the porch before him.

"Boy, Vermont, you look like the cat that ate the canary."

Roger blushed again and he hoped it wouldn't be noticeable in the dull light of the cloudy morning.

"Not still thinking about our meeting this morning, are ya, son?" Mrs. Miller said, and she and Beth began to laugh heartily as they stepped past him and entered the house.

All through breakfast Beth and Lorna (some time between Beth running off to the stables, and coming back to the house, Beth had begun to call Mrs. Miller by her first name) had laughed and talked as if Roger was not even in the room. Roger didn't mind, just as he didn't mind sitting silently in the car listening to Beth tell story after story. She glowed when she spoke, and Lorna had figured this out. She had a knack for getting Beth started, and Roger just sat there, at the end of Lorna's kitchen table, eating the last of the bacon.

The Nightcrawler

The kitchen looked like it could have been Ma Walton's. Everything in it seemed old. The wallpaper, covered with sketched herbs in green, was a dingy yellow, like a newspaper that had been sitting in the sun too long. The appliances were white, clean and well-cared-for but definitely 70's. Pots and pans hung untidily above the table. The dishes on the table were vintage, the pattern on them faded from many washings. It was clear that Mrs. Miller took care of what she had, but didn't feel the need to put on airs for any one who dropped in.

Taken by surprise when Mrs. Miller addressed him, Roger said, "I'm sorry," slightly embarrassed having not heard. "What did you say, Mrs. M..., I mean Lorna?"

"I said, you're awful quiet."

"Well, a man has to know when to speak and when to just sit and listen." He smiled at her, then at Beth and said, "Don't you agree?"

Beth laughed out loud. It was more of a cackle than a laugh. Then she said, "You are so full of shit, Vermont."

Lorna joined in with the cackling and added, "She sure is a force, son, are you sure you can handle her?"

Roger opened his mouth to answer but Beth jumped in before him saying, "Maybe you should take the fifth on that one, Vermont."

They all got a chuckle from that, and Roger indicated that maybe it was time they hit the road before his mouth got him into trouble. Beth got up and began to clear the table and Lorna said, "Don't be silly, Beth. You kids need to get moving, I'll have this cleared up before you get to the highway, now go on." Beth gave her a great hug, the kind you gave your favorite aunt when you knew you wouldn't be seeing her again for some time. "You're sweet to do that," Lorna said, "Now you better get moving."

Roger thanked Lorna for the hospitality and took Beth's hand to lead her to the front door. On the front porch Beth hugged Lorna once more and bounded down the steps on a run to the tent. "Let's go, Vermont. I thought you were in a hurry to get to the canyon."

Before Roger could follow Beth's lead, Lorna had grabbed his arm, squeezing tightly. Roger turned to look at her. The friendly face he had gotten to know and like was gone. In its place was a stern face, a much older face. Lines that Roger hadn't noticed until now had become clearly evident around her eyes and across her forehead. Her eyes, moments ago, warm and swimming with humor, were now cold and threatening. Roger looked back to the tent. Beth had climbed in unaware that Roger hadn't joined her. She had begun to pack up ready to stow things in the Jeep and would have the tent taken down in minutes.

"Mrs. Miller, are you okay?" Roger didn't think she was but he couldn't think of what else to say.

"There are bad things out there, son." The words came out in an almost whisper. "The red eyed dog is after you."

"I'm sorry, what did you say?"

"Beware of the red-eyed dog." Then as suddenly as Lorna's demeanor changed, she was back to her old self. "You gonna let her do all the work, son?"

Roger looked over his shoulder, Beth had begun to fold the tent and the big sleeping bag hung from a low branch of a nearby tree. "I guess you're right," he said trying not to sound too creeped out by what just happened. As he trundled across the lawn to Beth he called back, "Thanks again for everything, Mrs. Miller."

Within five minutes, they were both in the Jeep. Beth insisted on driving, which meant, as far as Roger was concerned, she had another of her detours in mind. He felt Lorna's eyes on him the whole time they were packing up and was glad to be in the car. Beth honked the horn then drove toward the road, as Roger looked back to the porch.

Lorna stood, hands on the porch rail, her eyes back to the steel grey cold that she had when she spoke of the red-eyed dog. The cold stare sent a shiver through Roger's bones but he couldn't look away. Until they had turned onto the road, his eyes were drawn to Lorna's, transfixed by them, expressionless and penetrating. He squeezed his eyelids together as tight as he could. When he opened them, Lorna

The Nightcrawler

wasn't on the porch anymore. Lisa was, his sister stood in the very spot Mrs. Miller had just been. With a slight jump that he hoped Beth would attribute to the uneven driveway, he closed his eyes again. This time when he opened them, the porch was empty. Roger turned away from the house. The sun had begun to burn away what remained of the clouds. Bright beams of light now streamed through and the summit of Scruff Peak was now visible. The trees lining the side of the mountain were greener than Roger believed possible. He fixed his gaze on the rays of light cascading down, his mood was sullen and he barely noticed Beth's voice, cheerfully recounting her morning with Lorna.

"You okay, Roger?" Beth had picked up on his gloomy mood and hoped to help if she could.

"What?" He didn't face her; his gaze was locked on the expanding sky. The clouds were disappearing at an unnatural rate. A small solitary wisp of cloud separated from the remaining cloud cover had floated across the blue sky that framed Scruff Peak. It moved slowly, rolling and changing shape. Roger's expression changed from sullen to morose when the small cloud seemed to take the shape of a dog. He was sure it would open its eyes and they would glow red.

"I asked if you're all right."

Tearing himself away from the sky, he looked at Beth. She had a deep concern on her face. Roger reached over and put his hand on her shoulder. "I'm fine, maybe I'm just tired."

He looked back to the gap in the cloud cover. The dog had broken apart. It was just a shapeless puff of white, not a dog, or a demon. Roger looked down at the ground, watching it disappear in a blur as Beth guided the Jeep along a narrow side road, or was it a path through the woods? With each passing minute, the path got tighter, an occasional tree branch clicking the mirrors as they passed. The surface of this road also got progressively worse. Roger would have given her the gears about the route she chose but he wasn't up to it.

It had seemed to Roger that they had traveled a great distance on this path less taken, but in reality it was barely any time at all. The road opened to a small clearing and Beth stopped, grabbed her pack from behind the seat and jumped out. "Come on Vermont."

She sprinted across the small clearing, and vanished behind some trees. Roger followed at a much less enthusiastic pace. Towering pines blocked the view of everything but the sky directly overhead, which had cleared to a dazzling blue. The air was completely still; the only sounds were the birds somewhere in the trees and water rushing over rocks. The ground was green, but no grass grew, just moss covered rock. At the edge of the clearing, just before the base of the pines, underbrush was making a feeble attempt to grow in the rock. Below the trees, brown dried pine needles covered the forest floor like a blanket.

When he got around the tree that Beth disappeared behind, Roger's heart sank low in his belly, as he frantically looked from left to right trying to find her. She was gone. He spun around, straining to see through the trees. He called her name, at first just speaking, then louder and louder until he yelled loud enough to strain his vocal cords.

A small brook was cutting its way through the rock, the sound of gurgling water he heard in the clearing moments before was much louder, blocking out the bird songs. It had a calming effect; the tightness that knotted his shoulders and went all the way to his nauseous stomach had eased slightly. He walked toward the sound, calling Beth's name.

The air smelled of pine. To Roger it smelled of Christmas in Vermont. Lisa had always insisted on a real tree. She always made such a fuss over their Christmas tree. Every year the whole family squeezed into Uncle Frank's pickup and went to Devon's Tree Farm to pick out the perfect spruce or pine. The first Christmas after Lisa was gone; they got in Uncle Frank's truck, headed to the farm but ended up at Walmart. A seven foot artificial affront to Lisa's memory went up that year. It was the same one that Mrs. Morris had put up every year since.

"Hey, Vermont, try to keep up, okay?"

Roger could not see her but trotted in the direction her voice. His eyes brightened, a smile blossomed on his face. The brook took a turn to the left and as he followed it, it began to be more of a ravine. On the

The Nightcrawler

far bank was a mill of some kind. A wooden water wheel had fallen from the side of the field stone structure and what was left of the wheel was broken and decayed on the edge of the water.

Steps cut into the bank and about a hundred yards up was a waterfall. Not Niagara by any means, at twenty feet high and six feet or so wide it was closer to an indoor water feature at some mall. A fine mist rose up from the pool at its base. With the sun just now rising above the top of the trees, a small rainbow seemed to hover overhead. In the pool at the bottom of the waterfall, the water up to her waist, was Beth. She was naked; her tanned skin a dark contrast to the white water cascading over her as she arched her neck back to let the water splash down on her face.

Roger stood, riveted to the spot. He felt like a perving Tom, even though he knew he wasn't. It was almost like being a kid again and peeking through the fence. He was embarrassed watching, but also very aroused. Beth moved almost in slow motion as she swayed slightly in the cold shower. Her nipples stood erect, caressed by the cold water. She straightened up; saw Roger standing on the bank watching her.

"Are you coming in?"

He rushed down the uneven steps, twice slipping on the damp stones, finally falling in an ungraceful heap. Through hearty laughter Beth asked him if he was hurt. Roger waved her off, got up and carefully tiptoed to the edge of the pool. He undressed quickly, his back to her, trying to hide his erection. He turned and ran in hoping the splashing would help conceal his excitement.

"Woohoo, it's freezing!" he screamed.

"Oh, you big baby. Come over her and I'll warm you up."

With the water rushing down on top of them, Beth put her arms around his neck and lifted herself up. With her legs wrapped around him, she made love to him. Her body moved rhythmically with his. Her eyes looking directly into his the whole time.

Back in the car Roger, seated in the passenger side watched the sky, mostly blue and spotted with billowing white clouds that seemed to be in a hurry to get somewhere. They quickly moved across the sky changing shapes as they went. On the road, Beth guided the Jeep along a path that no two-wheel drive vehicle could navigate. There were times when Roger was sure she had pushed her position on this path too far and they were sure to flip, or fall off the edge. Each time she squeaked by, the Jeep plopping down level on all four tires as they passed over obstacle after obstacle. This surely had been Lorna's shortcut to yet another of Beth's must see sideshows. He did not argue though, having thoroughly enjoyed the waterfall. After one particularly hair-raising climb over a fallen tree, the road seemed to widen and smooth out. They were also going downhill, affording them some of the most stunning scenery of the trip so far. A huge valley opened up in the distance and from this road, or path, they could see for miles.

With smoother terrain, Beth had picked up the pace, not as if they were on an interstate, but they were going thirty to forty, depending on the curves in the road. Roger sat quietly, looking from the scenic terrain ahead to the dense forest alongside the road. The sun was bright in the landscape ahead, but the road was still completely shaded. Pale underbrush and grass grew at the edge of the trees, but just beyond was the familiar carpet of pine needles. Three yards or so into the trees the forest floor turned first mahogany, then black, as the sun's rays were completely obscured. An odor, musky and damp, wafted through the trees.

Something caught Roger's eye, deep in the woods. Something had moved. He stared intently in the direction of the movement. Was it his imagination? He watched the blackness between the trees, looking for any sign of motion, craning his neck back as Beth continued to guide the Jeep along.

"What are you looking at?" Beth asked.

"I don't know, I thought I saw something moving in the trees."

"What kind of something?"

"I don't know, lions, tiger and bears, or maybe Bigfoot, oh my."

"You're so full of it, Vermont." She punched him in the arm and they both began to laugh, taking turns making growling sounds. "Did you ever hear the one about the bear who met a rabbit in the woods?" Roger did not say anything; he just looked at her while waiting for the punchline. "Well, the bear asked the rabbit if his shit stuck to his fur."

Roger's face was on the verge of erupting into an all out laugh. "And what did the rabbit say?"

"I thought you would never ask. The rabbit said no. So the bear picked the rabbit up and wiped his ass with it." They laughed as though it were the funniest thing they had ever heard. Of course, it was not but they were in a mood to laugh.

Roger was still laughing when his peripheral vision picked up motion in the pines. His head spun to see, and this time he was positive, something out there was moving. Beth told him to relax; lots of things lived in the woods. She began to rattle off animals, as though she were hosting a wildlife adventure show. Normally captivated by her voice he barely heard her critter roll call. There was something following them in the trees, he was sure of it. The tree trunks looked black. Very little of the brilliant rays from the morning sun made it through the thick canopy.

Roger leaned out over the edge of the Jeep, his head so close to the passing brush at the road's edge he could hear a whooshing as they whizzed by. He stared into the gaps between the black tree trunks, and there, maybe one hundred yards in, something white gleamed in stark contrast to the ominous dark that was the forest floor. Someone was out there.

"Slow down," he mumbled.

Beth barely heard what he said, but she slowed and began to pivot her head from the road to the woods, trying to see what Roger was looking for. It was almost like driving through a residential neighborhood at night trying to read the addresses on the dark houses.

Roger stared toward the figure he had seen in the shadows. Now, it was gone. He anxiously panned back and forth through the trees, and the figure reappeared, closer this time; it was a girl, it was Lisa. She was waving and his mouth curved up into a smile. However, it was an unhappy smile. He temporarily forgot where he was. Or maybe when he was. He wanted to run over and give his big sister a hug. He wanted to laugh and play with her. He was a kid again. Lisa was here and a sense of being safe seeped into him. Nothing bad ever happened to him when Lisa was around.

However, bad things did happen to Lisa, one bad thing anyway. She had drowned beneath the ice of a frozen pond. When Roger began to think about that his contentment at being a little boy with a big sister evaporated. He saw a huge dog, near the girl, its haunches taught, ready to spring. Before he could warn her it did spring, tackling the girl, both of them disappearing from sight.

"There, stop the car." Roger was excited and agitated, not aware of the militant tone he had used. Beth slammed the brakes so hard the car swerved sideways, skidding to a stop just under the outstretched lower limbs of a huge pine, the needles brushing the windshield. The musky smell was much stronger near the trees.

Roger was out of the car and sprinting into the woods before Beth could call after him to wait. Half way to where he knew his sister had been, he saw the dog again. It looked directly at him. Its eyes glowed red in the darkness of the forest. Roger was sure he saw blood dripping from the animal's mouth. He ran at the creature, which in turn retreated deeper into the woods. Roger stopped at the place where he was sure Lisa had been. There was no sign of a person of any kind, no blood, and no indication that the forest floor had been disturbed in ages. All he found was a smooth carpet of pine needles.

By the time Beth had caught him he was on his knees, running his fingers through the brown needles, sifting for some evidence that he wasn't losing his mind.

"Roger, let's go back to the car."

Without a word, he got up, turned to put his arms around her and held her tight. His eyes streamed with tears. He hadn't thought of Lisa in years and now he was seeing her every day and this was the second time in two days he had watched her come to harm.

Chapter Twenty-Three

A few hours after leaving Stew's Texaco, Scott ran into some bad weather. Nothing like the tornado back in Kansas, but with the memory so new and so very clear in his mind he became anxious. With visibility almost zero he pulled over to wait it out. The radio reception was as poor as the visibility and since all his CDs were packed away in the trunk, all he could do was sit and wait, his head back against the headrest, eyes closed listening to the rain and hail pounding against the Charger's steel roof.

The rain pounded against the car in a rhythmic symphony. Almost elegant, Scott thought. Over and over again the storm intensified, and then relented. The drone was hypnotic. Drained and sleep deprived he drifted away, away from the roadside, to a street somewhere in the English countryside. He was having a dream, the first pleasant dream since he ran into that bum. It was raining in his dream, but not like the storm that raged around outside the car. A gentle rain, pleasant even. The sun was trying to peek through the clouds above a hill in the distance. A thin fog hovered just above the ground in the valley below. Scott was standing in the rain, he was neither wet, nor cold, and he couldn't feel the drops. He could see them, but not feel them.

He heard singing, looked to the source and saw John Lennon standing beneath a large apple tree in full blossom. John Lennon, dead since Scott was a small child, standing beneath a tree singing a song about rain. After a while the voice became course, but the singing continued, it was as if he were listening to a radio and the station had drifted out of tune into a static fuzz.

Scott woke, groggy and confused. He wasn't sure if he was awake or still dreaming. The singing had not stopped. He was back inside the car, the storm had let up some but the rain was sill tapping lightly on the car. The singing he heard was a ghastly out of tune voice, still the same song, but definitely not John Lennon. The noise, yes it was noise not music, was coming from the backseat. Scott knew who was singing, he knew but he sat and stared through the windshield, watching the water running down, not wanting to confirm what he knew.

"God I love that song, don't you Scott?"

Scott turned to see Matt, or was it the Nightcrawler, sitting in the back of the car, beaming his toothless smile. At least the singing stopped, Scott thought. Maybe this was just part of the dream. He knew it wasn't, but he felt better thinking it was, wishing it was.

"Looks like the weather is on the mend, Scottie," an upbeat voice announced from the rear seat.

The rain had slowed to a sprinkle, the color had returned to the landscape as the clouds thinned and the sun began to burn through the gaps. Not that Scott noticed, as he gazed blankly into the distance, he could feel his heart pounding in his chest. His head felt foggy, and the muscles in his belly knotted. His whole body felt clammy. Suddenly he flung the door open, his guts wretched, vomit exploding from him with more force than he thought possible.

When he was sure he was finished, he sat up and wiped his mouth with the back of his hand. He dried his eyes on his shirt sleeves and slowly looked in the rearview mirror; there was nobody there. Streamers of sunshine were cascading down from the scattered clouds that remained. Mild sprinkles fell to the ground, tens of thousands of tiny prisms, creating a rainbow as brilliant as any Mother Nature had ever displayed. It was a glorious sight. A sight that on any given day would have lifted even Scott's most dire mood but this day he gave it a cursory glance then looked at himself in the mirror. His cheeks were stained with tears and dark stubble covered his normally clean shaven features. His hair was greasy and uncombed. Feeling thoroughly disgusted with himself, he stepped out of the car being careful not to step in his lunch splattered on the pavement. As dreadful as Scott felt, the cleanliness after the rain refreshed him some; he still felt like shit, but a bit better was better than a bit worse. He inhaled deeply from his diaphragm, inflating his chest with the fresh, clean mountain air. There was a smell, or was it a lack of smell that he wasn't familiar with. In Los Angeles, a person could see and smell the air. Not even a downpour like this one could banish the smog of LA. Here, he could see for miles and his lungs felt strong and satisfied. He inhaled again, even deeper, his vision began to fade and he put a hand against the car to steady himself. Slowly he let his lungs deflate and the swooning sensation in his head subsided, leaving only a weakness in his legs.

He walked around to the back of the car and stretched his arms out over his head. Eyes closed, enjoying the silent calm after the storm, he twisted right to left then right. The muscles in his torso loosened and Scott's anxiety eased. He followed his washing machine exercise with some leg stretches, touching his toes then leaning against the car to stretch out his calves.

Feeling better still but not great, he needed a shower, or at the very least, to splash some water on his face. The silence of the deserted Colorado highway was suddenly broken by a loud screech. Scott followed the sound, about two hundred yards up, a sign read, SCENIC LOOKOUT SIX MILES. Perched atop the sign was a large crow. The bird's feathers gleamed in the now shiny afternoon sun. Scott, overcome with an eerie sense of déjà vu, hurried back inside the car. He started the engine and began to drive along the shoulder all the while looking down at the ground directly in front of the car. Half way to the sign he finally looked up, the bird was gone.

With an audible sigh, Scott checked his mirrors then pulled out onto the highway. He accelerated to seventy-five in seconds and turned on the radio, Rain by the Beatles came from the high end stereo as clear as could be. Scott tentatively checked his rearview again. The backseat was empty.

"Fucking perfect," he muttered to himself. When the song ended the DJ came on. "God, I love that song don't you, Scott?"

Scott checked the backseat again. Still empty, but he felt odd, like he wasn't alone. The DJ was blabbering on about the storm that had just passed and something about a music festival in Pueblo on the weekend. Scott was oblivious to his shtick. He was equally unaware of the majestic peaks that flanked the highway. The median began to widen as the opposite lanes veered off and disappeared behind a towering stand of pines and granite boulders. The pavement widened as an exit lane to the Scenic Lookout opened on the left shoulder.

Scott steered the car along the exit ramp, the pines on each side created a tunnel leading to a white-washed cement block building. The roof was steep and painted green, evenly spaced rust stains ran down from the screws holding the metal sheets in place. Several RV's and trucks with camper trailers attached were parked along the length of the building, their hot engines tinkling as the metal cooled. Scott had to park fifteen spots past the restrooms.

Having retrieved a clean shirt and his overnight bag from the trunk he walked quickly for the men's room. Behind the building, a diverse group of tourists stood against a railing, pointing and snapping pictures. Scott passed the ladies room and swung open the next door, the hinges protesting loudly. Had he not already tossed his lunch he surely would have entering the men's room. He continued inside, where water ran in a urinal against the back wall, its white porcelain rust-stained worse than the roof. A single sink, mounted to the wall next to one of those plastic fold out baby change stations dripped steadily. A solitary toilet stall sat empty next to the urinal, its door missing. Scott wondered, would anyone actually squat there and shit, in this filth, no door, exposed like that. He just hoped his bowels didn't fuck with him now. Overhead, a florescent light flickered, on the verge of going out.

He turned both taps on full in the sink, those spring loaded taps that stay on for a few seconds then shut off unless you hold them. "Great," he muttered, thinking what ever asshole got the idea for these things should be shot. He removed his shirt, using a face cloth from his bag, wiped himself as clean as he could from the waist up. He tossed the cloth in the trash, thinking he would just get a clean one in his next hotel room. He pulled a fresh shirt over his head, stuffed the dirty one in his bag and walked out back to see what the attraction was.

The mountain air was stimulating, after the awful smell of the restroom. Scott felt rejuvenated. Tourists took turns snapping pictures in front of a stone carving of a Grizzly bear, nearly eight feet tall. It was as though the bear was standing guard, so overzealous photographers didn't climb the guardrail to get the ultimate picture of the drop. The view was stunning. Directly over the railing was a vertical fall hundreds of feet to a lush green valley. At the far side, two summits climbed to the billowing white clouds that reached down from the sky just low enough to caress each peak. The snowcaps blended with the white fluff becoming part of the sky.

Scott had little interest in sightseeing, so he flung his bag over his shoulder and walked briskly back the way he came. When he got to the Charger, there was a man pressing his face against the glass of the driver's side window. Scott was sure it was the bum again. He stopped in his tracks, ready to return to the sightseers if his fears were correct.

Before he could speak, or retreat, or even hide behind the minivan he was standing next to, the figure beside the Charger stood up straight.

"Hey, man, this your car?" The stranger gave a wolf whistle, like a horny construction worker. "My name is Denny, what's yers dude?" He was peppy, in his enthusiasm. Peppy would be the only word that could describe Denny.

Scott calmed at the sight of Denny.

Denny was by his own account, "nineteen, but very mature for his age." Scott didn't think he looked all that mature; his hair was reddish blond, and was in need of shampoo. His pale blue eyes seemed a bit dull for such a young soul and acne covered his face. Scott was sure he was gay. After all what straight, nineteen-year-old male wears a Backstreet Boys T-shirt? This kid was as queer as a three dollar bill and Scott wanted more than almost anything to get him away from the car. The problem was what Scott wanted even less than looking at Denny was another visit from The Nightcrawler.

Before he could stop himself, he offered Denny a ride. Within thirty minutes, Scott thoroughly regretted inviting Denny into his life. Much to his dismay, Denny was the male version of Ashley. A relentless barrage of meaningless chatter constantly spewed from Denny's mouth. He tried to imagine having Ashley back, seated where Denny was.

Then Denny, pimple faced, nattering, faggoty, Denny, would say something like, "Hey dude, where you at?" or "Earth to Scott, Earth to Scott." This would kill Ashley's image, leaving Scott alone with Denny. Alone with Denny and hating every minute of it.

As each mile dragged on, Scott became more agitated. He needed to get this little fag out of the car, even if it meant getting revisited by the bum. Even the fucking bum didn't grate his nerves like this little prick. Scott began to have visions of telling Denny to get the fuck out of the car, just open the door and jump out, at sixty plus miles per hour.

Denny began a new tirade, concerning some video game; "It was like so unfair," Denny began. "I spend a week getting to this point in the game and I get stuck." He checked to see if Scott was keeping up then continued. "I check five websites, to get past that spot. I did exactly what they all said to do and still I was stuck."

Scott was beginning to boil, it wasn't as though Denny's crap was any less frivolous than Ashley's, but he liked Ashley. To Scott, Denny's voice was like fingernails on a chalkboard.

"Denny," Scott said in a tone that shut Denny up instantly. "Denny, if you don't shut the fuck up I am going to kick your ass all over the side of this road."

Denny stared at Scott for a few moments, and then his lips slowly turned up. Scott was taken aback as Denny began to laugh, then, through his laughter he said, "Good one Scott." He shrugged his shoulders and continued the story of how he persevered and beat the game. At the end of his tale he laughed, and laughed. It was an awful laugh.

Scott had reached his breaking point. He could no longer take

Denny. He steered the car to the side of the road. The Charger fishtailed violently, coming to a stop, half on the grass beyond the shoulder. He got out of the car and ran to the passenger side. He pulled the door open and hauled Denny out in an adrenaline assisted fit of strength. Denny lay sprawled out on the grass fifteen feet away, tears welling up in his eyes. They were not tears of a child in pain, but of a man overtaken with fear. Scott glared down at him. His unshaven face glowed red. His chest heaved as each breath filled him with more rage.

"Don't you ever shut up?"

Denny didn't answer; he just looked up completely overwhelmed by what was happening to him.

Scott grabbed Denny's pack from the backseat and threw it with the same force he had thrown Denny. The pack struck Denny hard in the face, then careened over his head. His face burned scarlet from the force of the blow. Blood poured from his nose, covering his shirt, yet he made no attempt to stop the flow. Scott took a step toward him and Denny whimpered weakly then looked down to his lap. He had wet himself and when he realized that he pulled his knees up tight to his chest, wrapped his arms around his legs and began to cry. Completely deflated, the young man buried his head in his lap, his nose still oozing blood and sobbed.

"You pathetic little pussy," Scott said, then slammed the door he had just dragged the boy out of, walked around the car, got in and drove off in a spray of loose stones.

The 440's throaty hum grew higher with each passing second. The speedometer passed fifty in mere seconds, then sixty, seventy; Scott was trance-like, almost a zombie as the landscape of Colorado passed in a blur. The car seemed to defy gravity as it continued to accelerate up a steep incline, overtaking an occasional RV or minivan towing a pop-up trailer. At the top of the hill, a truck loaded down with timber and heading for the sawmill was at a near standstill in the right lane. The driver blared his horn as the streak of red, motor city metal flew over the peak of the hill nearly leaving the pavement. Hitting the even steeper downgrade, the Charger's suspension protested slightly then settled in for what must have seemed to Scott like a free-fall. Moments after blowing by the lumber hauler the needle was resting just past one-twenty.

Very slowly, Scott regained what remained of his sanity. A slight speed vibration had developed in the front end, and he gently eased off the accelerator. The speedometer was still maxed, but the ride smoothed the moment the car slowed. The grade leveled out and the needle retreated, a minute later the throaty drone had returned as the Charger cruised comfortably at seventy. Coming into view, a sign read, Wheeling 18 Miles. And perched on the sign was the crow, its head following the Charger as it passed. Scott's eyes were drawn to the bird as though it were controlling his will. As he passed, Scott was sure the crow winked at him. He depressed the gas pedal and didn't slow down until he found a filling station in Wheeling.

Wheeling was a small town very much like Staples, where he had lunch at Mollies, and gassed up at Stew's Texaco. Wheeling was a one-horse town about three miles south of exit 375 off I-70. Scott went through the familiar song and dance with Josh at the Mobil station. He got advice on where to eat, asked Josh to fill his tank, and he used the restroom. Josh had little to say; he told Scott that his only choice for food was The Gold Nugget about a half mile up on the right.

The Gold Nugget looked oddly modern in a town that was a throwback to an earlier time. It had a façade of red brick and the large windows in front were flanked by white shutters. Inside scarlet walls were adorned with an assortment of Norman Rockwell prints, and the tables were covered with brown paper, the kind you would use to wrap boxes for parcel post. Scott sat at the table nearest the door and pulled the menu out from between the stainless steel napkin dispenser and the red plastic ketchup bottle.

Moments later a plain looking, chunky young woman with a faded blue skirt and neatly ironed blouse approached, pen in one hand and notepad in the other. Before she had a chance to speak, Scott announced that he would have a steak sandwich, fries and a Coke.

The Nightcrawler

She smiled, and was gone as quickly and quietly as she had come. He put the menu back and looked around the room. A few tables to his right a grubby looking man in a soiled plaid short sleeve shirt and a Yankees cap was scarfing down a burger with the grace of a pit bull. Through the window behind the Yankees fan, a gleaming Volvo truck sat, no doubt waiting for the Yankee.

The only other table was occupied by a pretty young girl in her late teens or maybe early twenties, sipping from a coffee cup. She was sitting alone. The same waitress who took Scott's order cleared two empty plates from her table.

Movement at the far end of the room caught Scott's eye. It was him, that bum. This was the first time Scott had seen him while other people were present. This was the time to confront him. This was the time to end it for good. As Scott stood to face him, the waitress set his Coke down on the table. Scott looked at her, then back to the bum, but he was gone. In his place, a young man, tall and gangly, with short reddish hair walked toward the pretty girl.

"The restroom is over there, sir," said the waitress.

"Sorry?" Scott replied.

"I said the bathrooms are over there. It looked like you were looking for the bathroom."

"I'm fine," Scott replied in a far off voice.

He stared at the young couple as they crossed the room toward the exit. As if the young man felt the penetration of Scott's gaze, he turned and locked into Scott's eyes. The two men seemed to connect on another level. A Twilight Zone level.

The young girl nudged her boyfriend and said, "Hey Vermont, let's go already. He turned and they walked out the door.

Scott sat, head in hands until his meal arrived. His head had ached since waking to see the bum in the rear seat singing. Now it felt as though there was a bass drum pounding out the back rhythm for the Army Drum Corp. He tried to eat, picking at his food until it was cold.

"Is there something wrong with your food, sir?"

Scott looked up and shook his head, "Just not feeling great." He looked toward the door as if to make sure the coast was clear. "Is there a place nearby where I can get a room for the night?"

"Well, if you want to stay in a nice hotel you might want to get back on the interstate until you get to Grand Junction, maybe an hour and a half should get you there. If you don't feel up to that you could try Annie's."

"What's Annie's?"

"Annie isn't a what. She has a couple of spare rooms. She rents them out when she feels like it. They ain't much, but at least you won't have to drive if you don't feel well."

"Where is Annie?" Scott asked with a grimace as a searing pain shot through his head.

The waitress scribbled something on her pad, tore off the page and handed it to Scott. "It's just up the road on the right, number 18. You tell Annie that Teresa sent you."

Scott thanked her, dug a twenty out of his pocket, left it on the table and went to his car.

Chapter Twenty-Four

Scott stood in front of the car just after 7:00. Another restless night of bizarre dreams and fitful sleep combined with too much time sitting in a driver's seat had Scott dreading the inside of the vehicle. He was not up to getting back in the car, but he was less apt to enjoy a day in the town of Butthole, smack dab in the center of the less than great state of Nowhere.

His eyes looked a bit hollow and his face just a tad gaunt, but otherwise, he had showered, shaved and was wearing a somewhat wrinkle free golf shirt and shorts. His reflection in the mirror had given him a bit of a fright before he showered, but now that he was ready to hit the road, he felt a bit better.

Outside, the air had lost that mountain freshness. A weather front overnight had ushered in a dank pocket of humid still air. The temperature was in the low seventies but Scott broke a sweat before he had placed his bag in the trunk and slid into the Charger. Remembering his CDs were still in the trunk, he climbed back out to retrieve them. Then the all too familiar squawk from atop Annie's house, a large crow, THE large crow, sat like royalty on Annie's chimney. As always, a long worm dangled from its shiny black beak.

"What are you looking at?" Scott called to the bird, almost as if he expected it to answer.

The bird did answer, in a way. It took flight, dropping its breakfast, like a trained WWII bombardier. The worm came to rest, draped over Scott's shoulder, still squirming. Scott muttered a weak, "Ick." Swiped the thing off his shirt, then stood, mesmerized as it slithered toward the grass at the edge of the drive, the full length of its progress preserved by a milky slime trial. Scott looked from the worm back to the spot on his shirt where it had been, at least there was no sign of it on his shirt. When he returned his attention to the stone path that was Annie's driveway, the worm was gone, and with it the slime trail.

He got back in the car, forgetting his CDs and quickly fed the key into the ignition, the Charger's huge engine fired up instantly. The rear wheels began to spin on the damp stones as Scott depressed the gas pedal.

On the road the Charger fishtailed slightly when he accelerated, leaving two black snakelike streaks on the pavement. Not really feeling hungry, but not wanting to have to stop after getting started he returned to the Golden Nugget for breakfast. He sat at the same table as he had the night before. A tall heavy man with dark hair, streaked with gray, wearing a grease-stained white apron trudged up to his table and sat in the chair opposite. He filled the coffee cups in front of him, set the pot down on the table and asked, "What can I get you?"

"Eggs, bacon," Scott answered not bothering to engage him more than that.

"How do you want your eggs?"

"Scrambled."

"White or wheat?"

"Sorry, what?"

"What kind of toast would you like, white or wheat?"

"White, thanks."

"Okie-dokie then," he said and before he noticed that Scott had finally looked at him, he had left for the kitchen.

First, the dive bomber crow, now the okie-dokie monster is back. Scott was longing for the rude bustle of LA. If he had to deal with one more perky waitress, greasy cook, one more pleasant gas station attendant, or most of all, one more worm-toting crow, he was either going to go mad or puke. Maybe puke then go mad.

The Nightcrawler

A few minutes later the cook returned to set a large plate in front of him. On it was a mountain of scrambled eggs, flanked by toast, bacon and a healthy helping of home fries.

"There you go, sport," he said. Then, as though he was trying to set him off, he clicked his tongue while pointing a finger at him like a pistol.

Scott stared at him as he turned and went to greet an old man dressed in denim overalls and a John Deere cap. Scott picked up his fork and poked his food, moving his eggs around on his plate. What little appetite he had, had diminished at the utterance of "okie-dokie". Then it had been completely squashed when the greasy fry-cook clicked and pointed the same way the bum had a few days ago.

He felt queasy, wanted to leave but he was sure he would vomit if he got up. So, he sat, poking his slightly runny scrambled eggs. Oddly, it appeared that the more he poked them the runnier they got. They began to wiggle and ooze, turning his queasiness to nausea. He looked away hoping to regain some control, and when he looked back his eggs were a brown squirming mass. His bacon was gone, the toast was gone, and the eggs were no longer eggs. He sat, horrified at the sight of a wriggling plate of nightcrawlers.

Gathering all that was left of his sanity he jumped to his feet, his thighs banging the underside of the table, sending his plate and coffee crashing to the floor. He bolted for the door.

The cook hollered, "Hey, sport, what do you think you are doing?"

Scott stopped at the door, looked back to him, then to the upset table he had just fled. There, on the floor beside the table, was a scattering of scrambled eggs and fried potatoes. As the apron clad man started toward him, he took some cash from his pocket, peeled off a twenty, tossed it in his direction and dashed out the door.

The cook picked up the money, shook his head at the mess on the floor and announced, "They just keep getting nuttier every year."

Back on the road, he steered the Charger along the pavement by instinct. It was like his most basic brain functions, the ones that

Mick Ridgewell

control fear, or maybe the ones that preserve survival had taken control. Those brain functions that prevent you from going too near the edge of the pier if you cannot swim, or tell you to stop the car at a red light even though your attention has been distracted and you didn't really notice the light change.

The radio was on, Scott was only vaguely aware of it. A caller had phoned to discuss the bald eagle that had taken roost in a nearby radio tower. The local media had named the bird Clair, after the woman who first sighted the bird. The crew assigned to maintain the radio tower was tasked with removing Clair. They claimed they were doing it not only to prevent possible corrosion of the metal where the eagles' nest sat, but also to protect the bird. They claimed that Clair was at great risk of lightning strikes up there.

The caller, who said her name was Trudy, argued that only the tower was of concern to the crew, not Clair. That bird is a national symbol and should be left alone. She urged people to meet in the mall parking lot to sign a petition, blah-blah-blah. The radio host repeated Trudy's message, then chuckled and said, "Okie-dokie."

A commercial started, but all Scott could hear was okie-dokie, drumming in his head over and over again, like a base drum in a marching band, okie-dokie, boom-boom-boom, okie-dokie-okie-dokie. Soon the words took on the voice of the bum from Detroit. Scott's head throbbed, the drum's constant booming, he felt nauseous, fevered, cold, then hot, then cold again.

The Charger ate up the pavement, not going anywhere in particular. Scott was guiding it between the lines, keeping it on the road, but not navigating its progress. The odometer clicked off mile after mile, up steep inclines, around sharp bends, and s-turns, bypassing stunning views of towering trees and rock walls, all the while Scott's heart continued to race, and sweat beaded his face. The sky was a pale blue against the charcoal gray peaks that climbed through the trees. An occasional cloud briefly hovered near the summits, before being whisked away by the stiff currents of the upper atmosphere. The air rushing in through the open windows of the car smelled of pine and would have been pleasant were it not for the overpowering humidity.

The landscape could have been the painted backdrop of a movie set, except for the slight sway of the trees in the unseen wind, the scene was motionless. Scott didn't notice the highway was empty. The Charger cutting a path through the hot mountain air was the only hint of life. It was as if the whole of Colorado had closed after he entered. The only evidence of civilization was this paved strip winding through the mountains. He had not seen most of the signs at the highway's edge. Destination signs, signs advising trucks of steep grades, signs that gave warning of traffic merging from scenic viewing areas. Signs sparingly placed along the edge of the road zipped by on the Charger's right, unnoticed by Scott Randall.

The sign that did get his attention was an electronic radar sign. As the Charger approached the sign, a big red eighty-nine began to flash, followed by the words, PLEASE SLOW DOWN.

Scott took his foot completely off the accelerator and coasted, eighty-two, seventy-six, sixty-nine, sixty-five. Two hundred yards beyond the first electronic sign, a second sign lit up. Fifty-nine, TOO FAST, Scott continued to coast, the sign flashed again, fifty-three, then in the same big red letters, OKIE-DOKIE. With all his force, Scott jammed his right foot on the brake pedal. Blue smoke streamed out from beneath the scorching rubber, the pungent smell of the burning tires flooded the inside of the car. When the car came to a full stop he closed his eyes so tight starbursts began to explode from his optic nerve to his brain.

Apprehensively he opened his eyes; the sign was flashing TOO FAST. TOO FAST, but he was not moving at all. Then a loud squealing of a horn startled him back to where he was, parked in the right lane of a four lane highway. A white streak of a passing car, a high performance four banger whined in concert with the pitchy squeal of its foreign horn. The car was going too fast for Scott to identify the make.

The sign went black again and Scott resumed his course through Colorado. It was mid-afternoon and the Charger was sucking fumes. He settled into a steady fifty-five and squinted into the distance hoping to find an exit sign. Twenty minutes later, he was eating Fritos and drinking a Coke in a one-horse town just over the New Mexico border. He felt focused as he mapped out a plan to end this nightmare. He would drive through to Albuquerque tonight come hell or high water. Get up early; do lunch in Flagstaff, dinner in Phoenix. He would stay in a nice hotel in Phoenix and be home the day after.

It was a good plan, but sometimes, a plan doesn't always come together.

Chapter Twenty-Five

Beth hated the Interstates. Nothing interesting ever happened on the Interstate, unless of course you consider fatal car accidents interesting. The country should be seen from the county roads and two-lane highways, the ones that pass through the small towns, not by them. It was with some regret when she took the ramp from Colorado Route 69 onto I-25 heading south to New Mexico. She didn't like what was going on with Roger, she thought maybe the altitude might be messing him up, or even worse, maybe he was unstable and wasn't taking his meds. Did he have meds? Had she seen any since they met? Her mind began to conjure one unlikely scenario after another. Things like an escaped mental patient, or maybe a cerebral episode that had deposited a cast of odd characters inside his head.

Whatever the reason, she had hoped a change of scenery might be just the ticket. The Jeep labored up steep inclines, and then did rollercoaster type accelerations down equally steep declines. Beth stretched her luck speeding out of Colorado, and she didn't slow down in New Mexico. The mountains were not nearly so majestic, but still breathtaking at times. The trees became smaller and fewer, almost sparse, as they neared Santa Fe. The landscape seemed to lose color with each passing mile. The sky however, was as blue as she could remember. The air was clean and the wind was whipping her hair around in torrents. If her concerns for Roger weren't so all encompassing, she would be loving the freedom that was all around her. Beth studied the clouds passing the horizon. They danced across the blue backdrop moving along in an invisible jet-stream. It was almost like watching a time-lapse film.

She stopped the Jeep only long enough for quick meals, to get gas, or use the restrooms. Roger had been quiet, but he hadn't had any more hallucinations or visions or whatever he was having. She talked him into resting while she drove, but her real reason was to get as much mileage behind them as she could.

They had passed Albuquerque in the early evening and by the time it got dark, they were pitching the tent at a campsite on the edge of the Cibola National Forest. Roger had regained some of his exuberance and tested Beth's patience, commenting on her quiet demeanor during camp set up. She was exhausted, having done all the driving while at the same time dealing with the stress brought on by her imagination. Shortly after the tent was up, she crawled in and fell asleep before Roger had entered and taken off his shoes. He sat near the door and watched her sleep. Listened to her sleep was more like it. The moon was hiding somewhere behind the earth and the darkness inside the tent was almost absolute. Roger sat straining through the blackness trying to see the outline of her body rise and fall with each breath he heard. A chorus of chirping crickets filled the night with a haunting rhythm.

With growing unease, he unzipped the tent and crawled out into the night. The zipper's interruption of the silence stopped the cricket song almost as abruptly as turning off a radio. A howling in the distance, a dog, coyote, or maybe a wolf brought a sense of dread. Roger zipped the tent closed and stood surveying the night. The darkness was almost as oppressive outside as it was in the tent. He had the feeling of a shrinking room, the walls closing in from all sides and began to get angry with himself. There were no monsters, no boogey men. So what in the hell was wrong with him? Since when was he afraid of the dark?

He closed his eyes, took a deep breath, let it out slowly and almost on cue, when his lungs were empty, the crickets resumed their chirping. A scent of smoldering wood wafted through on the crisp breeze. It was a nice smell, a calming aroma and Roger followed it, not really paying attention to where he was going. Not that it would have

The Nightcrawler

helped in this darkness. The smell of smoke grew stronger, almost overpowering as he walked. Then a second smell began to permeate his senses. It was meat, like the smell of burgers on a grill, but not really like that at all.

Just past a stand of trees, Roger could see the faint glow of a campfire, about a hundred or so yards to his left. He stopped and stood, frozen as if his feet were set in cement. He wanted to approach the fire, to see who was cooking at this time of night, but something in his mind told him that might not be a safe thing to do. His curiosity got the better of his common sense and he crept toward the camp. He was trying to stay along the edge of the trees, which he hoped provided him some cover. The mild breeze at his tent had quickened to gusting winds, the trees swayed overhead. Whistling taunts floated down, then the wind would change direction, slow, or strengthen, causing the whistling to change to moaning.

The camp was set at the edge of the tree line. Roger cautiously drew even with the small tent; the flames from the fire easily illuminated the scene. Plumes of white smoke swirled through the top of the trees and quickly blew away into the night. He glanced around the area intently looking for the inhabitant but saw nobody around. A skinned animal, probably a rabbit he thought, hung on a makeshift spit over the fire. What little fat the scrawny critter had, dripped steadily fueling the dying flames. With each drip, the light grew brighter, the flames licking the searing carcass. The sizzling juices sent an inviting aroma through the night air.

The scent, although distracting, didn't ease Roger's apprehension. He turned to retreat to his own camp but tripped and fell over something in his path.

Roger's face was inches from the pointed toe of an old boot. He looked up from the boot to the face of a tall man. His back was to the glow of the flames, his eerie silhouette filling Roger's view.

The man stood motionless for a moment then said, "You should be more careful. Sneaking around a man's camp in the dark of night can be a dangerous thing." His voice was soft and had an accent that Roger didn't recognize. His words were crisp, his enunciation perfect. To Roger it didn't sound real.

The man offered Roger a hand and when he took it, the man hauled him to his feet with a swift heave that caught Roger by surprise. The man's grip on Roger's hand was vise-like and didn't release when the two stood face to face.

The stranger's dinner stopped dripping, the flames faded to a flicker. The dark folded over the two men. Still gripping Roger's now aching hand, the stranger said, "You have a heavy spirit, for such a young man." Then he released the younger man's hand and glided to the edge of the campfire.

Roger marveled at the large man's smooth gait. He appeared to be walking on air as barely a sound came from a single footfall as he treaded over the ground. When he got to the fire, he tossed a few bits of kindling into the embers, sending a dancing swirl of red sparks, spiraling up until the glow disappeared in the cool air.

With new fuel to feed the flames, the camp took on a glow that shimmered back to life illuminating their faces. For the first time Roger got a good look at the man. He was much older than Roger had first thought. His hair was long and almost white. He wore it pulled back and tied at the base of his neck where it hung down the center of his back ending between his shoulder blades. His skin was dark, slightly lined but otherwise youthful. His cheekbones set high, helped to frame dark eyes that gleamed with peaceful contentment. His clothes were tattered, but he wore them well, a red plaid shirt and blue jeans, frayed in the knees and seat. He was a tall man with striking posture and poise.

Roger stood motionless, not saying a word. He didn't know what to do or what to say. More than anything he wanted to retreat to his tent and to Beth. Beth he thought, this was right up her alley. She thrived on meeting new and strange people. As much as he wanted to bolt, Roger didn't retreat. He stood there unable to take his eyes off the old man, now sitting crosslegged at the fire.

Out of the silence, the melodic sound of the old man's voice put

Roger back on the firm ground of reality. "Would the young man with the heavy spirit please a lonely old man with his company?"

Roger's heart sank deep into his abdomen. He did want to join the guy, but he wished Beth were here to take the lead. She was better at these encounters. It was her thing, well one of her things. He was not sure why he was apprehensive, he had accepted rides across the country without hesitation. There was the fellow in the old Buick with the weird hair and the multitude of piercings in his face. Then the fat lady with the tattoo of a skull and cross bones on her neck driving a pickup with a cap on the back. She smoked big stogies and had a raspy voice that got worse every time she went into one of her coughing fits. He freely accepted a ride from a perv who began to masturbate while he was driving. Roger had threatened to punch his lights out if he didn't stop the car. Surely, this soft spoken old man was safer company than any of those.

The old man lifted the animal from the fire. While holding the makeshift spit in one hand, he wrenched one of its limbs off with the other and held it up in Roger's direction. It should have burned his hand but his grip didn't falter.

"My name is Storm Cloud, but you can call me Ike," he said with a grin. "Now come, sit by the fire and eat. She would want you to eat. You are going to need your strength to finish the journey you are on."

Roger wondered how he knew about Beth. Did he see them arrive at the camp? Maybe he was passing by when they put up the tent. That didn't make any sense; it was too dark to recognize anybody.

Ike was poking the fire with a stick, and couldn't have known the astonished look on Roger's face. "The raven is a very good spirit," Ike said, still looking into the glowing embers of the campfire. "If you heed her warnings you will be saved from harm."

Roger was completely confused now. He's talking about Beth, then he's talking about birds, then Beth. "I'm sorry, Ike, but I don't have any idea what you're telling me."

"Young people have a hard time listening to what is obvious to the elders." Ike finally looked up from the fire, his expression still soft, like a loving grandfather. "My people do not believe that we die. Our bodies pass, they dry up and blow away with the wind, but the spirit soars on for always."

Ike paused, his eyes dark but warm, studying Roger. He looked for a hint of comprehension. He glared as though his stare could reach deep into Roger's soul, to the heart of his spirit. "When our spirit leaves our body, it joins with an animal, watching over the ones left behind."

Ike held out the meat again and Roger took it, "Yeow, doesn't that burn your hand?" Ike didn't answer; he returned his attention to the crackling coals, watching the smoke swirl up and dissipate into the breeze.

"How do you know about Beth?"

"I do not know the one you call Beth." He looked up and again their eyes met.

An uncomfortable silence followed this admission. Roger was anxious about the whole discussion, and Ike felt his unease. The silence suddenly broke by a fluttering sound from the treetops. They both looked up, Roger squinting to see something in the blackness. "She is here," Ike, said pointing over Roger's left shoulder.

"Beth?" Roger called out.

Ike dropped a few more twigs onto the dying embers. They ignited immediately, flooding the camp with a pale, orange radiance. Perched high in a tree Roger saw a bird, possibly a raven or a crow he thought. Its eyes glowed red in the firelight.

"She has been watching over you your whole journey." Ike peeled a hunk of flesh from the carcass in his hand and tossed it to the ground, near the edge of the tree line. The bird swooped down and devoured the morsel as though it hadn't eaten for days. "She has also been watching the other one."

"The other one?" Roger asked, his voice cracking just a bit. "Beth? Is Beth the other one?" Suddenly a chuckle escaped his lips. "Beth put you up to this didn't she?" Roger spun around, "Beth, real funny, you can come out now."

Ike paid little attention to Roger, who was circling the camp sure he would find Beth hiding in the trees. Beth would be jumping out any second laughing her ass off.

Ike poked the fire some more and continued, "She has also been following the dog whose eyes glow red like fire." Roger turned back to Ike who continued poking the ashes, sending more embers and smoke billowing upwards. Ike studied the expressionless face of the young man opposite him. Gently, as if not sure Roger was ready for this conversation, Ike continued, "You are familiar with the dog I speak of?"

"I, I had a dream."

"You had a dream of a dog with red eyes?"

"Twice, actually." He looked to Ike who was no longer looking into the fire. He was looking at Roger. "Well, the second time wasn't really a dream." Roger walked slowly, warily toward the fire. His legs felt weak, and his head felt foggy. He was moving like a man decades older.

"You had a vision," Ike said. He made it sound like a question, but really it was a statement.

Roger squatted across from him, and unconsciously picked up a twig, with which he poked at the embers. "I'm sorry, what?"

"When a man sees what isn't there, he is either dreaming, hallucinating, or he is having a vision." Ike sat across from Roger, "Watch the smoke rise from the coals," he said, motioning his right hand toward the sky. "My people used to send messages from across the plain to the people of the mountains using the smoke."

Roger craned his neck toward the sky trying to see a message in the swirling mass. "Just looks like smoke to me, Ike."

"Sometime smoke is just smoke. It is only when the spirits shape the smoke into a message that it means any more than a sign of fire." Ike produced a pipe and a small pouch from the breast pocket of his old shirt. "Sometimes the smoke needs a little help," he said with a slight grin. He reached into the pouch and pulled out a pinch of tobacco, at least Roger believed it to be tobacco until the old man lit it.

The smell was pungent and sweet at the same time. First Roger thought it was the odor of pot, but it wasn't. It wasn't pot and it wasn't tobacco. Ike took two deep pulls; both times he exhaled directly into the base of the fire. The embers glowed red the first time then popped and sparked the second.

"The flames need your help, young man of heavy spirit."

"You can just call me Roger and I don't smoke."

"This is the only way to find out what the other one wants of you," Ike said extending his arm over the fire offering the pipe to Roger. "She might also give you guidance. She likes the girl that you travel with. She thinks this woman will do anything to keep you safe."

"Who the hell is *she*?"

"Draw from the pipe and the answers may come"

Roger swept his hand to Ike's and took the pipe. The pipe was hot and burned the palm of his hand but he didn't flinch. He just gripped it tighter and followed Ike's lead. Twice he drew the smoke from the pipe into his lungs, and then struggled unsuccessfully against the urge to cough. The smoke burned his throat, his chest wretched in protest. A tear ran down his cheek, yet he continued. Twice he coughed the smoke into the glowing embers. A swirl of red sparks spiraled up from the ashes almost before he finished. His lungs were on fire, he wanted to cough again, but he wouldn't let himself. The aroma of the pipe seemed more pervasive and less sweet as tears continued to well up in his eyes, blurring his vision. His throat felt like he had swallowed a mouthful of the sparks that danced over the fire. It was queer, the way they hovered before his eyes.

Roger's head began to spin; he wondered where his common sense had gone. A man he just met, a man he didn't know at all, offers him a pipe, and he smokes it. Who knows what was in that thing? "What was that shit?" He was looking at his hands. They were shaking. Not just a shiver, they were violently shaking. He tried to stand but his legs would not lift his weight.

When he looked back to Ike, Ike was no longer sitting across from him. Roger was alone, except for the raven. The bird looked up at Roger from the spot where Ike stood moments before.

"Hey, old man, where the hell are you?"

Roger was near panic as he called out into the darkness. The bird squawked. The noise was deafening in the utter silence. The wind howled through the treetops sounding like an animal in the throes of death. Roger gazed to the source of the sound and saw the branches sway in a motion that appeared to give them a collective life. At that moment he could almost believe in monsters.

The raven again let out an ear splitting caw and the sound appeared to linger unnaturally in the exhaust from the campfire. The smell of the pipe permeated the whole of the campsite, Roger's eyes burned. Tears streamed down his cheeks. His face glistened, and he felt his chest strain to inhale as though a huge weight were crushing his ribs. His legs felt paralyzed, his arms like lead. He cried out for Ike, but the only answer came from the bird. Sparks and smoke continued to thicken as the bird spread its shiny black wings. As the great wings began to flap the turbulence brought crackles as the oxygen starved embers glowed bright red breathing in the fresh air. The raven rose into the air above the flames and was consumed in a blinding flash, and what was left behind was Lisa. She was grown up, but there was no doubt that it was Lisa. Roger instantly relaxed, just like he had a hundred times as a boy. Beth was right; Lisa was still his guardian angel. He melted in her gaze. It was like looking into his mother's eyes.

Lisa smiled down at him and all his anxiety faded. He felt safe and relaxed. Lisa had always had that effect on him. Nothing bad ever happened to him when she was near. The apparition above the flames held out a hand but Roger's arms were too heavy to reach out to her. Lisa's lips appeared to move, but the only sound came from the swirling wind sweeping the uppermost tips of the towering trees. On the ground, the air was still.

"Lisa, I can't hear you, say it again."

Her lips moved again, and Roger heard the words, but the sound came from above the trees. It was like sitting in a movie theatre with a bad sound system. What he heard scared him, the voice came in a whisper, "Stay close to Beth, she is your guardian angel now."

Roger squeezed his eyes shut, took a deep breath then slowly opened them. Lisa was still there, but she was eleven again. She was wearing a coat, hat and scarf that appeared to blow in the wind, but it was a wind that had no effect on the flames, or the smoke.

Lisa had white skates on her feet, which dangled just above the fire. Her eyes were sad. They were the eyes of someone saying goodbye. With all his might, Roger leapt to his feet calling out her name.

"Stay close to Beth, she will keep you safe."

"Lisa, don't go."

"I'll always be here if you need me, Roger."

His sister disappeared into the ashes, a bright flash erupted and a pillar of red sparks and white smoke swirled upward in concert with a scream he would always remember. Roger looked up, his gaze following the ghostly white column, the tiny red embers within, like hundreds of eyes staring out of the dark, hypnotizing him. Then the tree tops began to move slowly, circling above him. The ground beneath seemed to fall away from his feet. His view of the sky narrowed as if he had backed into a dark tunnel and was moving ever farther from the entrance. He now wondered what was in that pipe. Then all was black. No sound, no light, and no thought.

Chapter Twenty-Six

Scott Randall was no longer the man who rewarded himself with a new set of golf clubs back in Detroit. There were dark crescents below his eyes, shadows cast by his cheekbones over his sallow face, and light creases over his brow were all obvious outward signs of his decline. There was more striking evidence however. His athletic posture looked weakened by a slouch of his shoulders. His once confident stride was now the foot dragging gait of a cowering high-school outcast. Most telling of all was the blank stare where his once overpowering gaze had been. It was as though his arrogance, his mojo, had just seeped from every pore and evaporated.

The surge of energy he felt by laying out the rest of the journey so neatly at the filling station faded with the first hitchhiker he passed. It could have been any college kid hitching home for the summer. Things can seem so harmless in the distance. Up close the college kid was far from that. Not a college kid at all. The bum was standing beside the road. Just standing, his finger cocked like a gun, the few teeth in his maw glowing yellow in the desert sun.

The bum was everywhere, changing the tire of an old VW on the shoulder of the road near Albuquerque, yet sitting in the passenger seat of that same VW. A Chevy pickup passed the Charger while Scott had let his speed drop below fifty. In the back of the truck, with a stalk of hay held between his lips, was the bum. Again the cocked finger in tandem with a mocking wink. He was behind the counter at the Mobil station near Gallup; Scott refused to look at him but he knew the bum was there. There was no mistaking that offensive smell. As always the clicking noise came from the bum's mouth, as he feigned the finger gun. Scott didn't look up to see the gesture, but it was there, he just knew it was there.

Somewhere just over the Arizona border, Scott pulled into a truck stop for a bite. The bum was filling up the tank of an eighteen-wheeler. The rig's engine clanged that awful diesel drone. Blue haze rose up from the twin stacks over the cab. The air was still and thick with exhaust. Scott avoided eye contact with the man pumping fuel into the truck. Inside the restaurant, the air was as thick with tobacco smoke as the parking lot was with diesel exhaust. Blue swirls billowed up from most every table occupied.

"Sit wherever you like, hon," came a voice that was surely female but raspy enough to be confused for a man's.

He didn't look to see the source of the she-man voice; he just slunk to a table that was as secluded as possible. He felt that everyone in the room had stopped what they were doing to watch him. Don't look at them he told himself, they are just a bunch of truckers, no bums, no demons, no worms or crickets, no creepies in here. They are just a bunch of truck drivers eating fried food and smoking their way to coronary disease.

The owner of the raspy voice set a cup of coffee in front of Scott and asked, "Know whatcha want, hon?"

Without looking at a menu, or the face the voice came from, Scott asked for fish and chips. Most every truck stop, roadhouse or greasy spoon served fish and chips. He managed a quick look at the waitress, not her face, but the rest looked okay enough. White Nikes on tiny little feet, gave way to athletic looking legs. Her skirt was short enough to bring attention to muscular thighs, but not so short that her ass would be showing if she bent to touch her toes.

"You betcha, hon," she said, turned on her heels with the grace of a ballerina and glided away from the table.

Scott watched her until she disappeared behind the kitchen door. She was a pleasant distraction. Her butt swayed just enough to be sexy without looking slutty. She wore a red T-shirt that fit just right. Her hair was short, dark blonde, with highlights that glowed then dimmed then glowed again as she walked under the lights. As soon as the door swung closed behind her, Scott resumed his examination of the tabletop. He couldn't see anything bad if he just looked down. How many times had he heard someone in the movies yell, "Just don't look down!" Well this was the exception to that rule. This was the time to not look up.

He sat trying to think of anything but the bum. He replayed the meeting in Detroit, the dinner with Sarah, the afternoon with Grace. He thought about taking Max to the beach as soon as he got home to let her run in the surf. Few things gave him as much pleasure as seeing Max run flat out across the sand as the waves broke along the shore. The sun, the surf, a boy and his dog.

Scott had almost made the mental trip to the ocean when a plastic glass full of ice water clunked on the table in front of him. "Your food will be right out sugar," the raspy voice said.

He said thank you to her ankles, noticing a small tattoo just above the top of her shoes. It looked like a lizard at first, maybe a chameleon or gecko. She seemed to be hovering as he stared intently at the tattoo. It didn't have legs, he was sure there were legs but now it looked like a snake, a serpent, or even a Chinese dragon.

"My name is Maggie," she began. "You sure don't fit in with this bunch."

Scott was barely aware she was speaking. He was trying to get a better look at the tattoo, sure that if he got a look from the right angle he would see the legs of the lizard. "This is just a summer job for me," the voice went on. "I'm a student of drama at UCLA."

He watched the ankle as she rambled on about almost being in a commercial in LA, and almost getting the lead in the biggest play of the season at school. She would have been the first junior to get the lead role in years.

While she spoke, her leg bent at the knee. She was twisting her toe on the floor as if she were putting out a cigarette butt. It gave Scott a clear view of her ankle. At the tattoo, the worm tattoo. He recoiled but found it impossible to look away. Why would anyone with such beautiful legs mess them up with a tattoo of a worm? It wasn't just a worm; it was a thick, brown nightcrawler, a thick, brown, fucking squirming nightcrawler.

This wasn't going to be the eggs on the floor scene again. He fought the urge to run screaming from the room. Tattoos can't squirm. It was all in his head, his stupid sick, insane head.

Still, that worm was crawling up her leg. Spiraling around her calf, like it was on one of those train tracks going up a mountain in a cartoon.

Using the calmest voice he could, Scott asked her if she might check on his food. He wanted to get back on the road as soon as possible. She didn't seem to take offense to his interruption, just said, "Oh sure", and went back to the kitchen as elegantly as she had the first time he watched her. She paused at the swinging door to the kitchen and Scott chanced another look. Not only did he not see any worm, he didn't see anything at all on her ankle.

"You are fucking losing it, Scott", he said louder than he realized. A young couple with two kids in tow walked past on their way out. The dad, who Scott refused to look at, told him to watch his language. Scott apologized, absently his eyes fixed on the Formica table, studying each scratch in the faded gray surface as if they held the clues to the secret of life.

His dad often told him the secret of life. The problem was the secret was different with each situation or point his dad was trying to make. If he was sending little Scottie to his room it might be, *cleanliness is next to godliness*. If the lesson was on sportsmanship, it might be something like, *it's not if you win or lose, it's how you play the game*. Of course, he only used that one in winning situations. What was always between the lines with his dad was, *winning is the most important thing*. In losing situations he might use, *you only get out what you put in*.

Yes sir, if you wanted advice that was sure to send a little boy straight to a therapist, Zach Randall was your man. Scott sat quiet on the outside, but screaming deep inside, screaming for something worthwhile from all of Zach's charm lessons that might put him right. The only thing that came to him was, *Scottie, quit being a baby. If that smelly fucking creep comes back you show him who's boss. If he opens his mouth to speak, you put a fist in it. If he gets all manly and puffs his chest all big, well you put a hole in it.*

"I'm not being a baby. The prick isn't real, he's a spook, a ghost or something. How can you kick his ass if he isn't real?"

"I'm sorry, are you talking to me?" Scott hadn't realized that Maggie was putting his food on the table and again was unaware that he was talking to himself.

"What, no I was just, just, I was just."

"Are you all right, sir? You don't look too good."

He didn't answer. After waiting a minute or so, Maggie shrugged, turned and glided back to the kitchen. He began to poke at his food. The greasy smell of deep fried fish and chips, combined with the cigarette smoke and pots of aging coffee steaming behind the counter gave him a sudden urge to flee. He could feel his stomach churning. The hunger was beginning to twist the muscles in his belly. He needed to eat. He had enough sense left to know that if he didn't eat he was surely going to break down. Both physically and emotionally, he would simply begin to fall apart. Hell, he felt he was already headed down that road. On the other hand, if he ate he was sure he wouldn't keep it down long enough to get to the door.

A single worm slithered out from under one of Mrs. Paul's fish fillets. Scott's stomach tightened and his breathing quickened. He squeezed his eyes shut so tight they began to hurt, and his head started to pound. Without thought his hands came up to cradle his head. He rocked forward and back, forward and back, "No, no, no." He repeated that one simple word over, and over again as though a verbal denial would make everything alright.

"Mister, are you okay?" Maggie had returned to his table with genuine concern. "Can I get you something?"

Scott opened his eyes and the worm was still there. It had crawled off his plate and slithered over the Formica table leaving a white, glistening slime trail in its wake. He looked up at Maggie, she had to see it too, but Maggie didn't see it, that much was sure. She looked at Scott, her eyes wide open, tears on the verge of welling at the corners. She was a truly nice person who was scared and concerned for a man who was having a breakdown, or worse.

Scott's gaze returned to the table, the worm was at the extreme edge. Behind it a trail of slime was illuminated by the ceiling lights. Scott mused that it glowed almost like a neon sign, and then horror stuck him as he realized the slime trail spelled out something.

He read aloud the words spelled out on the table. "Okie-dokie."

"I'm sorry?" Maggie asked backing away slightly.

Scott began screaming, "Okie-dokie, okie-dokie."

The room was silent, except for his screams and the thumping of his feet on the tile floor. Scott jumped from his seat, his chair flying out behind him and ran from the restaurant.

Chapter Twenty-Seven

Crossing the border into Arizona was like an instant cure for whatever was bothering Roger. They were wearing straw hats Beth had picked up at a souvenir shop near the Petrified Forest National Park, and Ray-Bans she produced from her backpack. In the distance the sun reflected brilliantly off the heat shimmer that was always just out of reach of the Jeep. They resumed their quest to enjoy the country away from the Interstates as much as they could. The Grand Canyon was hours ahead; it was as if they could both feel the breeze at the rim and anticipate the scorching heat of the canyon floor.

Roger felt no need to recount his experience at the campsite and when Beth asked why he didn't sleep in the tent, he just told her he was watching the campfire and fell asleep. Since he woke on the ground next to the smoldering embers of a small fire next to their own tent, he wasn't sure it all wasn't a dream. It's not like he hadn't had his share of those on this trip. He couldn't explain the fire, since he didn't remember building it. Behind the wheel, the top off and the wind blowing through at fifty-five, all the weird shit that happened since they left Nebraska was best forgotten.

Beth had picked up a few supplies at the souvenir shop where she got the hats and they were stopped beside a small river for a picnic. The sky was the lightest, brightest blue. The desert was so different from the green hills of Vermont. Roger was awestruck. A slight breeze did little to cool the one hundred degree air. The sparse trees and sundried scrubs were reluctant to rustle in the weak wind. Water gurgled over stones rounded by a millennia of erosion at a nearby river. The only sound to break the serenity was the crunching of their footsteps on the parched surface and the occasional caw of a large black bird perched atop a sole saguaro cactus, towering twenty feet over the desert.

Immediately after eating, Beth stripped down nude, grabbed a small package from the Jeep, and waded into the water. It was only waist deep, cold enough to keep a six-pack chilled if they had one and the current was more than enough to sweep away a small child. She waded in undeterred by the cold water or the uneven surface beneath her feet. She let out a slight squeak when the water reached her tummy but didn't slow her progress.

Roger watched with pleasure and just a bit of anxious tension, thinking that any minute someone might come along. No passersby were near however and Beth took soap and shampoo out of the small pack. Roger joined her just as she dunked her head in the icy water. He wasn't quite so brave as she. He timidly undressed then tip-toed across the same path to the edge, wincing and grimacing with every step on the hot rough ground.

"Don't be a baby Vermont," she called enthusiastically splashing him with both hands.

In a futile effort to shield himself from the frigid onslaught, he held his hands out in front of his chest. Then surrendered, realizing the futility of his efforts. He turned his back to her, arms held out, his back and neck arching back toward the water and splash. By the time he was able to scramble to his feet the current had taken him twenty feet downstream. Beth had washed and rinsed before he made his way against the force of the rushing water back to where she stood. She tossed him the pack with the soap and shampoo and left him standing in the water shivering. He hurriedly washed himself and scurried out of the water, where Beth tossed him a towel from the back of the car.

It was at least two hours before they got back on the road. The heat felt good after the cold bath, and for a while, lying in the sun just seemed right. Eventually they made love and then it was back in the water to cool off. They didn't speak much during this time; he was still trying to make sense of the fireside chat with Storm Cloud. She was just happy to have Roger back. No demons, no nightmares, just sun and laughs and nothing but good times ahead.

As the afternoon passed, Beth began an endless monologue regarding Bobbie's many skinny-dipping episodes. Surely, she had been trying to get Jack's attention. Beth never understood why she felt the need to use shocking activities to get his attention. He was a busy man but he always made time for his kids. Of course Bobbie brushed her off with, "Sure Bethy, easy for you to say being Daddy's little girl."

Her stories about Bobbie were interrupted by the sight of a car on the shoulder of the road. It was big and red, the make of which neither recognized at first. When they got closer Roger said, "That's the car from that Dukes of Hazzard movie."

"Should we stop?" Beth asked.

"Sure, it's not like we're in a hurry."

She stopped alongside the General Lee. On the opposite side a disheveled looking man with dark hair was holding the passenger side door open, screaming at nobody to, "Get the fuck out of the fucking car."

Roger and Beth both craned their necks but could not see anyone else in the car.

"He's crazier than you are, Vermont."

Just then the crazy man noticed the Jeep and began yelling at them, "Hey, you two."

Beth was not about to wait for the worst to happen and she sped away leaving the crazy man to grow smaller and disappear from her rearview mirror.

Scott Randall, looking into the car saw the bum, as filthy as ever. He was smiling up at Scott with a casualness that infuriated and repulsed him. It was a smile that was dotted with blanks and the teeth that were there were gray, or yellow, in fact they were about any color but white.

Scott grew angrier; he leaned in with the intention of hauling this prick out of the car and kicking the living shit of him. Yes, he was going to show this creep what he was made of.

Before he could get close enough to grab the filthy coat, his mind began to reason. *The coat. It's mid-summer in Arizona and this prick is wearing a coat.* Immediately after that thought passed, a breeze wafted through the car, sending the rancid stench into Scott's face. Scott recoiled, stepped back and tripped over some scorched vegetation, falling to the ground scraping both elbows on the hard pan that covered the landscape as far as the eye could see.

"Damn Scott, that looked like it hurt." The grin had not faded, if anything it grew slightly broader.

"Listen," Scott said looking up into the car. "I don't know what it is you want from me, but whatever it is, I don't have it."

"If you don't know what it is, how do you know if you have it or not?"

"I'm not in the mood for riddles, and I'm not in the mood for you, so get the fuck out of the car, and fuck off."

"I used to be a lot like you, Scott. The last full year I worked, I pulled in two-fifty. I was better than everyone, if you had asked me I would have told you exactly that." Then he took a golf ball of all things out of his coat pocket. He tossed the ball up, caught it, tossed it up, caught it again, and then tossed it at Scott who nonchalantly caught it in the palm of his right hand.

"Yep, two-fifty. That was when it happened. Do you remember, Scottie?"

"Remember what? What the hell are you talking about?"

"It was about nine years ago. I was visiting my little brother in Vermont. I went to try to convince him to come and work with me in Detroit. He was too good to be living, at best, a mediocre life. The only thing he had going for him was Millie and the kids. However, he said he was happy in Vermont. You ever been to Vermont Scott?"

Scott didn't answer. He just sat in the dirt staring up at the man seated in his car.

"Anyway, it was winter and I'd taken my niece and nephew

tobogganing at the park. While I was helping my nephew up the hill, I lost track of his sister Lisa. She had been coaxed up the wrong side of the hill by some teenage boys and sent whooshing down the snow covered slope and didn't stop until she was right out on the middle of the pond. Then the ice gave way and she disappeared."

He stopped talking and wiped a tear from his cheek. Scott looked on in horror at the hobo. His head shook slowly from side to side as though the mere gesture could shield him from anymore of the man's tale.

"Those cowards ran right passed me when they fled. I grabbed the smallest one. He looked into my eyes. He was crying, just like you are now, Scottie."

"What does this have to do with me?" Scott said, his voice pleading to be left alone.

"Scott, Scott. That was you I grabbed by the coat running from the park that day. You punks didn't even have the guts to try and help the little girl."

"Nobody could have helped," Scott screamed back. "I told them to leave her alone, but they wouldn't listen. Then when the ice broke, it was too late. There was nothing we could do. Nothing I could do." His voice had trailed off to a whisper.

"I got a neighbor to take Roger home. I never left that park until they brought that poor little girl up. She was blue and her eyes were still open. I see that face every night in my dreams. Can you imagine that, Scottie?"

Scott buried his face in his hands, his shoulders jerking between sobs. "Would you just leave me alone. Just fuck off."

"It got so I was afraid to sleep and tired men make mistakes. At work I made a decision, you don't need the details, but three men died as a result of that decision. They were good men, with families and friends."

He sat quiet for a moment picking at his coat as though he were removing pet hair. He probed in the pockets then examined his empty hands when they emerged. Scott continued to sob into his hands until the man continued. His voice had changed, not the sound of his voice but the tone he used.

"It wasn't really my fault, at least people tried to tell me that. I knew better though," the bum said. "You see, Scott, I didn't think those men were as important as getting the job done and I was too damn exhausted to see the error I was making."

Scott had finally regained his feet and stood on the spot where moments ago his ass had been. "What the hell does any of this bullshit have to do with me? The girl was an accident and you killing a few men is not my fault."

"And that in a nutshell my friend is why I am here," the bum said.

He went silent. Staring off across the horizon, extreme melancholy filled his expression. After a few moments, he blinked and returned his attention to Scott.

"Sorry about that, Scottie. Now where was I? Yes, yes, people, all people have something to contribute."

"Anything you have or may have had is in the past means shit to me, now fuck off and leave the world to those of us who can still do something with it," Scott shouted. He did seem remorseful while he listened to the story of Lisa's drowning but had to get this prick out of his car and out of his life.

Scott had begun to step forward and lowered his eyes to make sure he didn't trip over the same thing that caused him to fall backward. When he looked up again the car was empty. He was startled by the bum's absence, almost as much as his presence had spooked him not long before.

"You are one loony fucker, Scott," he told himself as he slammed the door shut. He could not bring himself to consider regarding him by a name. The Nightcrawler was no name for a man. Matt is a name, but was it his? Was there even a "him" to give a name to? The biggest reason not to regard him with a name was the importance of not validating his existence. Better to be crazy than admit that creatures like that were part of his species.

Back on the road, windows down, the hot wind blowing through the car, Scott was still repulsed by the stink left behind by the bum. If he was not real, then how could he leave a smell behind? The flipside of that, if he was real, then how could he disappear into thin air? How could he have made it from Detroit to Arizona without a car? There is no way he could hitch, who would pick him up? Even if he got someone to stop, they would leave him standing at the side of the road as soon as they got a whiff of him.

Scott's mind started to do laps around these questions. The speedometer slowed slightly, seventy, sixty-eight, sixty-three. He was completely unaware of his speed until a couple of kids in a rusted out pickup rumbled by, the engine thundering along unrestrained by any exhaust system. The noise from the V8 brought Scott back from his thoughts; the speedometer was now dipping below fifty.

Ahead, the sides of the truck bed wobbled violently, the rust-weakened steel barely able to hold them in place. Scott's foot slowly depressed on the accelerator, and the Charger blew by the rust bucket like it was tied to a fence. He looked over at the driver on the way by and almost drove off the road. It was him again, the bum, driving the pickup. He stuck his tongue out at Scott, but it wasn't a tongue at all. It was a nightcrawler, long, shiny and brown.

Scott's foot hammered the gas pedal and in seconds the old truck was barely a spec in his rearview mirror. He replayed it over in his mind, the truck, the driver, the tongue. He was unable to resist and his skin crawled. The speedometer was steady at one hundred.

When the truck was completely gone from view his cell phone rang. He slowed to sixty, and rummaged for his phone in his pants pocket. He was anxious to hear a friendly voice, someone from the office, hell even Thomas would be an improvement over the bum. He found the phone, flipped it open and held it to his ear, "Hello."

"Driving a bit fast Scottie, you'll get yourself killed like that." Scott's face went ashen and he tossed the phone out the window. It was 'his' voice, how could he call him on the phone? Scott looked at the seat where the bum had been. If someone, anyone, had sat there why wasn't that bag of chips crushed? But, if nobody sat there then why did this car stink like the street vermin from Detroit. His thoughts began to spiral in his mind like the twister. His fingers gripped the wheel so tightly his knuckles went white, the muscles in his forearms burned and the veins in his wrists bulged. An involuntary scream welled up in his chest and exploded from his throat.

Roger and Beth both jumped with a start as a red blur swept by on their left. The passing car was going so fast, the sound of the engine didn't arrive until the car was lengths ahead.

"That's the weirdo we stopped for back there," Roger said.

"He's going to kill himself before the end of the day," Beth said, in a voice that was almost a whisper.

"He won't make it that long if he doesn't slow down."

"Billy used to drive like that all the time," Beth started with a grin. "He came home one day and Daddy went ape shit." She laughed aloud. "Daddy got a call from Judge Ross down at the traffic court, he was one of Daddy's poker buddies and Billy was in his morning session."

"That was lucky," Roger said, thinking that any help you can get in traffic court has to be good.

"Lucky my ass. If he had another judge he might have been found guilty, but Daddy may not have found out."

Roger watched Beth with adoration as she told the story. Beth had an ability to draw the listener into her anecdotes.

With an expression that said, 'Wait until you hear what happened next' she continued. "Daddy was so mad he told Billy he couldn't drive any of the fleet cars." She burst into a fit of laughter and stuttered through the next part. "B-B-B-Billy said, 'How am I going to get to work?' And guess what Daddy said?" she asked Roger looking at him wide eyed, anxiously waiting his reply.

"I don't know, take a cab?"

"Come on, Vermont, how many cabs do you think are going to drive 30 miles to the ranch to pick Billy up?"

"So, what did your dad tell him?"

"Daddy said, 'Ride a damn horse if you have to but you better get there'."

They both laughed hysterically, imagining the horse that Billy rode into the dealership, tied to the fence behind the service bay.

"No way your dad made him ride a horse to work."

"Yes he did, for a whole week."

Their laughter bellowed out of the Jeep, then stopped abruptly at the sight of the red car, again on the shoulder of the road. The cars hazard lights were flashing and the crazy man who had passed them a while back was standing between the taillights frantically waving his arms as though he were trying to take flight.

"Should we stop, Roger?"

Roger knew as much by the tone of her voice, as the fact that she didn't call him Vermont that she didn't want to stop. That she was really creeped out by their earlier encounter with the man in that car.

"It's over a hundred, Beth. If nobody else comes along he'll die out here."

She stopped the Jeep alongside the Charger.

"I ran out of gas. Can you help me out?"

"We don't have any in the car but when we get to the next store or gas station we'll send someone back for you," Beth said before Roger had a chance to offer the nut job a lift. She then drove off, leaving Scott Randall standing alone in the scorching Arizona sun.

After what seemed like several hours of sitting on the ground in the Charger's shadow, Scott was more than happy to pay twenty dollars for the five gallons of gas the tow truck driver delivered. He wasn't at all interested in the driver's tale of how those nice kids just caught him heading out the door. He couldn't care less that the driver was on his way home for dinner. He shook his head to acknowledge the man's appreciation for Thomas' car but said nothing.

The driver must have figured Scott wasn't the chatty type and poured the gas into the car, taking great care not to spill any. When the can was empty he wiped the fender near the gas cap with a rag he pulled from his back pocket.

"There you go, mister, she should start up now."

The car turned over for what seemed to Scott like an eternity then roared to life.

"Yes sir, that's a mighty fine car. Pete's is a little ways up on the left. You can fill up there. You ought not try to go any further. Might not make the next station."

Still wiping the top of the fender surrounding the gas cap, he said, "You tell Josie that Tucker sent ya."

"Thanks," was all Scott said.

He handed him a twenty without ever looking at Tucker. Then he got in the car. As he was pulling out, he heard Tucker's reply, barely audible over the crunching of the gravel beneath the tires. "Okie-dokie."

The sun was setting when Roger and Beth crossed the parking lot of Duke's. It was a huge orange ball, the bottom half hidden below the jagged line of the distant mountain. Duke's was a saloon right out of a Hollywood western. The whole place was a tribute to John Wayne. Pictures from every movie he had ever been in adorned the walls. The giggles had started when the waiter asked, "Can I start you pilgrims off with a drink?"

It was the worst possible John Wayne impression. Not that Roger and Beth would have known; they had to ask who was in all the pictures all over the walls.

Roger's laughter stopped abruptly, followed by a small gasp as though he had been kicked in the belly by a pack mule. Perched on the driver's side headrest was a raven. Roger was sure it was the same bird he had seen at Ike's camp the night before.

"What's wrong?" Beth asked, following his gaze through the big picture window to the Jeep. A bit startled she timidly asked, "What's with this car and frickin birds?"

The Nightcrawler

She took his hand in hers and began to walk out toward the car. Roger pulled her back, released her hand, at the same time stepping toward the car. The air was still, Duke's air conditioner hummed behind them. Crickets chirped across the road. Roger's shoes made little sound on the gravel but to Beth, each footstep was thunderous.

She didn't know why an onslaught of fear now surged through her. She had no fear of birds. She was, of course kidding herself. The fear was of Roger, or for him. Roger was walking toward the car and the bird and the way the bird watched him was scary.

The silence was shattered by an eighteen-wheeler speeding past, on the otherwise deserted highway. The calm air was replaced with the gusts from the truck's slipstream. Roger's straw hat flew after the truck spiraling to rest on the center line of the road. It was an odd looking island, on a sea of asphalt.

A shrill caw came from the Jeep as the raven took flight. Her wings flapped only long enough to get airborne then she glided to the ground next to Roger's hat. The bird took the brim of the hat in her beak, and then spread her wings. The wingspan was half the width of the road and glimmered in the quickly fading dusk.

"I think it wants your hat, Vermont."

Their giggles had returned as Roger began to stride across the pavement to retrieve his hat from the bird. The raven gave a loud caw, released the hat and with wings spread and jumped at Roger, who jumped back a step.

Beth's laughter reverberated in the still air, but this time Roger didn't join in. She didn't see the anxiety welling inside him as she called out, "Let her have the hat, Vermont, I'll get you another one."

The last of the sun had slipped behind the peak of the mountain. A buzzing sound came from a track of lights that illuminated a billboard across the street. The billboard invited everyone to The Mad Dog Saloon for the coldest beer in a hundred miles. A giant black dog snarling through a mouthful of jagged white teeth stared out with blood red eyes.

243

Roger's jaw dropped as he looked to the source of the light. Lisa had warned him of the red eyed dog, Mrs. Miller had warned him in her weird trance-like voice of the red eyed dog, and didn't Ike make mention of it?

Scott guided Thomas' car along the road in complete solitude. His phone was somewhere on the pavement fifty miles back. He hadn't dared to turn on the radio for fear of an Okie-dokie, or some DJ calling himself The Nightcrawler. So there he sat, in the cockpit of the Charger, traveling sixty-five miles per hour, with nothing but his thoughts, and the sound of the wind coming in through the open windows.

Scott had always liked the desert. The dry air, the topography, the way the day could be hot enough to bake your brain right inside your skull, yet the nights were cool enough to give you chills. It had been a while since his last Nightcrawler sighting, and he had settled into a calm, almost sedate stupor. He marveled at how quickly the sun sets in the desert. The purple sky was all that remained of the brilliant orange sunset of moments ago. The only other light came from the car headlights that he didn't remember turning on casting a puddle of light a short distance ahead.

Scott's eyes were drawn to a glow that appeared out of place in the middle of the desert. As he drew closer, the light split in two. The road seemed to split the light. He thought of Charlton Heston parting the Red Sea. A few moments later and it was clear that the light on the right was a small building he assumed was a gas station or corner store. On the opposite side of the road was an illuminated sign or billboard.

Something deep inside urged him to turn on the radio. George Thorogood belted out "Bad to the Bone". The volume was deafening, the calm state he had enjoyed only moments ago, replaced by panic. Moreover, there standing in the middle of the road was the bum, the Nightcrawler, Matt, the vermin from Detroit.

The speedometer slowly climbed, sixty-eight, seventy-two, seventy-six…

"Roger, there's a car coming, get off the road," Beth screamed. Her eyes filled with horror as the oncoming headlights fixed on Roger like the eyes of cougar stalking a fawn.

The terror in her voice tore his attention from the billboard. He spun on his heels and there it was. The big red car, the car that was old and new at the same time. How often had he seen it in his dreams? Sudden realization dawned on him. The car in his dreams was the car that was out of gas. The man in the dreams was the crazy man driving that car. It was the same car. With the quickness he showed Jack Walker in the outfield, Roger charged for the side of the road.

Eighty-seven, ninety. "You won't get away you stinking fuck." Ninety-two... Scott fixed his eyes on the bum as he ran for the edge of the road. Ninety-five...

"Roger, hurry! He doesn't see you."

Roger could only hear the car. It was almost on him, he wasn't going to be off the road in time. Beth's screams grew more shrill with each call of his name as she ran toward him.

"I got you now, you prick," Scott yelled through maniacal laughter. He saw the bum make a final effort to dive for the gravel at the edge of the road. "Too late," Scott chortled.

There was a sickening whack, like the sound of a hardball meeting the homerun swing from an aluminum bat. The bumper of the Charger struck Roger's right leg half way from his foot to his knee. His feet were knocked flying over his head sending him cart-wheeling through the air. The pain he felt was like nothing he had ever experienced. He felt the bones in his ankle explode on impact. His knee had bent at an angle it was never meant to go. It seemed like electricity was shooting up the length of his leg and erupting in his groin. He saw Beth running toward him then she was gone, replaced by sky, gravel, the red-eyed dog and then she was back as he pin-wheeled through the air.

The silence that had engulfed her was then obliterated by the far off sound of anger, or was it hysteria. "Got you, you piece of shit," Scott yelled back through the window as he slammed on the brakes locking all four wheels. The Charger squealed to a stop, the cloud of blue smoke from the charred tires drifting off through the air in front of the car, ghostly in the headlights.

Roger's ass came crashing down on the gravel, followed in a wave by his back, his shoulders, and then his head. When he came to rest he felt nothing, his eyes focused on the glowing red eyes on the billboard. Then everything went black.

Beth sprinted toward him, "No, no, no," she whispered to herself. Stopping, next to his motionless body, any control she had was gone. "Roger, Jesus Christ Vermont wake up." She kneeled beside him, tears streamed down her cheeks, her words barely discernable through her sobs.

His left leg came to rest splayed out slightly. His right leg looked worse. His knee angled inward toward his left. Half way between his knee and ankle blood flowed from a wound where the shard ends of his fibula and tibia, exposed, glowed a reflective red in the light from the billboard. A crimson pool formed beneath the mess that was Roger's leg.

"Roger, oh shit, Vermont?"

She stroked his cheek and his head turned away from her, exposing the back of his skull, which was matted with blood and dirt. The night had gone completely silent. She could hear her heart pounding in her chest. She had never felt so alone, so very far away from anyone who could help. She needed Daddy; Daddy always knew what to do.

"Wake up, Roger, you have to wake up." She was stroking the side of his head, her hand now covered in the blood that flowed from the laceration in his scalp. Her vision was impaired by torrents of tears, yet she strained to see why her hand felt wet.

"Oh Jesus, Roger, you're bleeding, you're bleeding bad."

Beth began to scream toward Duke's, until something caught her eye. It was the red glow of taillights. The car that hit Roger was just sitting there. Why won't he come back and help? The hum of Duke's air conditioner and the vague rumble of the car's idling engine were the only sounds, just white noise in otherwise total silence.

Scott put the car in reverse; he had to make sure it was over. *Bad to the Bone* still echoed around inside the car as Scott skidded to a stop just inches from Roger and Beth. Triumphant, he got out of the car and strutted around the car to witness the end of The Nightcrawler. He looked down at the kid sprawled on the gravel, then into the streaming eyes of the girl trying to shield the boy from any further attack.

"What's your fucking problem, man?" Beth was near hysterics but this time her voice was clear.

Scott looked down at her, then at Roger, lying broken and bleeding in the dirt. His head was shaking back and forth, his mind unable to comprehend what he was seeing.

"No, it wasn't him. I didn't do that. It was the bum I hit." Scott was terrified. Had he done this?

He pleaded with Beth, "Where did that bum go?"

"What are you talking about?" She was screaming at the top of her lungs. Hate flared out of her eyes burning into Scott Randall.

"What the hell is going on out there?" Beth and Scott both turned to see the silhouette of a man holding a rifle, standing in the doorway of Duke's.

Beth resumed her desperate plea for help. Scott was frantically trying to explain about the bum, but nobody heard a word over Beth's shrieks for help.

"You stay right there, fella," the man in the doorway hollered in Scott's direction.

Scott began to back up fearing that gun might just go off by accident, or maybe not by accident. He bumped into the open driver's door of the Charger, and before the guy with the gun could utter, "Stop or I'll shoot," Thomas Andrew's beautifully restored, 69 Charger was just a pair of disappearing taillights in the darkness of the desert.

Chapter Twenty-Eight

Tears streamed down Scott Randall's face as he sped away from Duke's. The night was now completely black. Only the instruments on the dash and the fanned out illumination of the headlights broke the darkness. There was no moon overhead, not a single star was visible across the desert sky. The Charger's 440 droned a hum as it hurled the car at a speed that would be extremely hazardous in the light of day. In this blackness it was suicide.

Where did that kid come from? It was the bum; the bum was the one standing in the road. Why did that kid look familiar? Scott began to have a myriad of thoughts stream through his mind. Ashley, how was Ashley doing? Jesus Christ who cares about Ashley, she is probably fully recovered and back at home with her mother. Her mother, Ashley made living with her sound like a real summer vacation didn't she. Who gives a shit, that kid back there looked like he might be dead. Christ of course he's dead, the fucking car was going over a hundred when it hit him. No, when I hit him. The car didn't do anything, I did it.

While the banter echoed around in his head, the speedometer registered a steady one-ten. In the glow of the instruments, his face unshaven, his hair mussed, his eyes pink, cheeks tear stained, Scott Randall could barely be mistaken for the man who walked out of C.S. and T.'s boardroom just days ago. His six-hundred dollar suit packed away in the trunk, he now wore shorts and a golf shirt, both wrinkled and smelling of two days wear.

He's dead, he has to be dead. I have to go back. Maybe I can help. Shit, what could I do? Didn't I do enough already? They'll come looking for me. Even if they didn't get the plate number, how many mint 69 Chargers are on the road? What are you talking about? Christ, you have to go back. It was an accident. Sure. That's why you ran off. They will all say that. If it was an accident why run?

Some how, in the middle of the longest debate, possibly the only debate he had ever had with himself, Scott's father's advice popped right in. *Scottie my boy, not matter how bad you screw up, no matter how much trouble you think you will be in, you have to take responsibility for your actions. Sure trying to cover things up, or denying them most times seems like the easy way out, but every time you do that you add a chip of guilt into a little space in the back of your mind. Eventually the space will fill up and rupture, leaking evil that will corrupt everything you are.*

"Sure, Dad, easy for you to say." They are going to throw me in prison for this. That kid is dead, and that girl thinks I did it on purpose. The look in her eyes, there was hate in her eyes. I have never seen that look before, but it was easy to read. It was hate, hate as deep as the deepest abyss of all the oceans. She didn't see me as a guy who had an accident, or even a man who made a mistake. She looked at me like I was evil.

The Charger crossed the solid double lines as the road curved slightly to the right. The Uniroyals squealed their protest as Scott corrected his position on the road. When the road straightened, the center line disappeared, again total blackness took over. The speed dipped below ninety-five through the bend in the road and leveled off there.

Reluctant, but not wanting to continue his nonsensical rationalizations for going back or running away, he turned up the radio. His hope was that music would steal his mind away, calm his thoughts so he could come to a logical decision. Static hissed out like an angry snake, Scott hit the seek button, a Walgreens commercial ended followed by the drawling voice of a woman. "We just got word of a hit and run out near Duke's Restaurant, anyone in that area please yield to emergency vehicles. Now here's an oldie from Blue Oyster

Cult."

Scott's fingers began to tap the wheel. Tension began to ease, as if he had turned a valve, and the stress escaped his mind with each breath he exhaled. The desert didn't look as dark and the future, less bleak. Of course he could return to the scene. He is a respected man of means. It was an accident; he didn't intend to run down that kid. It was the bum he was aiming at.

He felt a chill as the night air rushed in, so he rolled up the driver's side window, as the Cult continued.

As he reached across the front seat to close the passenger side window, the speedometer dropped to ninety. He fished for the knob to close the window, unable to find it. A brief glance at the passenger side door and his hand was on the knob. He turned the crank, the window began to rise in that uneven way that crank windows do.

When his attention returned to the road, the car had slowed to eighty-five. An odd figure to his left drew his gaze out over the desert. Double solid lines suddenly broke the monotony of the darkness and the hypnotic broken single line. At eighty-five mph, it was only seconds before the lines that warned of a bend in the road actually curved to the left.

The road curved harder than Scott was prepared for and he had to fight to keep the car on the pavement. His eyes concentrated on the white lines down the center of the pavement.

The speedometer now settled at seventy, the road straightened, the center lines disappeared and Scott's concentration on what was directly in front of the car expanded past the radiance of the headlights. The figure he had seen moments before was closer; he squinted into the darkness to make sense of it. His distance perception, compromised by the blackness of the desert night. Before he could react, he was right on top of the strange figure.

Scott Randall had just enough time for his eyes to send the image of the figure to his brain before he reacted. The image was so out of place he should have known it wasn't real. What he saw was a little girl, twelve maybe thirteen years old, standing in the middle of the road. She was wearing a winter coat, snow pants and ice skates. No way there was a girl alone out here at this time of night. Even if a twelve-year-old did find herself out here, she would have enough sense not to stand in the middle of the road. The most surreal of course was the clothes and skates. This was the Arizona desert in the middle of summer, triple digit temperatures made ice-skating impossible.

At seventy, Scott didn't have time to reason those facts out. He didn't have time to tell himself that little girl was just another hallucination and to just plow through it. At seventy the only thing he thought to do was turn the wheel hard to the right. The front tires instantly hit the gravel shoulder; the whole car shuddered at the sudden unevenness. Scott fought for control of the car as the drone of the engine was replaced by the thumping and groaning of the suspension. He caught a brief glimpse of the girl as he passed her. She was waving and smiling.

An abrupt quiet replaced the noise of the tires and the protesting springs and shocks. The only sound now was The Cult, coming from the radio. The ride was suddenly smoother than any fine luxury car on brand new pavement. Scott jammed both feet down on the brake pedal. There was no change. That's when he realized the car was airborne. He looked down to the ground from the side window, straining hard, trying to see how far down it was. He saw nothing but black.

His hand gripped the wheel like a vise, he looked through the windshield, waiting for the lights to give him a sign that he was landing. He didn't get any sign, the car crashed down on the hard pan of the desert floor with such force that the steering wheel spun like an airplane propeller. Both of his wrists broke instantly, his body thrust forward crushing his ribcage against the steering wheel. His spine sent electric shock waves across his shoulders and down his arms as his head was snapped back, then thrust forward splitting his chin on the wheel, shattering his jaw. The impact forced the floorboards up, driving his left knee into the steering column shattering his kneecap.

After the initial impact, Thomas Andrew's car left the ground again, turned over twice and came to rest on its roof. Steam billowed from the engine compartment, the freewheeling rear tires continued to spin at high speed, the left front tire was gone and the right was bent up inside the fender at a ninety degree angle. The cloud of dust raised by the impact hovered over the car and the glow of the one remaining headlight made it look more like fog.

The car now at rest was no longer a prize piece of Detroit muscle, but a worthless pile of broken glass, broken plastic, and twisted metal. When the car crashed down on its roof, Scott was hurtled down onto the roof with a force that was nearly impossible to survive. On impact with the roof two of the ribs, which broke when he was thrown into the steering wheel, punctured his left lung. His left leg bent at an unnatural angle at the knee, his left foot quivered outside the car. The right side of his face, gashed open when he collided with the dome light, gleamed scarlet in the dim glow from the instrument panel.

"I told you this afternoon that you were driving too fast."

Scott looked out the window from which his left leg protruded and saw him. He was sitting cross-legged, his elbows on his knees, his chin on his hand. Scott had no reply, his brain wanted to get up and kick the fucker's ass all over the desert but his body would not co-operate. He tried to scream but nothing came from his mouth but a gurgling sound and a foamy mixture of blood and saliva.

The bum straightened up, tapped his knees, smiled his grin of gaps and black teeth and said, "Criss cross apple sauce."

Scott's respiratory rate increased with the added anxiety of Matt's appearance. A wheezing, whistling sound now accompanied each exhale. Coughing came at increased intervals sending small eruptions of crimson ooze from his mouth.

"Gee Scottie, you don't look very good at all. I was really hoping we could continue our discussion. You know, the one about all people adding value to society. But you know what, Scottie old boy. I don't think you have the time."

Blue Oyster Cult had been followed by an endless commercial

break. Everything from tonight's lineup on Fox, to Beater Boyz. Scott's breathing had quickened, his entire body shivered violently. The commercials continued on the radio. The metallic taste of blood and the pungent smell of the foulness he spewed out with each coughing fit now combined with the odor of his own urine brought an urge to heave. His eyes, filled with tears, locked on the blurred figure sitting outside the car.

"Damn commercials, eh Scottie?" The bum reached into the car, Scott saw the exposed skin on his wrist. It looked slimy, like the figure back at the Best Western. Scott's breathing stopped; his eyes bulged out in terror. The bum hit the seek button on the radio, Elton John filled the air with "A Funeral for a Friend". "That's much better, don't you think?"

When the bum withdrew his arm from the car, Scott's rapid breathing continued. He looked from the wrist to the face. It too was a shiny writhing mass.

"Well Scottie, time for me to go. Don't get up, I'll see myself out." He cocked his now glistening, sickly hand into a gun, and made that clicking sound. The bum collapsed into a writhing mass of earthworms, no they were nightcrawlers. The worms flowed in a ghastly wave into the car. They moved with a collective purpose. The initial wave left him covered to the waist and he tried again to scream, bringing on a spasm of coughs, producing a flow of blood that didn't end with the coughing. At the same time the electrical system in the car failed, the light was gone, and the radio fell silent. Complete darkness enveloped him and the worms. The desert was completely silent but for Scott Randall's wheezing and a very faint oozing sound.

Chapter Twenty-Nine

When Roger regained consciousness, he was lying in a private hospital room in Phoenix. After Beth had gotten over the initial shock of the accident, she completely took charge of the scene. She instructed the man with the rifle to call an ambulance. When he came back, she got her cell phone and called Jack. She was very calm, fighting off the urge to cry at the sound of Jack's voice. Jack told her he would take care of everything.

Jack Walker didn't forget any details when he took care of things. Ninety minutes after he got off the phone, Roger was in surgery after being airlifted to Phoenix and his parents were on their way to the airport. Before sunrise, Billy and Bobbie were heading out to retrieve the Jeep and get it to Phoenix. Hotel rooms were booked near the hospital. By just past 7:00 am Jack and Nora were striding arm in arm through the hospital corridor to Roger's room. Just ahead of them and leading the way was Dr. Rex Cooder, long time friend of Jack Walker and head of Orthopedic Surgery. Probably the key detail Jack had taken care of was to arrange for Rex to meet Roger's chopper on the roof of the hospital and personally take charge of his medical care.

The impact his head took on the ground didn't cause any serious damage. He suffered a concussion, and the laceration took sixteen stitches to close. Rex had the chief of neurology view his films and confirmed that no permanent brain injuries were evident.

"The boy took quite a bump on the head and may have some headaches for a week or so, but I expect he'll be right as rain in no time," said the chief.

Roger's knee and ankle were a much bigger story. Rex and his team spent four hours adding screws to bones and reattaching tendons and ligaments. Rex told Jack that the boy will walk fine, he may even run, with a noticeable limp of course but he won't be playing ball at the college level again.

When the trio entered Roger's room, the young man was looking around the room with a confused, *where am I,* look on his face. Beth was sleeping in a reclining chair that Rex had an orderly bring over from his office.

Rex explained to Roger where he was and looked over the boy's chart. In hushed tones he explained the details of his surgery. Roger took the news well.

"I never thought I'd play in the majors anyway," Roger said. "But I don't know what this will do for my scholarship."

"If that crazy sumbitch's insurance doesn't cover your college, you let me know, son," Jack said. "Even with the limp you'll still be the best man on the field at next year's slow pitch game."

"Daddy," Beth jumped out of the chair and all the control she had the night before was gone. She wrapped herself around Jack and began to cry. Nora put her hand on Beth's shoulder for support but Nora new it was Jack that Beth needed. Billy and Bobbi would always come to her first but Beth and Jack had a closeness that Nora couldn't get through.

With Beth sobbing uncontrollably on his shoulder, Jack looked over at Roger. "How ya feeling Rodney?"

Roger grinned in spite of the pain at the back of his head and numbness in his left leg. "I think I'm gonna pull through, Mr. Jenson."

"Kid's got brass ones, don't he, Jack?" Rex said, then hung Roger's chart back on the bed and left the room.

At the same time Rex was leaving the room, two Arizona State Troopers were cautiously approaching an overturned car matching the description of the hit and run vehicle from the previous night. The sun was already beating down on the desert. The cool sixty-five degree overnight temp was now closing in on eighty.

"Michigan plates. That has to be the car," the first officer to reach the Charger announced.

"You think he got out of there, Ted?"

When Ted made his way around to the side of the car, he stopped in his tracks, making an odd grunting sound.

"What the hell?" Ellis Wilkes, Ted's partner had come around and they both stared in disbelief.

A white running shoe lay next to the car. A brown blanket of something started at the shoe and continued inside the car. They both squatted, hands on the butt of their guns as they did. The entire inside of the car was carpeted with what looked like brown freeze-dried spaghetti, if there was such a thing as brown spaghetti.

"Whad'ya reckon?" Ellis asked Ted.

"Got me."

Ted took out his night-stick and poked it into the mass inside the car. The brown crust fell in on itself and both officers fell back on their asses in shock. They sprang up and backed away from the car with their weapons drawn. Both officers peered into the car with incredulous disbelief. The dried brown crust was gone leaving nothing but the skeletal remains of what was just hours ago a dying Scott Randall.

"Son of a bitch," Ted uttered as he crept back to the broken Charger.

"What the hell is that stuff, Ted?"

Gently stirring the brown material with his stick, Ted looked back at Ellis and said, "Looks like dried up worms."

"Worms? How'd they git out here?"

"Hell if I know, but that's what they look like."

"Well that can't be the car from last night, the hit and run was only nine hours ago, give or take," Ellis said keeping a safe distance from the horror in that car.

The Nightcrawler

"I guess they were hungry worms," Ted replied then flicked some in his partners direction and laughed a nervous laugh.

Ellis scrambled back further and said they best call it in.

"Okie-dokie," Ted said. He stood and followed Ellis back to the cruiser.

Two hours later, Thomas Andrews answered the phone in his office, "Sarah you better have Scott on the phone."

"I'm sorry, am I speaking to Thomas Andrews?" The voice wasn't Sarah's and it sounded muffled and far away.

"Yes, and who am I speaking to?"

"My name is Patty Freeman. I'm with the Arizona State Police." She paused, waiting for a response, when there was none she continued. "Mr. Andrews, are you still there?"

"Yes, what can I do for you?"

"Sir, do you own a red Dodge Charger, license plate CST VP?"

"Yes, was it stolen? "Let me talk to Scott. Is he there with you?"

"No sir, it wasn't stolen that we know of. It was involved in a hit and run last night. The driver of the vehicle appears to have lost control and was killed in a single vehicle accident."

After another long silence, "Sir, are you still there?"

"Scott's dead?"

Patty went on to tell Thomas all the details that she could. They hadn't identified the driver yet. Next of kin would have to be notified. She got his insurance information. The rest of the details were lost on Thomas. He seemed to have shut down.

When she finished Thomas hung up the phone, stood up, walked out of his office, down the hall and across the same lobby where he and Scott had stood just days before. With no expression, he told Sarah he was leaving for the day. She exchanged a worried glance at Jane the other C.S. and T receptionist. The elevator door opened and Thomas left without any explanation.

He needed some air; instead of going to the basement to get his car

257

he went down to the main lobby of the building. He felt flushed, Scott may be dead and his car was a write-off. He didn't think he had enough insurance on the car, shit he should have taken twenty for it last month when he had the chance.

Thomas exited onto the sidewalk in front of the building. It was hot and humid, the sky was clear and the sun was blinding. Then the smell hit him. What was that smell?

Before he could go back inside to the parking garage, Thomas heard something he was in no mood to hear. Not that he was ever in the mood to hear it.

"Can you spare some change, friend?"

He turned and was face to face with the source of the offending odor. A filthy homeless man stood grinning his toothless grin directly between Thomas and the door to get back inside.

"Jesus Christ, when is this city going to clear you people off the streets?" Thomas waved his hand in front of his face in an attempt to fan the smell away. "Get the fuck away from me."

"Shame what Scottie did to your car, huh?"

Thomas felt his heart pound in his chest, the hair on the back of his neck stood up, starting a quiver down the length of his spine. He took his cell from his breast pocket, "I'm calling the cops, now you better fuck off before they get here."

The bum just cocked his finger, pointed it at Thomas, clicked his tongue, and said, "Okie-dokie."

About the Author

Mick Ridgewell lives with his wife, Lynn, son, Cory, daughter, Lauren, and Savannah, their rescued greyhound, in Southern Ontario, where he is currently working on his next novel.

Look for Mick Ridgewell on Facebook or follow him on Twitter @mickridgewell

Only one priest can battle the ultimate evil!

Evil Eternal
© 2012 Hunter Shea

An evil as ancient as time itself has arisen and taken root in New York City. Father Michael, the mysterious undead defender of the Church, answers the call to action from the Vatican, while Cain, a malevolent wraith that feeds on fear and blood, has taken the life and form of the city's mayor and readies a demonic army to ignite the apocalypse.

With an unlikely ally, Father Michael will prepare for the grim confrontation as he grapples with his sworn duty to God and the shreds of humanity left beating in his immortal heart. The time is ripe for Cain and the fulfillment of dark prophecies. Father Michael must battle Cain and his horde of demons in a final showdown that could very well herald the end of mankind.

Available now in ebook and print from Samhain Publishing.

Enjoy the following excerpt from Evil Eternal...

Cardinal Gianncarlo walked briskly to Pope Pius XIII's office, his black robe billowing behind him. The sound of his quick and heavy footsteps echoed across the vast, marbled hallway. The day was bright and filled with promise, in stark contrast to the roiling cloud that had descended upon his fluttering heart.

The Cardinal was normally a stern man, authoritarian to those beneath him, unflappable in his sense of duty to the Lord. His parents, Italian citizens who had made the mistake of openly sympathizing with the Jewish plight during Word War II, had been murdered before his very eyes. At the age of seven, he had been placed in a Nazi death camp, managing to survive two years in brutal captivity until the Allied forces freed them all. He vowed to live the rest of his life in service to God and had done so with unequaled integrity and passion, earning the confidence of the leader of his blessed church.

The email from the lone priest of a small Vermont parish had turned his skin the color of spoiled milk when he had been urged by his secretary to open it just minutes before. With a knot of dread cramping his stomach, he sped off to the Pontiff's study. Time was of the essence. Time and—

He reached the library that doubled as the Pontiff's main office and study, and with unsteady hands rapped loudly on the massive oak door. Like the architectural design of the entire Vatican Palace, the door was a study in elegant simplicity. The wizened voice of Pope Pius XIII beckoned him to enter.

"Sorry to disturb you, but something urgent just came in that I think you should see," Cardinal Gianncarlo said with a slight stammer.

The Pope looked at the Cardinal and knew. The exact details of the message were still a mystery to him, but the outcome, of that he was sure. The Cardinal thought he detected a slight flickering of the light, the fire that had made him one of the most dynamic popes in centuries, behind his old friend's eyes.

Pope Pius XIII unfolded the printout with trembling, liver-spotted fingers and read the extensive message. When he was finished, he looked up at his old friend. Deep lines of great sadness etched across his brow.

"So, the inevitable has come back to hound us," the Pope said.

"As much as it pains me to say, yes."

With a heavy sigh, the Pope slumped back in his chair.

"How long has it been since the last appearance? Twenty, thirty years?"

"Nothing since Jonestown. Well over two decades of praying the evil was finally gone forever," the Cardinal answered.

"What has no life can never die, my friend. I had hoped to have passed on to our Father's arms before this office was faced with such a situation, but we both well know life is never quite what we plan it to be. I'm an old man now. Do I have the strength to go through this again?"

The Pope shrugged, the weight of time and responsibility bearing down on his brittle, sagging shoulders. He had served the office of pope for over thirty years, no small feat. He recalled his days as a young man, fresh from the seminary in his first parish in Bergamo, Italy. That young man would never have even dreamed to be what he would one day become. And no one could have guessed the true secrets that lay in store for his discovery when he ascended to the papacy.

"Would you like me to get Father Michael?"

Cardinal Gianncarlo had to resist the urge to pull him close, offering comfort for a man who had dedicated his life to bringing peace and comfort to millions. They were different men the last time, when the beast within Jim Jones was sent to hell, but not before so much had been lost; terrible choices forced to be made, too many lives lost. It had changed them, added years and unbearable pain to their souls.

The old Pope shook his head.

"That is my duty. At my age, it will surely be my final call. Let the burden of the nightmares rest with me. I only ask that you sit and pray."

The Cardinal settled into a plush leather chair and the Pope offered his hand across the large, neatly arranged desk. In silence, the two men prayed while life outside his windows carried on, ignorant to the dark shadows gathering at the earth's edge.

SAMHAIN
PUBLISHING

It's all about the story...

Romance

HORROR

Retro ROMANCE

www.samhainpublishing.com